ASTOR'S MAIDEN CRUISE

AROUND THE WORLD

1987-1988

ASTOR'S MAIDEN CRUISE AROUND THE WORLD 1987-1988

Mauritian Adventure

Jackie Veerabadren

authorHOUSE®

AuthorHouse™
1663 Liberty Drive
Bloomington, IN 47403
www.authorhouse.com
Phone: 1-800-839-8640

Published by AuthorHouse   05/15/2012

ISBN: 978-1-4685-7902-4 (sc)
ISBN: 978-1-4685-7903-1 (e)

CONTENTS

PART 3

PROLOGUE

In the year 1987 unemployment was at its peak on Mauritius and many young people leaving secondary school with a Higher School certificate have no other alternative than to work in the textile industry. The textile industry being in full expansion it was the only place where it was possible to find a job. The numerous positions in the production chain, helper checker or machinist which provided pre training was paid about fifteen rupees per day. That year a bright star shines for many of them in the form of a brand new cruise ship built in the shipyard of Kiel HDW (Howaldswerke Deutsche Werft).

Owned by an American company the Astor II is leased by the British Morgan Leisure Company to cruise the world in luxury. Flying the neutral four coloured Mauritian flag would be giving her easy access to many ports where other flags would have brought about controversy. Consequently, the crew of one hundred and fifty are handpicked amongst the staff of the luxury beach hotels around the tiny island of Mauritius found in the Indian Ocean where high class tourism excludes charter flights.

Exceptionally a charter flight is organized to transport the Mauritian crew to Hamburg in Germany. The tropical climate of Mauritius consists of a temperature of positive thirty five degrees centigrade during the summer months of December to March; 'Cold' for the Mauritian, means the temperature of the town of Curepipe situated on the high grounds in winter, fifteen degrees centigrade, in order to feel warm again, a woollen sweater is enough.

Overnight, suddenly the air chills out; it is neither the usual five degrees decrease in temperature from the coast to the highlands nor the ten to twelve degrees fall on the thermometer between summer and winter months but a drastic decrease of sixty three degrees centigrade. This January 1987 is one of the coldest of European winters, the mercury having descended twenty seven degrees below zero.

Leaving Mauritius where cooking is still done on coal and wood fires in most households and where the wash machine is still almost unheard of, the crew's lifestyle undergoes a radical change. Moving from a third world country standard they get into a world of highest available luxury aboard this five star cruise ship. On the Astor many learn to operate the modern domestic appliances, use the wash machine and even the dish washer.

The abundance of the variety of luxury products and food cause some to become overweight while others, plagued by seasickness or unable to adapt to European food rapidly lose weight until they are only skin on bones. This wonderful adventure around the world is unanimously enjoyed by everyone who has the opportunity to sample the atmospheres in different lands, fifty countries and one hundred and fifty ports of calls is on the Astor cruise program.

Mela, Bianca, Nicoleta, Juliette and many others bring us with them on their adventures in and out of the ship. Their tears and despair in front of the hard work that is done with the shackles of horrible seasickness alternate with their smiles of wonder in front of the generous tips brought by their hard work. Their laughs of delight in the ports where they visit shops for a good buy and sample different food from Portuguese Pizza to Turkish delight.

They leave the waves to ride on the roads, horseback, camel, donkeys and bicycles and motorcars, buses and trams.

But as all dreams, even those which do come true, have to come to an end, the wonderful Astor Adventure finally dissolves sending our friends to their other destinies.

Mela

September 1986

The ring of the bell announced the end of the working day at leisure Garments. The workers gathered their bags and walked to the exit where they opened their bags to be checked by the security officers.

'Hurry up or we shall miss this five thirty bus and shall have to wait for six to catch the next bus!'

'Come on, give me time to get ready, do you think I can get out on the streets in this state, I need comb my hair and put on some face powder and lipstick."

"Oh no do not tell me you will do all this again"

'Of course I am and you'd better do the same, you look like a scarecrow with your hair in all directions and your appearance like an old hag!"

"Don't waste your breath you know I won't bother"

Since she finished school Mela had been working in a textile factory where pants and jackets were manufactured for the American market. Despite applying for all the jobs which were advertized, the only answers she received were polite acknowledgement letters; she was getting desperate finding the daily factory routine unbearably boring. During the trip home on the bus she was only half listening to the endless chatter of her colleague telling her about the next dress she would get herself stitched. A hard slap on the back brought her out of her reverie.

"I am talking to you if you do not want to listen just tell me and I shall shut up!"

"Do not get angry on me but I am so desperate to find another job, I am losing spirits and feel as if I am going to rot in this factory forever!'

"Do not be stupid, you have gone to school and with your certificates you will finish by finding a better job, stop worrying, anyway if you keep on neglecting your appearance, something worse is going to happen to you, you will not find a husband."

The wet august afternoon was cold and windy and they had to hurry in the mud and water of the bus station over the footprints of other hundreds of travelers. The trip from the high plateau town of Curepipe down to the Capital city of Port-Louis lasted one hour. It was warmer near the coastal area but the rain was still falling.

A nice smell of fish stew and boiled rice with the strong and hot aroma of coconut and green chilies chutney floated around the house. Mela was tempted to take her plateful of rice and fish stew to eat right away on entering the kitchen. Instead she decided to first take a shower and get into her nightdress before enjoying her favorite dish. She would eat the fish head and its teeth and eyes and brains and when she would have finished with it the poor dog Rebelle, would get only the hardest fish bones, the ones her teeth would not be capable to crush. It was half past six and already dark out in the yard; she went to take her shower in the dark corrugated iron outside bathroom and hurried inside to get out of the strong wind.

"There is a letter for you there on the table."

With the number of deceitful letters she had had during the past three years, Mela preferred to take the joy which was available and certain first. She would for a change leave the usual bitter pill of deception for later. She first soothed her soul with the simple pleasure of a fresh up with cool water, a fresh change of underwear and a nice warm meal for her stomach. A smile lighted face as she looked at the letter, it was from a shipping company and she felt a surge of joy and hope and thought of the job she had applied for a few weeks previously on a cruise ship.

The day of the interview she walked to the wharf and entered an imposing stone building. The company was recruiting hotel staff as the ship would be a five star cruise liner, and people with experience in the five star hotels of Mauritius would have priority to the job.

Mela, who had only seen the interior of a hotel once when she had been invited with some Italian friends of her sister for an evening, was shortlisted only thanks to her mention of being able to speak German. The Ship captain conducting her interview was a very handsome Franco Mauritian, who introduced himself as Captain de Gersigny. Mela felt awkward in this impressive office furnished with heavy mahogany furniture and decorated by various navigating instruments as well as all sorts of sea routes framed upon the walls.

"Have a seat mademoiselle."

"Why do you want this job?"

"It was always my dream of sailing the high seas as I love the ocean."

"This ship is a five star floating hotel and we recruit people with experience in the hotel industry, we have chosen you as you mention speaking German and there will be a lot of German passengers aboard, could you please tell me a sentence in German?"

Mela who had learnt German through a book and had never been speaking the language was worried but her desperation to find the job made her gather enough courage to say "Please tell me what you wish that I say in German?"

"What do I know, well, hmm, okay tell me that the weather is beautiful today?"

Mela thought for a moment and said "Das wetter ist schoen heute."

Captain de Gersigny burst out laughing and Mela was panicked thinking she had said it wrong. He pursued "I do not understand one word of German miss, but I can tell you your dream will come true. You applied for the post of cabin stewardess and I see you have a Higher School Certificate, you could if you wish take the post of wine stewardess, and you will be given training for what you are supposed to do."

Mela thought about the job of wine stewardess who would serve at the tables and that of cabin stewardess who would have the hard job of both cleaning cabins and act as hostess welcoming the passengers and taking care of room service. She finally opted for the job of cabin stewardess as she did not feel capable of doing a frontline job being directly in front of the guests having to be neat and well groomed at all times. Mela could not believe her luck; she felt her heart bursting with joy in her chest and had to take deep breaths to be able to contain her joy.

The process of recruitment went on with another interview with the ship's German hotel Manager Hans Zuchold. Mela took her German book and practiced all she could on the subject of ships and hotels. She was tensed about the interview with the German and was relieved when she got through it. The recruitment was done during the month of September and the next three months the new employees would have to undergo sea training, firefighting and first aid courses to satisfy the international standards mandatory for people working on ships. Mela was really happy to attend sea training school in Port-Louis where the future seamen learnt theory in the class room. One hundred and fifty people had been recruited from Mauritius to work as hotel staff and seamen. The practical classes were done in the Port-Louis Harbor and in the fire brigade headquarters on the wharf.

The whole Mauritian population, from the two percent Franco Mauritians to the sixty seven percent Indo Mauritian as well as the twenty eight percent Afro

Mauritians and the four percent Sino Mauritians and the rest were represented in this batch to sail the seas as part of an international crew of four hundred people from Germany and Great Britain. Mela met the other members of the crew during training and she came to know how other people like her had had their dreams come true.

Bianca

Bianca was a mother of two little girls and was having a terrible time with her violent husband who was making a hell of her life with his paranoia. He had made her lose her job many times by made scandals on her work premises due to his jealousy. She had finally opened a small enterprise and sewed bags to sell. She had found a very nice young woman to work with her who also helped in her household chores. Each day in her prayers she begged God to take her away from this mad man. When she saw the advertisement for post on the ship, she quickly and secretly applied and persuaded her husband Luke to accept her departure for she would send him good money for finishing the construction of their house.

Nicoleta

Nicoleta was a woman about the same age as Bianca and her life had been a real struggle. She was married to Phillip who was a scoundrel who had given her three children, two boys and a girl. She had been the one to bring the home bread while he was always after some other woman or gambling away all of the little money he had. As a vampire, he was sucking her blood by living off her sweat. Nicoleta had been like a housekeeper and cook to a Franco Mauritian family for many years and her employers were very happy with her competence. She had started as a maid and had become the right hand of the family with all the other servants and gardener under her orders. She had once won the national lottery. She used the money gained to buy a little house near the beach at Grand-Bay, one of the most popular touristic villages of Mauritius. She planned to create a little guest house of her own and be self employed one day. Her rascal of a husband had sold the house for gambling without her knowledge and this had been the drop to overflow the vase. She had left him and taken her children to her mother. Her employer whose son was a sea Captain in charge of recruiting staff for the Astor found this job of cabin stewardess for her. Nicoleta took this opportunity as a compensation for the bad turns life had played on her.

Juliette

Juliette was a woman of Afro Mauritian origin; she was quite a fleshy woman of about thirty. Her life had been very difficult as her mother had left her and her brother and sisters to her grandmother who had raised them. She had found a job in a hotel near her house, her perfect and meticulous cleaning had made her the favorite of the housekeeper. She met Seeven, an Indo Mauritian man who fell in love with her and regularly visited her at home. Gradually he started living with her and gave her all the treatment a husband gives to his wife. He provided for their household and bought training school; some were distant and kept their rank of purser while others were more friendly, she came to know Vania, Mea, Michele Madge, Annick, Catherine, Veronique, Arianne, Michaela. As they were paid during the training many ordered their travelling bags from Bianca, a set of three nylon bags would cost only three hundred rupees. The hotel staff was formed by Bhima and Yvon who were waiters from Le Touessrok hotel, Harmon who was waiter at the La Pirogue Sun and, Satish, Hans, and Suresh who were barmen and the bar waiters Patrick, Norman, wine stewardesses Corinne, Martine, Doris and Corayssa. Gaulette, a man of huge corpulence was the bosun in charge of the sailors George, Sylvio, Gervais and others and a tiny man similar to a gnome called Constant. The utility boys were President, Shorty, Vincent, Badal, Alain and Serge. The laundry guys Cokpi, Ajay and Raj who were under the supervision of Bhurton. There was Ravi the storekeeper and Rickey the printer. The crew had first aid and firefighting classroom theory at the sea training school in town, for practical classes they were brought out, in the harbor to learn to handle a boat and on the wharf in the fire brigade headquarters to learn to handle a hose. Mr. Malabar, the teacher in charge of the training also named 'bosun' was a tiny man with very dark skin, while bosun Gaulette who was the one in charge of the eight sailors of the ship was a huge white skinned man. While doing the demonstrations to make the future seamen learn how to put safety boats out to sea, Nicoleta who was always ready for a laugh told Mela and Bianca "Have you seen Laurel and Hardy?" pointing with her head towards the two bosuns.

The contrast of the picture formed by the two such opposite types of men made the girls giggle a lot. The first aid classes were very interesting and the whole class was quiet while the teacher taught them how to save lives, in the eventuality of having to face dangerous situations on board the ship. When it was time to learn how to give artificial respiration, the men started to choose their practice partner saying out loud the name of the girl on whom they wanted to practice. The teacher quickly dissipated the awkwardness for the female crew whose names were being said by saying "We can only practice artificial respiration on somebody who has stopped breathing and thanks God we do not have such a case here. However there is a very nice unconscious lady ready for anyone to do artificial respiration." He left the class and came back with a plastic dummy which made everyone burst into fits of laughter.

Firefighting was the most difficult of the practical lessons to be done as one had to hold and learn how to handle a water hose with an enormous pressure jet on a fire. Many of the girls and even some quite strong men were thrown off balance as soon as the powerful water jet came through the hose. There was also the exercise of entering a building which was in complete darkness with potential hazards like live wires and noxious gases, on hands and feet with breathing mask on and try to find out possible survivors. During the process of training the Muslim woman who was fat and heavily dressed in her traditional clothes found it impossible to strip down to the necessary attire to do the training properly. She had to give up the hope of travelling the world as she did not want to give up her head cover and could not do any of the more than strenuous exercises demanded. Juliette soon lost all the kilos that she had gained during her convalescence and she became so thin that she had to buy clothes two sizes smaller. Mela was still quite fleshy in spite of all the exercises they had to do as she was compensating by eating big plateful of rice each evening. The training which started in October finished in December and the departure was scheduled for the sixth of January 1987. As most of the crew was also going on their first flight, their maiden flight, they had to have their passports, and all the necessary vaccination required done. Mela was a bit worried when she learnt that it would be necessary to pledge some value in order to get the necessary papers to travel. She was wondering if her mother would consent to pledge their house. She lost her sleep on the day she heard that fearing to see her dream vanish so near the destination. Fortunately most of the crew had nothing to offer in way of guarantee and the company decided to stand for them, such a relief to all. Miss De Boucherville was the secretary of Captain Goileau and she took care of every single detail for each and every person of the crew needing a passport, and vaccination. To celebrate the end of the training and the future departure a soiree was organized at the seaman's club where all the crew of the new ship was assembled. They were given more information about their work and were introduced to the Managers of the project and all those who would be part of this great adventure.

The Sega, the Mauritian folklore was played by the little band formed by Yvon and other members of the crew. On that night, Mela and Nicoleta, together with most of the crew members danced the Sega, heads full of hope and fantastic dreams of a wonderful princess of the seas. They decided to form a group to show the Mauritian Sega to the people on the ship. Mela who loved dancing the Sega put her name down on the list of volunteers.

PART 1

Chapter I

Cold Mauritius and Freezing Kiel

The year 1986 was wearing away, receding to give way to 1987. Mela spent the New Year's Eve with a heart full of hope at the perspective of an exciting life ahead instead of the depressing prospect of seeing the inside of the factory day after day as in the previous three years 1984, 1985 and 1986. She went to shop for necessities to bring on her voyage and as it was told it would be cold in January in Germany they were to bring warm clothes. Mela had been born in Port-Louis where the temperature rarely went below twenty four degrees even in the heart of winter in the months of July and August. Cold for Mela meant the temperature of the Highlands of Mauritius where she had rarely stayed, not lower than fifteen degrees centigrade. She therefore bought a couple of sweaters to ward off the cold. Her aunts and cousins came to say goodbye and they had a happy dinner together and helped to pack her bags. She had one large, one medium and a small bag, from the set bought from Bianca. She would carry mango pickles and Kraft cheese and octopus vindaloo in the big bag which was to be put down in the haul. On the fourth of January Mela was having her hair cleaned of lice and nits from her mother when she heard her mother sniffing from behind her. She was annoyed that her mother should cry at such a happy event for her.

The Sabena plane chartered for the crew of one hundred and fifty Mauritians was scheduled to leave Mauritius on Monday the sixth of January. On the eve of the departure day the summer rains flooded the whole island, things did not get better on Tuesday and the plane was unable to take off in such weather. Mela was so disappointed to have to spend another night in Mauritius and not on the plane, she got angry and let off her frustration on her mother "What did you have to cry for, you see because of your tears which brought ill luck the plane cannot leave. Do not let me catch you weeping again!"

The plane was finally due to leave on Wednesday the seventh of January, the company having given a van to pick up the crew; her family was to come by taxi to bid her farewell.

They went to pick up people from the upper Plaine Wilhems, first stopping at Quatre-Bornes for taking on George, then at Vacoas to fetch Bianca and finally to take the little sailor who resembled a gnome in Curepipe. The man got on the van and when he saw Mela, he kept on looking in her face so intently that she felt creepy. Fortunately she was seated next to Bianca and he could not come to sit next to her. At the airport Mela, impatient to be at last on the move, quickly kissed her family goodbye and hurried inside. The crew embarked on the charter plane which took off at eight o'clock in the evening for an eleven hour flight to Hamburg. During the flight, Anita the youngest of the crew got airsick and vomited all her meal in the sickness bag. The Captains, Goileau, De Gersigny and Bellepeau and the latter's young son Nicolas were escorting the crew to Germany.

The Astor ship had a smaller predecessor named the Arkona, built in 1981 also by Howaldswerke Deutsche Werft, she had also been also named Astor at a point in her life.

A consortium of German investors had conceived her to be the "**Dream-Ship**", taking German cruise passengers around the world. Three years later the dream ship was sold to the South African ship owner Safmarine which had organized series of voyages between Europe and South Africa and cruises to the Indian Ocean and the waters of Norway and Greenland. The falling South African economy made Safmarine decide to sell the ship and invest in a larger more versatile and improved version of the dream-ship. The order called Hull2eighteen in HDW gave birth to the new Astor. Safmarine however could not continue with the project due to the decline of the South African economy and the insecure political situation of the country. The future of Hull2eighteen was in jeopardy until several of the senior managers involved who believed strongly in the ship's future began the quest for new investors and the necessary finance required to establish a new Europe-based passenger ship. A few months later the ship was ready, owned in Panama, she was registered in Mauritius and flying the red blue yellow and green colors of the Mauritian Flag. The ship had to maintain the highest standards of service cuisine and hospitality. The ship being a Mauritian ship, the majority of its service crew was handpicked from the International high standard hotels of the Island. Together with the British and German officers and hotel staff, Astor would be the only ship with fluency in English, German and French, the main languages of Western Europe. The Morgan Leisure Company which had loaned the boat had given the responsibility of recruitment to a Mauritian company called Island Leisure. It was essential that each and every seaman had the required international norm training for the job.

The forerunner of the new ship had been the first Astor which had been built in Hamburg HDW. Valuable experience gained on the earlier Astor had contributed in the making of the new Astor and apart from the length which was twelve meters more. The new Astor would use similar construction methods and configurations having been proved right on her predecessor. The four considerations with regards to conditions and prospects in marine tourism were maximum safety, economic operation of ship and services, lowest possible maintenance costs and modern layout. The new Astor had been conceived to cruise all over the world, mostly for cruises between one and three weeks, draught having to be limited to about six meters in view of the increasing number of ports of call in modern marine tourism. The external and internal form of the ship was extensively influenced by the need to comply with both owner's specifications and survey regulations and requirements of various national and international authorities such as Leak proofing, fire protection, rescue and firefighting equipment and so on. The overall length of the ship was one hundred and seventy six and a half meters, the length at waterline almost one hundred and fifty two meters, the width at frames nearly twenty three meters. Lateral height to freeboard(C deck) was eight point ten, the lateral height to promenade deck was sixteen points zero five meters; the maximum draught was six hundred and ten meters.

The approximate carrying capacity was three thousand nine hundred and fifty tons, along with an engine power of fifteen thousand and four hundred kilowatt, the approximate speed of the maiden voyage would be two kilo knot. Approximate registered tonnage was twenty point seven BRZ. German Lloyds regulations and supervision had been used to build the ship. Allocated class symbols were as follows Hull + 100 A 4 ELS with freeboard 2.0m Passenger ship. Engines + MC EL AUT, the construction of the ship itself used the symbols as below + Built under the supervision of Lathe ship it has been calculated to maintain buoyancy in the event of ingress of water .100 A 4 the construction of the ship complies in all respects with GL requirements. Major surveys are conducted at four yearly intervals. With freeboard 2.0m, the ship possesses greater freeboard than is laid down by regulations. For engine parts + constructed under the supervision of GLMC Engine and Electrical system are designed in accordance with GL regulations. It has EL Category 1 anti-ice stiffening of certain submerged parts of drive system and AUT Installations for automatic engine room allowing the engine room to remain unsupervised for at least eighteen hours a day.

British (Department of Trade) safety regulations as well as other regulations such as USA Coast Guard regulations are to be observed where these are relevant to the areas in which the ship was to operate. A SOLAS (Safety of Life At Sea) rule is a compilation of regulations issued by the International Maritime Organization demand that all passenger ships be divided along their length into main fire sections not exceeding forty meters in length. The six Fire sections of the Astor are demarcated by particularly well insulated steel bulkheads capable of containing any fire preventing it from spreading over the ship.

The plane landed on the Hamburg airport at seven O'clock in the morning Mauritian time, but because of the time retardation, Germany was still fast asleep as it was only four in the morning. The crew walked down to the tarmac where the ships agents were waiting to transport them by bus to Kiel HDW where the new ship had been built. In the month of January 1987 the temperature on Mauritius was about thirty three degrees centigrade and the sixteen degrees on the plane had been freezing to the Mauritian crew.

When they were hit by the cold on the tarmac they did not know what was happening as they suddenly felt as if being whipped through the bones with an icy jet. The ships agents had fortunately brought heavy black woolen coats which they distributed to the crew who were relieved to be able to get some warmth. They were directed to two long buses where they took place quickly and they were carried from Hamburg to Kiel on a four hour trip.

The heavy coat kept the upper body warm but the head and feet still felt the cold Mela was fascinated by the landscape where the snow had covered nature in white and the trees were bare of any leaves. The front seat she had taken was exposed to draughts and her toe was burning from the cold but she was oblivious to the pain as the joy surging in her whole being for having at last crossed the oceans and reached this wonderful continent.

The buses reached the Kiel HDW where the brand new ship was waiting for its crew. The crew was taken to the mess where breakfast had been set ready. Mela was very hungry and like all her compatriots was glad to have this energetic breakfast of tea coffee with bread, butter jam and cold cuts of ham. It was the first time she had come across ham and she ate some cuts to calm the hunger in her stomach.

The administrative officer Mr. Mead allocated the cabins and each one went to the room which would be their home for the next six months. When reaching C deck to look for her cabin she met Bianca who was also in search of her living quarters.

"Do you know where to find cabin 210?"

Mela looked at her keys and saw that she had been allocated this number also.

"That's wonderful, I am so glad to have you with me Mela, I was afraid to be put with some girl and not be able to adapt to her. I hope you are happy to be with me too?"

Mela was delighted to have Bianca as cabin mate as she had come to know her during the training and had grown to like her calm and gentle manners very much. She kissed Bianca and told her how nice it was to share a cabin with her. The higher grades officers 'cabins were situated at the entrance of the C-Deck while the cabin stewardess quarters was found at the far end. The cabin was luxury to Mela who used to share her four rooms house with three brothers and sister with no privacy and nothing for herself. There was a bathroom and toilet between every two cabins with a door entering from each cabin. When entering the cabin the door to the bathroom was immediately to the left, with the beds on the right. The lavabo with a cabinet above holding a compartment for each occupant stood opposite the double door wardrobe and at the end of the cabin was a long sofa and a table in front of the porthole. Mela chose the upper bed and it suited Bianca who preferred the lower one as she was afraid to fall from the high upper berth during her sleep. They started unpacking before the meeting at four with Mrs. Edith Dryburgh the ship's housekeeper. When opening her luggage, Mela was appalled to find all her clothes smelly with the pungent smell of pickles and octopus vindaloo. During the handling and the long flight and bus ride to the ship, the oil and spices from the jar of pickles and vindaloo had lost all the oily yellow mixture of spices all over her clothes. Some of her clothes were so damaged that they had to be put in the waste basket. There was a meeting with the ship's housekeeper in the auditorium on B deck for job description and rules and regulations. The twenty four cabin stewardesses filled the auditorium where the house keeper, a tall, slim woman of about fifty was looking at a pile of papers.

"Good morning girls, I am Edith Dryburgh but I will not mind being called Mrs. D. First of all let me welcome you all and congratulate you for having been chosen to be part of this great Astor adventure. This ship will carry a five star hotel and I want all my girls to become five star cabin stewardesses. I know many of you have been working in big hotels but from now on the things you have learnt must be forgotten to make place to the standards of the Astor. You will be given all the information you need to know on the ship in due time by the responsible persons, but my duty is to make you all be aware of the expectations that the management have of you all. You will be given an intensive training about the job and we want excellence from you, the passengers of the maiden voyage will be paying one million pounds sterling for three months and they will expect value for money."

Copies of the job description where the responsibilities of the cabin stewardess are stated in details were handed out cleaning of cabins and suites, service to cabins (meals and drinks, etc), cleaning of alleyways and assisting passengers at all times, including emergency drill and any extra duties assigned by their superiors.

Mela took a bath in the nice bathroom and settled on her upper berth to spend her first night on the Astor. Her sleep was disturbed by spells of itching of her hands and feet and soon she felt all her limbs numb and swollen. She was wondering what had caused this, at dinner, the food being hardly palatable to her; she had eaten almost nothing. When thinking back she found out that the culprit was the cold pork cuts that she had eaten for the first time in her life. In the middle of the night she could do nothing more than to stare at her limbs transformed into stiff reddish columns by her furious scratching. She did a secret prayer swearing never to eat any pork products again.

On Friday ninth of January the whole day was taken up by the lectures delivered by Mrs. D in the Auditorium. The stewardesses were briefed at length about the minutiae of passenger cabin cleaning, bathroom shining, pantry and alleyway maintenance and the special duties of extra cleaning and the reputedly famous polish night. The work sessions were broken up only by short breaks for lunch and tea time as only one day had been allocated to theory classes. Interesting video lectures followed, where typical dos and don'ts played by actors could be seen on the screen. This part of the lecture was appreciated as it brought many laughs even to those who could not really understand the dialogues. Mrs. D released the girls at twenty to ten at night, all were exhausted and sleepy. Back in the cabin Bianca and Mela discussed shortly about the warm things for their bare head, hands and feet that the day after they would buy out in Kiel.

They took a taxi to the shops in Kiel and Mela tried to practice her German for the first time in a real German environment. She was very happy to be able to help translate for her friends with her little German vocabulary. That night Mela could not find her cabin keys and had to wait for Bianca to enter the cabin fortunately when undressing she found the keys in her jeans small pocket. They had a cabin inspection with Mrs. D and walked around the ship until eleven thirty in the night. The senior stewardesses had been demonstrating the cleaning of the cabins. They were doing the mirrors when Birgit, suggested that using toilet paper to clean the mirror gave wonderful results. She had taken a great quantity of paper and cleaned the mirror to show the girls.

"I would not do that as the toilet paper is destined for no other purpose than to be used in the toilet for its original function. We do not want the storekeeper complaining that unusually large amounts of rolls are used by the Housekeeping staff. So please girls use your cleaning cloths and window cleaner." Mrs. D pointed out.

Engrossed in the training, nobody noticed that in the meantime the ship had sailed to Denmark. Only at night when she was in bed did Mela feel the rolling of the ship, she told Bianca "It feels so nice as if you are dancing in the arms of a powerful handsome man!"

On Sunday the cabin stewardesses started to clean the brand new cabins under the supervision of the German senior stewardesses Doris, Brigitte, Marion and Beate.

This morning Mela and Bianca get up at five thirty and get ready to have breakfast, eggs and fruit juice, tea and toast before going to work. The day uniform is a grey dress buttoned in the front with two pockets and a belt. The master keys which allow the stewardesses to open the cabins hang from the waist belt. Each cabin stewardess has her own cleaning pail with the necessary cleaning apparel for cleaning the twelve cabins under her responsibility. Today they would have to work till midnight to finish doing the cabins and Mrs. D has made it clear that absolute perfection was requisite of their cleaning. The senior stewardess of each section brought the stewardesses in their section to demonstrate the way things need to be done. They demonstrated how the beds are made by lifting the mattress to tuck the sheet squarely and cover neatly with day covers, the sofa bed made and then put back in the sofa style by manipulating the levers.

They showed how all mirrors and surfaces are cleaned and polished. Mrs. added "What about, those surfaces, they would collect dust and need to be regularly polished."

She showed the doors and porthole surfaces, the window ledges, pictures and opened the cupboard and drawers even the pugs and sockets. The curtains and blinds have to be opened and checked to remove any dust there and on the ledges.

Each day the stewardess has to clear away crockery, replace drinking water and fruits as required, all ashtrays and dustbins are to be cleaned. It is not allowed to throw anything from a cabin without the passenger's prior permission. Garbage is to be separated in three groups; items to be crushed, like bottles, those to be incinerated like paper and plastic. Linen is to be changed every three days in cabins and every two days in suites, and of course each time the sheets were soiled.

All electrical apparatus is to be checked daily to report any faults for maintenance. Water is to be changed daily in flower vases and the entire cabin is to be vacuumed and any carpet or furniture stains be cleaned or reported if unable to remove. It is vital that each cabin has one life jacket per berth. The mini bar in the suites needs daily checking for the necessary equipment, a set of glasses for the different sorts of drinks, two Brandy, two Beer, three Highballs, and three Whiskeys, four Wines and champagne as well as the stock of required free issue before arrival of the passengers. Daily supplies of ice in buckets and tongs, flask of iced water and bottle opener need to be provided. The fridge is to be defrosted and cleaned after disembarkation and glasses need to be spotless and pass the light test, with no marks or spots or cracks when held in the light. The team has to maintain absolute neatness and hygiene in their respective pantries. Dishes have to go into the dishwasher as soon as there is enough to load the machine. All garbage have to be removed before each shift, the different garbage bags to be brought to the crusher on C deck and to the incinerator on D deck. Extra cabin cleaning is necessary to keep the cabin neat and clean. Air conditioning vents and air vents on the doors, the doors to be cleaned inside and out as well as skirting boards, vacuuming under the beds and inside the divan should also regularly be done to avoid accumulation of dust. Shower curtains are to be changed as soon as it is dirty and always before taking in new passengers. Spring cleaning is to be done in all empty cabins keeping them ready for next cruise. The walls have to be cleaned of any marks and the outside of cupboard to be polished, inside the lamps as well as light and fittings are to be dusted. Mattresses are to be turned every three weeks or as directed by the senior stewardesses. The bathroom cleaning is demonstrated as the most difficult and important part of the work for a cabin stewardess is to maintain the bathroom of passenger cabins spotless in spite of all the incidents which occur and the nature of the place being for the concentration of human dirt. Mrs. D looks at the girls above her pince-nez glasses and says "Mind you girls that my bathrooms are so clean after you have been inside that one can eat his dinner in it! I want daily scrub of the shower and drying of panels and floors. The shower curtain is to be changed at the slightest spot.

The metal surfaces have to shine, the bathroom floor is to be cleaned everyday and the bathmat changed. The tooth mugs have to be thoroughly washed inside out. The toilets need to be cleaned inside and underneath and hinges to be cleaned and disinfected, the toilet brush and holder are also to be kept spotless. Do not forget to dust around the air vent and empty and clean toilet bin. Please make sure there are sufficient tissues, sanitary bags and soap. There is nothing more annoying than being seated doing your bit of business and then when finished not finding any paper on the toilet paper roll!"

On Sunday cleaning of the cabins starts and Mrs. D tells her staff that if needed they would perhaps have to work till midnight. Mela goes with Doris a very nice and beautiful German girl who had worked on the first Dream-ship and had a deep nostalgia of her first ship. She compared everything possible with her first Dream ship and kept on repeating "Of course on the first Astor things were much more beautiful, one will never revive those dream days."

Under the supervision of the senior German stewardesses, the Mauritian stewardesses clean the cabins and as soon as they have finished their section they move to other sections to help their colleagues. Mela does cabin 420 and 428 with Doris before lunch and cabins 474 and 476 after lunch. Then she goes out to help Lina in cabin 453 and Annick in cabin 500.

With this cooperation the stewardesses have finished doing all the cabins at ten thirty.

It would require considerable roaming about in this huge building before getting one's bearings on this ship. The cabin crew had only seen C deck and the auditorium on B deck since their arrival. On Monday while they were doing the training a call was heard on the loudspeaker that all the staff was to go to C deck. The provisions for the ship were being loaded and the maximum staff was required to help carry them inside on a rolling table which came from outside the ship in the containers. The crew was to assist the rolling tables by manually pushing the boxes of various articles from cleaning stuff to food and drinks inside.

Chapter II

Sailor's Feet

That winter had been one of the coldest in Germany and in Kiel HDW where Lady Astor had been built the temperature was of minus twenty seven degrees centigrade. The air stream from outside was making the temperature inside where the goods were being loaded very cold. The Mauritian crew who did not know the meaning of winter, were not equipped with either boots or gloves and had only their hair covering their heads. A difference of almost fifty degrees centigrade is indeed much for a human being who has never seen nor dreamt of snow. The German crew who were suitably dressed for the cold went on the front line while the Mauritians were placed behind them in the line for pushing the goods being loaded in the ship. Soon their hands were freezing and numb and they had to go fetch the heavy coat given to them on their arrival by the ships agent. They sang and tried to be merry by making jokes but the cold soon entered their bones and dulled their good humor. They ran for short breaks to the mess to sip a warm drink and get back to the loading. The amount of things being loaded seemed never-ending, beyond imagination. Mela and her friends wondered where all this stuff would go, how large must be the store to contain such heavy volumes of all sorts of goods, sparkling and plain mineral water, soft drinks, juices and boxes of other drinks, milk and liquor.

Juliette got into a fury as she noticed that a stewardess pretended to go for coffee breaks but disappeared for more than one hour. "Some people think that they can go and have warmth in between their legs while others are having their asses freezing. We would all be glad to also have something warm in between the legs instead of freezing our hands on those icy rollers."

On Tuesday morning after breakfast the stewardesses meet in the auditorium for putting duvets and pillows in their cases to have them ready to put in the cabins. Once more all the staff had to go to the loading station on C deck when the containers of stock arrived. The Mauritians came with all the clothes they could put under the heavy coat but it seemed the weather had anticipated their defense as it got even colder. The loading was done for the whole day with short breaks closely monitored by the superiors. It was already eleven o'clock at night when Mela and Bianca went back to their cabins. After they had removed the wardrobe they had on and showered it was already midnight.

On Wednesday morning Bianca and Mela were fast asleep when they heard knocking on their cabin door. It was Annick one of the stewardesses who had come to wake them up "It's already five past seven and everybody is already in the auditorium waiting for you Mrs. D has sent me to fetch you."

Work started at seven o'clock, not having time to take a bath they dressed up in haste and hurried to the meeting point. At ten o'clock trembling of hunger and thirst they rushed to the mess for a tea break but breakfast food had already been cleared. They had to drink some hot tea to appease their hunger until lunch time at twelve o'clock.

That night the chief utility steward Albert was celebrating his birthday by giving a party in the crew bar. The girls dressed in their beautiful clothes and made up their faces and went to enjoy it. Mela chose a beautiful black dress but found the party quite boring, she ate some of the snacks and drank a couple of canned coca cola and went back to her cabin. She went to the laundry room facing her cabin 201and washed her clothes while writing in her diary.

On Thursday after her duty doing the cabins Mela came back to her cabin, she was sweating and could not wait to refresh herself with a shower. She had already undressed and clad of her panty only she turned the handle of the bathroom to get into the shower. The occupant of the adjoining cabin 203 was using the shower and shouted "There is somebody in the shower,"

When the door opened, Mela saw Nicoleta with a towel around her "Oh it is you who are my next door neighbor; it is already four days since I moved in here and it is only now that I meet you, I am really pleased that we are so near to each other."

Nicoleta and Mela were to become the best of friends and they would tour the world and the ship and live many exciting adventures together. As Bianca was not yet back, Mela went out with Nicoleta to have dinner in the mess. There was cauliflower and roast veal on the menu; the veal was edible but the boiled cauliflower was hopelessly plain to them as due to their spicy eating habits, the absence of chili and spices made this food dull.

The year 1987 was the advent of the AIDS (Auto Immune Deficiency Syndrome) a disease which had appeared in the homosexual community of San Francisco and in parts of Africa as a result of anal intercourse between human males and with animals. It had been found that this virus could spread through sexual contact or blood and all the crew of the Astor were being tested for the disease. In Mauritius the disease was still practically unknown and people did not know its origin or meaning. The crew from Mauritius were sent to the ship's hospital for doing the AIDS 'test as in their country there was not yet any means of examining blood samples to detect the presence of the virus.

In the hospital waiting room was a poster about the AIDS disease and the various means of contracting the disease was listed. Nicoleta and Bianca who were not so well versed in written English asked Mela "What is the meaning of anal and oral sex?"

Having heard about homosexuals before she told them that anal sex was what men did to each other having intercourse through the anus, but she was puzzled at oral sex as she knew the meaning of oral as talking. She explained to them that oral sex means talking about sex.

"How can talking about sex transmit the disease?" enquired Nicoleta.

"Maybe it tempts the people to have risky sexual practices." replied Bianca.

On Friday Mela went out with Bianca and Maizie another Mauritian girl who worked as purser for a walk outside in the town of Kiel. They walked to the shops over the snow covered ground, fascinated; they kneeled down and took some snowflakes in her hands. The sensation of the freezing soft snow was special and Mela caught a few snowflakes that he popped into her mouth. Back home in the tropics, they had to wait for the 'Icecubeman' to get this freezing sensation in the mouth when he grated pieces from a big block of hard ice cube and sprinkled colored sweet syrup on it. One got all sticky and sweet after eating such an ice whereas these flakes of snow were so nice and pure with such soft melting taste.

On Saturday seventeenth of January, the ship leaves the Port of Kiel on its way to Southampton on the British coast. After dinner the whole crew meet for a party on pool deck. Mela and Nicoleta with Eva and Kristy Ann, other Mauritian girls from the purser department danced the Sega wearing orange colour Sega costumes consisting of a large skirt worn under the navel and a mini blouse tied below the breasts. The first cruise is celebrated by a nice party for the crew and officers given by the Captain Ivan Currie an Irishman of about sixty with a white moustache and serious face. The crew assembles on pool deck to watch the departure of the Astor, the very first movement of the ship with its crew. The snow is everywhere, falling heavily onto the sea and covering the sea and the ship in white. Eyes cannot leave the magnificent picture of this huge ship making its way on the frosty waters of the Kiel Canal embedded in a sky of snow, as if it was sailing on snow. The time in Southampton being one hour ahead of Kiel the clocks are put one hour forward and before going to bed, the crew is instructed to change the time on their clocks and watches to one hour later. On Sunday the alarm clocks ringing one hour before the usual time, the crew finds it hard to wake up and prepare for going to the mess for breakfast before taking duty. Tons of towels are transported from the stores on D deck to be loaded by hundreds on the trolleys and put in the lift for being stocked in the pantries. Mela is sent to deck suites to help Nicoleta in the suites 231 and 233. After that she goes one stair below on B deck to help Bianca to make the beds on the B forward deck for cabins 411, 413, 415, 417, 419 and 429 until past midnight. Both go to bed exhausted, grateful to have an extra hour to sleep as they were going back to Kiel and the clocks were to be put one hour back. That night Mela was so tired that she found it hard to sink into the sweet state of lethargy prior to fall asleep. She had been walking on the ship in the remote places which seemed to her so mysterious and creepy but could not help giving in to her curiosity. She had entered a corridor and walked inside a dark room when suddenly the door closed behind her. She found herself in complete obscurity, panicked, she tried to feel the surroundings with her hands and feet and braving her fright she stepped ahead in the dark. Suddenly her body fell in an abyss and landed in a tight spot where she found herself unable to move even a finger. It was as if she had been locked inside a coffin without any space to move. She wanted to shout to scream for help but no sound came on her lips, she was petrified and her heart was beating like a drum, so loud she could hear the sound of its beat.

A crashing noise startled her, she opened her eyes to see Bianca coming out of the bathroom and greeting her "Good morning girl, get up and get ready today we shall be having the first passengers!"

The closing of the bathroom door had saved her from that horrible nightmare where she had been locked in a coffin in utter darkness unable to budge.

At breakfast Lina was telling about her encounter with the beast of seasickness during the voyage from Kiel to Southampton.

"I have been throwing up most of the night, it was awful, my head was spinning and I felt hot flushes. I did not know what was happening to me until I heard Brigitte retch, and then I told myself, this must be the beast of seasickness."

On hearing this Mela was secretly rejoicing to think that not having felt any discomfort, it meant that she had the sailor's feet and would cruise without any worry.

The first passengers had been embarked at Southampton; they were travel agents and journalists, those who would sell the cabins to paying passengers. There were lots of television crews who had come to present the Astor to the world. For these very important trial passengers the cabins and suites had been outstandingly prepared to promote the ship to prospective rich passengers around the world. A sort of rehearsal was to be done with these passengers who had been chosen to play the part of paying passengers. At the workstation stewardesses are instructed to collect the fresh flowers delivered by the utility boys for the vases on the small glass tables in cabins and suites. After having adorned the cabins with fruit baskets and all the necessary brochures and various documents required for the mini bar, room service cabin service and laundry, the cabin stewardesses go to change for welcoming the new passengers. They have to wear the appropriate uniform with jacket, long sleeved blouse and bow tie and make up to play the part of hostesses. Mela, dressed in the cleaning uniform, a grey dress buttoned in the front and flat heeled shoes, had been running to and fro to put new items in the cabins since morning. Even though the cleaning had already been done before, she was feeling so tired when dressing up for welcoming the passengers in the high heeled black shoes and panty hose. The incessant walking to guide the passengers brought by the utility stewards to their cabins had made her feet sore. The brand new shoes were pinching at the back and in front setting her toes and ankles aflame. She smiled in front of the passengers and scowled as soon as out of their view to relieve her discomfort. That night the weariness had entered their bones and their feet burned from the all day long standing and walking. The cabin crew were glad to embrace their pillows and even the latest of the night birds were in bed leaving the crew bar almost empty. The hotel staff had all gone to bed after such a hectic and tiring day, the crew bar was unusually deserted and silent. Only the sailors and officers on the night shift came to have a drink in the bar to have a look at the female staff but this night no woman was out. Tonight the ship is sailing to Amsterdam and the clocks are advanced by sixty minutes which means getting up one hour earlier. More passengers are embarked on and the day is spent cleaning cabins and attending to pantry duties. In the evening the senior stewardesses teach their crew how to do the evening duty. After the passengers depart to have dinner in the ship's main restaurant the Waldorf, the beds need to be turned down neatly, removing and folding the day cover to reveal the immaculate sheets and pillows on which the nightshirts and pyjamas are to be placed without forgetting the chocolates on the pillows. The ashtrays have to be cleaned and the used crockery and glassware removed and replaced if needed and daily programmes and any forms put on the table. Tonight they place also on the pillow, the card which reminds the passenger to change the times on their clocks and watches to one hour earlier as the ship is going back to Southampton the time goes one hour back. In this lot of passengers Mela finds a sample of the passengers that she was to get in the cabins in the following two years. The man in cabin 308 was rarely seen and his cabin was hardly disturbed when he left. The man in cabin 316 left his cabin in absolute chaos, socks and shoes all over the place, the bathroom floor was littered and under water and the toilet not flushed after use. In 304 there was a couple with a beautiful baby, they were nice people and kept their cabin tidy. In cabin 318 was a very nice woman who was kind and friendly with Mela and talked to her asking her about her country.

The duty hours for cabin stewardesses was from seven in the morning to one in the afternoon where they had to maintain twelve passenger cabins allotted to each of them. They had a break for lunch which needed no supervision from the seniors as the stewardesses could go off only once their twelve cabins done. They all made the repast as fast as they could and some even went without lunch on days when they wanted to finish early for going ashore. In each pantry a stewardess was to stay on one to three o'clock duty to tidy the pantry. She has to pack away all dishes from the dishwasher and clean and polish all surfaces and floor. She then has to bring down the garbage bags to the crusher on C deck and the incinerator on D deck, bring up the towels, face cloths and bath mats, passenger laundry and cleaning cloth from the laundry on D deck, deliver the passenger laundry to the cabins and fill in the laundry book. Any cabins not yet done where a 'Do not disturb' sign had been placed on the door in the morning was to be done by the stewardess on this shift.

The stewardess on tea duty dressed in the evening uniforms, black skirt and white blouse and bow tie would take over from her at three for tea duty which was paid one hour overtime. As each day lavish tea buffets were set up in the different restaurants and bars on the ship, the passengers would mostly only order tea in their cabins in case they were seasick or unwell and could not stand or walk due to the unsteady floor on rough seas. During tea duty the towels are folded and placed neatly on the racks to be used in the cabins during evening duty and for next day cabin cleaning. Any bar and tea orders are to be attended to and no sandwiches are to be served between two and four thirty. Signed order forms for cabin meal service have to be sent to the galley and a copy kept for the housekeeper. General pantry cleaning is also done during tea duty, polishing of the coffee machine, urn kettle, cleaning of the fridge and polishing the glasses, cleaning the store room, tidying the linen. Any other duties assigned by the senior stewardess like collecting the stores from the provision master on C deck and preparing ice buckets at stipulated times by the passengers is also done in this time. The tea duty stewardess also had to serve early dinners after informing housekeeper and set trays for early morning tea or coffee.

Bianca and Mela spent time in their cabins when they were off duty at sea chatting from their berths until one or the other fell asleep.

On Thursday in Southampton after morning duty Mela not having any other duty before evening duty starting at six in the afternoon goes out to try and find better walking shoes as these shoes which pinched her feet had given her fever on that first day itself. Outside it was so cold that they had to enter shops every other metre to warm up before going on. Her toes were burning from the cold, even in the heat of her hometown Port-Louis under the tropics when the shot sun almost melted the coal tar on the streets had she felt this sort of burning as if her toes would explode, it hurt so much that it brought tears down her cheeks. She bought some postcards and a few dates and cakes to make up for the dull food on the ship. As soon as she got in her cabin Mela started to write on the postcards. She wrote the one showing the Hydrofoil at side of the Royal Pier Southampton for her brother. For her sister who was a great fan of lady Diana she wrote a postcard of the first official photographs of his Royal Majesty Prince Henry of Wales showing Prince Henry Charles Albert David with his mother Her Royal Majesty the Princess of Wales, she also bought a large poster of the Princess with her first son HRM Prince William. Having no time to go to the mess for dinner, she ate a few dates and went to do the evening service until nine and then went in the crew bar where she danced the Sega with her colleague Vania until one o'clock the next day.

On Friday the ship sailed towards Hamburg and after lunch Mela felt dizzy and queer, her head started to register a dull pain and soon she was hot and flushing, her stomach was overflowing in her mouth and she threw up not only the lunch she had eaten but white bitter liquid which seemed to come from the inside of her tummy. She felt the undulating movement of the ship which made her head whirl. She had to stagger, zigzagging along the alleyways to her cabin. She was wondering how she would manage to put the key in the lock to open her cabin with her trembling hands and this unsteady floor under her feet. The door was flung open with the displacement of the ship, and she found Bianca who had also been throwing up sitting inside with swollen red eyes.

That evening during the duty Mela had to help doing turn over as other cabin stewardesses could not even manage to stand up in this rough sea. The nice woman from cabin 318 was also sick and lying in bed, Mela brought her some Bosemine tea and a couple of Zwieback. This was her very first encounter with a very long series of painful spells of seasickness.

The next morning they arrived in Hamburg and the passengers left the ship thanking the crew by giving them a couple of French Francs and German Marks as tips. That evening Bianca invited her cabin mate to go out with her and boyfriend Hervey who worked in the machine rooms and a couple of other girls to the nightclub. Strolling along the streets of Hamburg at night in the famous Reeperbahn area, they could see the sex shops with beautiful girls almost nude on display.

The nightclub was packed and full of cigarette smoke, the music was deafening. Mela, who felt suffocated in this overcrowded atmosphere, was thankful when at one thirty they decided to return to their floating home. On Sunday the ship reached the port of Travemunde on the German coast, the seasickness had ceased but hard work was in store as new passengers were arriving and all the cleaning needed to be done again. Mela was having only a tummy ache, no dizziness and only very minor nausea. She was on tea duty and her period had come with its fanfare of pains and stomach cramps. On Monday she had lentils and rice with vegetable curry for lunch. Her stomach cramps got worse; from the age of thirteen she had suffered acute dysmenorrhoea, serious stomach cramps by her periods. She had yelled in pain but stoically refused to take any pain killer as the truly efficient one called Baralgin was reputed to cause sterility. As she wanted to have a lot of children she did not want to risk putting her fertility at risk. But now she found herself with no other choice as working would be impossible with this pain which had her winding in bed for hours, throwing up and breaking in cold sweats. She resigned herself to take a Baralgin tablet and in spite of having used up about six sickness bags until the evening she willed herself to go for dinner as it was chicken curry, her favourite dish on the menu.

"I shall eat the chicken curry no matter if I need to throw it up after." She ate and threw up half an hour later.

On Monday the twenty seventh of January, the German television crew was doing a shot for an advertisement on the ship. After her morning duty followed by a lunch of a delicious fish curry of which she had two servings, Mela went to enjoy a nice long sleep in her cabin before evening duty. When Bianca who had been on tea duty came to the cabin to wake her up after having had dinner, she asked in a sleepy voice "What is there for dinner?"

"It was veal meat in some sort of white sauce, as usual the plain British style!"

Mela did not feel like even looking at meat and went for evening duty where she took some milk in the pantry. At around ten the Sega band was playing in the Lido bar and they danced the Sega for a show and Mela was interviewed by the German Television.

They then went to give another show in the Astoria lounge where a big cabaret was on.

Having had no dinner she felt hungry after all this dancing, fortunately one of the girls who danced with them whose boyfriend worked in the crew mess had saved some fish for her; she shared her fish with Mela. Each morning Bianca gets up at five for her daily exercise pacing the alleyways; she wakes up Mela when returning to the cabin at six thirty. The rough seas make it difficult to move with the receding floor and everyone is praying to reach land again. On Wednesday when reaching Hamburg Mela goes ashore to phone the family back in Mauritius but nobody answers the phone there. They then go to the shops where Mela sees rolling staircase for the first time, they buy giant bottles of Nivea creams, as the cold and the air conditioned ship makes it essential to moisturise the whole body after each bath to avoid the skin becoming so dehydrated that it forms painful sores. On the last day of January almost a month since they left home, the bigger part of the Maiden voyage passengers are embarked in the port of Hamburg and the crew is on their knees with weariness after the hard work; once more the crew bar is unusually quiet, deserted of the hotel staff. On the first of February the ship leaves Hamburg to sail to Southampton in order to embark the rest of the passengers before starting on the maiden voyage. The sea is still rough and as usual Mela is sick and unable to eat, everything gives her nausea, she sees the black German bread and decides to try it, the taste is horrible, but she forces it down thinking it would do her good but like the pork cuts it does more harm than good and tonight the sickness bags are filled with the black German bread which Mela swears never to eat again.

The great day has come, day D for Lady Astor, the great day of her maiden voyage.

On Monday the second of February 1987 the Astor starts on the three months Maiden voyage from Southampton through Miami, Manaus and Abidjan to Genoa. People have crowded on shore to watch the ship sail with its colourful streamers cascading from ship to shore, while the polish band plays on and champagne flows over the sounds or rather the signs of goodbyes from friends and family. In the alleyways the loud speakers resound with the different news on the life on board, announcing meal times and informing passengers about the daily activities and night entertainment. As the ship gathers speed, the swell makes it way to stomach pits and churns the contents into bitter bile cocktails which are expelled without warning. Mela who, like many on the ship, had started feeling the seasickness, tried to brave it, and went to dinner. She had been told by her colleagues who had gone to the crew mess that there was fish on the menu and was hoping for a nice fried fish in a hot tomato and garlic chilli sauce. The huge chunk of boiled fish filet drowning in a white floury sauce was awful and after a few mouthfuls she gave up and went back to the pantry for night duty. Things were getting worse and people were getting sick, when cabin 208 asked for a bottle of Fachinger water over the phone she was relieved that it was not somebody who had been sick calling her for cleaning. Instead the passenger to whom she only brought a bottle of water for which he paid tipped her five dollars. She was feeling even worse with like a load of iron on her stomach but she made it until nine, the end of night duty. She quickly removed her uniform and tried mounting the steps to her upper berth. This was a difficult task on account of the moving ship which made her miss the steps which seemed to move away each time her trembling legs tried to step on it. She let herself on the bed, glad to have reached this haven where at least her trembling legs were resting. This was not the end of her troubles as the iron weight in her stomach was still oppressing her and she could not get any sleep and kept tossing in bed. Suddenly something shot out of her mouth and went all the way over the sheets wetting her. The sour smell of vomit was all over her face and on her berth curtains. She climbed down her berth with on trembling hands and feet and went into the adjacent bathroom to wash away the dreadful smell of vomit and get into clean things. With her relieved stomach she fell asleep at once and did not hear the alarm clock, Bianca had to shake her to wake her up. On Tuesday morning Mela gets a tip of ten dollars while bringing breakfast to cabin thirty-four. Still seasick and unable to swallow anything, she does her cabins with much difficulty and finishes at almost one o clock. She is on one to three o'clock duty and has to stay on in the pantry. Having not have time to go for lunch, she was feeling dizzy from hunger and seasickness and her gloom brought tears to her eyes. The days change but the sea remains as cruel, even the passengers in her section are down with seasickness. The lady in cabin 212 is very sick and has soiled her bed linen with vomit, which means linen change before three days and two dollars of tips. Fortunately the passenger in cabin 314 is staying in bed and only wants the bathroom done. When she goes into cabin 312 she wonders if there was a passenger there as it seems undisturbed even the bed has been done. The only evidence of a presence is the passenger's toilet things in the bathroom. Mela only had to put the day cover and do some polishing in the bathroom mirror and put the cleaning stuff in the toilet bowl.

CHAPTER III

Virgin Voyage

After three days and four nights at sea the passengers and crew especially those who had been tortured by seasickness were relieved to wake up on the ship anchored in the port of Lisbon in Portugal. The clear voice of Karin the shore excursion manager was heard over the loudspeakers, announcing the different shore excursions in five languages English, French, German, Italian and Spanish.

'Passengers for the city tour of Lisbon are requested to proceed to C deck for embarkation on the buses in fifteen minutes.'

"This is the last call for passengers going on the tour to the Castle of Queluz former summer residence of the Portuguese king."

The Tour Department coordinated the departure of the various shore excursions. Escorts from the ship accompanied the shore excursions tours guided by a local guide.

The crew went ashore as soon as their job had been completed; Mela and her friends leave after morning duty. Mela changed thirty dollars against three thousand Portuguese Pesos. She paid one thousand nine hundred and twenty five pesos for a doll and four hundred and fifty for a collection of stamps. After buying a drink she is left with a few notes and coins of pesos, she would keep that as a souvenir of Portugal.

During evening duty when the ship starts moving, Nicoleta and Mela start vomiting unable to hold even a drop of water on their stomach. They go to doctor for seasickness tablets, but these should have to be taken a few hours before sailing. He recommends them to eat zwieback and drink tonic water if they could not drink normal plain water to prevent dehydration.

The loudspeakers are announcing the excursion programme for the next day half day tours to Funchal and full day tours to other sightseeing places in Madeira. The sound of the loudspeakers is blurred by the sound of vomit in her ears as Mela uses one after the other sickness bag to relieve her churning, burning and sour stomach.

As she is on one to three o'clock duty In Madeira, she would have no time to go ashore but intends wandering outside in the port area. The only thing she wants to do after her duty is to go to bed as she is exhausted will seasickness. She does not even go on the decks to watch the land. The ship leaves Madeira to sail through the Atlantic Ocean covering the distance through the North Atlantic Ocean to the Caribbean Island of Antigua. The following seven days and eight nights at sea would be the longest and most difficult times of this cruise. Crossing the waters of the Atlantic at top speed, huge waves lap at the ships sides engulfing it in mountains of sea water crashing on the forward decks. The ship goes on a crazy ride plunging its lower decks inside the ocean, and emerging from the waves in a gigantic mist.

Passengers spend these days at sea discovering the inside of Lady Astor in her splendour of the grandest of grand hotels. They marvel at the elegant style and supreme comfort of the ship with its light and fresh general décor. Rich mahogany and colourful paintings, restful pastel colours and light woods harmonising with stronger touches of dusky pink, smoked lavender, mulberry and burnt orange are a pleasure to the eye. They take time to wander around the ship discovering this vessel which raises nine storeys above the waves. The lowest is E deck where is found the powerful machine rooms, most passengers had till now only seen the embarkation deck on C where they had entered the ship and been brought to their respective cabins. The Medical centre found on the first part of portside aft of C deck is visited by the first victims of seasickness and the passengers needing other medical assistance. Further forward, is the Fitness Centre flanked on one side with the massage and sauna and the swimming pool and Gym on the other side, then follows the Beauty salon facing the restrooms and the foyer. Staircases aft of the restrooms go up to the B deck forward foyer next to the lift. Interior cabins 500 to 516 on portside and 501 to 517 on starboard side are found On B deck forward, odd numbers on starboard and even numbers on portside. Exterior cabins with portholes 400 to 446 are situated on portside and 401 to 447on starboard, aft of the lifts is the ironing room and the Auditorium which adjoins the crew stairs from C deck which leads all the way to promenade deck. Cabins 518 to 528 on port and 517 to 529 on starboard On B deck mark the beginning of B aft. The foyer and exterior cabins 449 to 495 on starboard and 449 to 496 on portside follow further aft. Next to the foyer there is the lift forward of interior cabins 530 to 546 on port and 531 to 547 on starboard with stairs at the rear leading outside on the aft from B deck and A deck. Up on A deck the foyer is more spacious as above cabins 428 to 432 and cabins 429 to 431 the space is taken by the foyer, in the space of the next two cabins is suite 226, then cabins 224 to 200 forward and same thing opposite on starboard where suite 227 and cabins 225 to 201 are situated. Interior cabins on A deck are numbered 300 to 318 and 301 to 319, next to the lift which has in its aft the cruise office and reception inside cabins 320 to 326 and 319 to 327 on A aft are flanked by the suites 228 to 242 on port and 229 to 243 on starboard. On A aft cabins 244 and 245 stand either side of the foyer, suites 247 and 248 or cabins 248 to 270 and 249 to 271on the exterior and cabins 328 to 344and 329 to 345 on the interior. Most of the main social rooms are situated on the Promenade Deck where expansive portholes to port and starboard give panoramic views over oceans and Ports. The seven hundred and ten metre square broad and spacious central Astoria Lounge is the largest room aboard. It offers four hundred and twenty three fixed seats and a further one hundred and twenty five chairs can be brought in to comply with the requirement for all passengers to be able to take part in entertainment at the same time; it takes the whole width of the ship at the forward end. In the middle of the passenger area is found the social deck with seventy eight seats on one hundred and sixty metre square, wide glass doors lead to the promenade galleries with glass partitions showing the whole area. The lift is in its aft next to which is the foyer adjoining the library and card room. Further aft is the stairs and shopping centre followed by the Hansa Lounge, a piano bar next to galleries. Aft stairs and lift lead to the magnificent Waldorf, the main dining room, a fully equipped restaurant where daily two sittings are served for lunch and dinner and lavish midnight buffets are set for late birds. Square tables' numbers one, three and five on starboard and two, four and six on port as well as square tables for six numbers seven to thirteen and eight to fourteen before the lifts and stairs occupy the forward side. Towards the aft round tables for six numbered fifteen to twenty-seven on starboard and sixteen to twenty eight on port are situated next to the portholes with a square table for four number twenty-nine on starboard and thirty on port, the series then continues towards forward with a rectangular table for six number thirty two on port and thirty one on starboard and another set of square tables for four bearing numbers thirty four to forty two on port and thirty three to forty one on starboard. On the inside are tables for two numbers forty three to fifty one and forty four to fifty two.

In the middle stands the huge buffet; on either side are found round tables for four numbers fifty three and fifty four; six seated round tables fifty six to sixty four with sixty being a round table for four on port and fifty five to sixty three with fifty nine equally a round table for four on starboard. In front of the buffet two rectangular tables for two number sixty five and sixty six and aft of the buffet is the last series of rectangular tables for four sixty seven to seventy and the last but not least table is the huge Captains table number seventy one seating ten.

The stairs lead up one level to the sea air and sunshine on the boat deck first of a trio of sun decks. In its forward is housed the Conference centre forward of which are interior suites 100 and 102 with exterior suites 102 to 110 and 103 to 111 aft of the forward foyer are found cabins 112 to 132 and 113 to 127 giving way to the aft foyer and lift. Next on starboard side is found the night club equipped with its own bar, band and disco while the pool bar opening on the outside swimming pool is situated on port side.

Up one more flight of stairs is the bridge deck taken in the centre by the life boats and life rafts where the passengers and crew need to assemble for regular boat drills. In its forward are found the lifts and the wheelhouse and chart room while the Albany pub and children's deck are found in its aft.

Mela is getting more and more seasick and painfully finishes her work and spends most of her free time in bed, while the other crew members like her friend Nicoleta try and fight the nausea with Bacardi coke and Bianca in the arms of a sailor from the engine rooms.

She avoids the dining room as the odours of food are so repulsive to her; she uses only water for bathing unable to bear the perfume from the soap which makes her stomach heave. She always walks around the ship during duty with a couple of sickness bags in her pockets. The doctor having warned her against dehydration, she forces some bitter tonic water down her throat and tries to munch zwiebacks while working. In the evenings while they wait for the passengers to leave the cabins before night service she stands with her colleague Vania in the pantry watching the glamorous ladies and Gentlemen go to dinner.

"Mela come here quick, I have something to show you." says Vania.

Mela comes in as fast as allowed by her frail health to be caught in a wisp of a fragrance that made her run to the restrooms and throw out her zwieback and tonic. Unaware of what had happened, Vania said "Did you smell this perfume on that woman? It is called 'Poison' and costs a fortune. It is on sale in the Boutique but it would need a couple of months pay to buy it, I would die for a drop of it!"

Mela retorted "Now I understand the name, this poison has made me so sick I have hurt my throat with the nausea it gave to me, I have been throwing up until my throat bled."

The following days the passengers were particularly nice to Mela and each little thing they asked from her was lavishly rewarded by nice dollars. Mr. Wagner, the German passenger of cabin 208 who regularly tips her when asking for Fachinger water bottles orders the last six bottles of his trip and gives her thirty dollars. Mela has been practicing her German making the passengers laugh at the mistakes she made like saying 'spielen' instead of Spiegel for mirror when 'spielen' meant playing. It was great fun talking German and she had to try as most of the passengers were old people who did not speak any English. The old German lady who always says "hello hello' the only words she knows in English often talks to Mela in German giving her a chance to practice her German while at the same time, for a short time keeping her mind off the rolling ship and sea sickness. She thus learnt that on Friday thirteenth of February the weather in Germany had been ghastly and they were glad to be away from it and sailing to sunshine. They tipped her generously and regularly which was considerable motivation to work in spite of all the pain.

The ship has docked this Saturday fourteenth of February 1987, Valentine's Day in the port of the Caribbean Island of Antigua. After morning duty, Mela and her friends quickly grab some lunch as the steady anchored ship allows her and the seasickness victims to have a decent meal of rice and whatever is given in the mess. When she walks down the gangway she is delighted to see the land colourful and warm like her own Mauritius, in fact the place reminds her of a village in her country called Mahébourg, the same colourful and warm atmosphere. She selects a few one dollar notes from the dollars from her tips, and goes ashore where she buys herself a pair of shoes and coral and shells jewellery. Wandering downtown, basking in the sun she is filled by the happiness and well being she usually feels at home in the sunshine. When she comes back up the gangway and turns the circle on the board with her number from the red colour she had displayed when leaving, to the white indicating she was back, most of the circles were already white meaning most of those who had left were already back. She dressed for dinner and had another meal before going for evening duty.

Mrs. D had chosen that day when everybody was in high spirits to announce that tonight was polish night with thorough cleaning of the pantry and the equipment which would keep the stewardesses busy up till midnight. They all help cleaning and polishing, emptying the fridge and linen, shelves, washing all crockery, cutlery, glasses, cups and saucers and teapots The ice machine is emptied and cleaned and all other electrical equipment, dishwasher, coffee machine toaster are cleaned and polished Air vents are dusted and bulkheads and doors as well as alleyways and skirting boards. This night the crew goes to bed with the head and heart full of joys and the stock of sunshine from Antigua with the wonderful prospect of waking up in yet another sunny island next morning. The cruise office has spoken of the Virgin Islands of St Thomas a haven of seventeenth century pirates, now a peaceful place with beautiful mountains and woodland scenery with delightful palm-fringed beaches. They invited passengers to book for the tour to visit the underwater observatory at 'Coral World' or three hundred year old Bluebeard Tower in Charlotte Amalie.

On Sunday it is hot and sunny in the port of St Thomas where the boat drill is done with real winching off the boats from their stands getting in the life boat and doing a boat tour in the harbour which is indeed welcome by the crew. For the cabin stewardesses the drawback is that the boat drill starting at eleven in the morning considerably delays the completion of their work. It was frustrating not being able to finish the cabins early to go ashore especially as for once most of the passengers are out of the cabins. Another two days and one night at sea would get them to Nassau in the Bahamas. A festive atmosphere is in the air, forgotten are the miseries of life at sea and everyone seems taken with the infectious good humour and joy in the air at the bustling port of Nassau. The whole day and evening the cruise bureau announces departures of the shore excursions featuring the dazzling white beaches of Paradise Island and Cable beaches lined with luxury hotels or to the sizzling nightlife with spectacular and sophisticated entertainment. In Mela's heart the joys of Nassau has been multiplied by lots of letters from home brought by a new crew member from Mauritius.

On the twentieth of February the ship reaches the port of Miami, it is disembarkation day and many passengers would leave the ship leaving their cabins to other cruisers. The cabins will be freed at nine in the morning and by four in the afternoon the new passengers would be arriving. Saying farewell to the passengers brings tears to the eyes for those who have created bonds. Plenty of gifts in the form of dollars and luxury articles are given. As soon as all the passengers have left, the cabins are all stripped bare of all but the cabin fixtures to be cleaned polished and replaced. Mela is so busy working that she did not see night falling and went for a meal at eight thirty instead of her usual five thirty.

After evening duty while they are getting ready go out in Miami Mela says to Nicoleta "Wow, Miami I cannot believe I am in the town of the Television series 'Miami Vice' with the two actors I idolized!"

Mela is ready in a couple of minutes having only showered and dressed in a pair of jeans which has become too big for her and a T shirt and tied her long hair back.

She goes to the 202, Nicoleta's' cabin but her friend is still in the shower, after ten minutes she comes out enveloped in her towel looks at Mela and says "Why are you standing there like a fool go and get dressed, the night is wearing out!'

'I am ready can't you see?"

"Do you intend to go out in Miami dressed like a tramp? You better go and get something decent on you and comb that birds nest properly; I am not going to Miami with a 'Gana la cote."

The expression 'Gana la cote.' was used in Mauritius to describe people who were without town civilization and lived in the remote places on the coasts of Mauritius long ago and were almost savages. Mela knowing her friend hurried back to her cabin and chose her best outfit a black crepe raglan dress studded with coloured rhinestones forming an inverted triangle on her breasts. She only combed her hair once more and tied it up. They went out not without Nicoleta insisting that she wear some lipstick and eye shadow and let her long hair loose. It was already past nine thirty and they took a taxi with two other crew members intending to have a good time and live the scenes of 'Miami Vice' in one of the town's discos. The black taxi driver asked them if they wanted to tour the town before going to the nightclub. He takes them to at least ten nightclubs which are all desperately closed. They toured the town while anxiously watching the fare increasing on the speedometer as they sped along. After almost one hour they became restless sitting in the car and asked him to bring them to the disco. He started to preach on the evils of night life for Christians and telling them about Jesus Christ.

Nicoleta told him; 'Bring us back to the ship please."

The speedometer was already showing over fifty dollars and apart from a few backstreets they had seen practically nothing.

"But we have not been to the disco . . . ." Mela started to say. But Nicoleta told her 'Close your mouth and listen to me, can't you see this rogue is cheating us, let's get out of this bloody taxi before I lose my temper, I do not trust myself to resist slapping this hypocrite, talking about God as if he wants to save our souls by deciding our money should instead be spent on going to one closed disco after the other. I am sure he intends to have us spending the whole night in his taxi. Closed discos in the town of Miami, my ass, the son of a bitch!"

They returned on the ship relieved to be rid of the taxi driver but sad to have missed their dream of dancing in Miami. When they reach the ship Nicoleta says "You know I am really pissed off with this rogue, especially as I could not slap his black face, let's go to the crew bar and have a drink."

They were sitting with their drinks in hand and Mela said "Nicoleta why did you not beat him blue, I would have helped you, as I took so much pain getting all made up to sit in a taxi and pay for listening to a stupid and false preacher.'

'What is the matter with you, do you think I am stupid and want to get raped by the gangs of Miami which are surely friends of that rogue?"

They were discussing their ill luck when a Mauritian crew member who had had a few drinks too much came to invite them to dance. They politely refused saying they had just come back from the discos and their feet were hurting from dancing. The guy insisted and this annoyed them and they said no again. The poor man did the mistake of taking their hands to force them to get up and dance. They both turned all their frustrations on him and insulted the poor guy who had to apologise to them before they left the bar.

As soon as they were outside they both looked at each other and started laughing. They laughed till their sides hurt and tears were running down their cheeks. People going through the corridor stared at them wondering what madness had taken to them. Soon the crew would be used to seeing those two in fits of laughter.

CHAPTER IV

Dutch Curacao & French Haiti

Mela spends the twenty dollars received from Mrs Beindorf as a present for shopping in Miami. When ship sails out of Miami at four in the afternoon, it is a day at sea for Mela in every sense of the term. She wakes up at twenty to seven in the morning and barely has time to dress to take morning duty at seven. Having had only a cup of tea and a banana for breakfast, she believes that her nausea and trembling limbs is caused by hunger. She finds to her dismay that her monthly period has appeared with its contingent of symptoms from nausea to severe cramps and weakness. She goes down in her cabin and tries on the tampon which a passenger had given her but she is not able to put it inside as it hurt so much, she has to give the box of tampons to Bianca. She could not find her master keys when she tried to open the door of a cabin to do the cleaning. While she was looking for it everywhere breaking into a cold sweat, a passenger called to report that her swimming costume was missing. She went down to the laundry to look if the bath suit had gone down with the towels; fortunately the dirty linen had not yet been put into the wash machine. She had to shake a whole pile of dirty linen but fortunately she succeeded in retrieving both the bath suit and her set of keys. The going up and down the laundry and pantry enhances the severe cramps in her already sore abdomen. Sailing in the waters of the Amazon River is very hazardous due to the risk of catching malaria fever due to the dense vegetation and abundant water. Every stranger approaching these regions needs to be protected against the disease. Today is the start of the malaria prophylaxis which would give them protection in case of an attack of malaria. The bad day finally ends on a good note in the evening as her friend Lina comes to her cabin with wonderful pictures of Antigua and St Thomas that they had taken there.

Bianca the early riser, is the one to wake up Mela each day, on that morning after getting ready they both went to have breakfast in the mess. Not a sound could be heard from the corridor, they found an empty room with chairs placed upon tables and shutters still closing the kitchen entrance. They rubbed their eyes and looked at the clock; it was half past four in the morning almost two hours before the opening of the mess. They thought of lying down the sofa and try to take a nap until it was time for breakfast but decided to go for a sleep back to their cabins.

The ship anchors in the port of Port Aux Prince in Haiti at eight in the morning, the usual announcements of the shore excursion bureau filling the corridors indicate that the ship has anchored. People circulate from their cabins to the dining rooms and back getting ready to go ashore. The locals have already crowded the port area with wooden sculptures that they are selling for a couple of dollars. The sculptures represent all sorts of different objects, lithe human figurines and busts or heads and various sorts of animals. Haiti, like Mauritius, was once a French settlement, populated by African slaves who invented the Creole language when trying to speak French to their French masters. Mela delights in speaking to the natives in her native tongue the Creole, derivative of french language to the sellers; she buys a wooden sculpture representing a red fish carved on a brown plate.

A cyclonic wind blowing on the next day at sea causes the ship to rock even more. Mela, feeling queasy and hot in the face, hurries up the sundeck, sensing danger ahead. She was hoping to counter the sickness by fresh air but she slips and falls on the deck and hurt her heels. She has to go and sit quietly in the crew bar where a video on Mauritius is on show while crunchy hot samoosas, a Mauritian snack made of curried potato inside a casing of crusty pastry deep fried in oil is being passed. She cannot resist munching a couple of the hot snacks despite knowing that at sea she is only allowed zwieback and tonic. That night she throws tons of samoosas and bile and goes to bed miserable and in pain.

Curacao was a Dutch colony like Mauritius from 1634 and the influence of the Dutch colonization can be seen in the characteristic Old Dutch buildings of its Capital town Willemstad. Here, passengers are invited to try the traditional dishes of the land and to travel to the east coast to visit Cho lobo where the famous

Curacao liqueur is still produced today. They end the day visiting an old farmhouse and an aquarium with countless varieties of fishes.

Mela goes ashore with Lina, they stroll around the town to see the shops on the boulevard. After buying lots of five and ten dollar articles she realises that she has spent ninety dollars on clothes. They then find a hotel where Lina lends Mela her red and yellow striped bikini to dive in the hotel pool. They take many pictures diving in the pool with Lina's camera. The misery of seasickness is forgotten in the welcoming warmth and sunshine of this wonderful Island. Back on the ship they are immediately noticed by the sun tan which has brought a blush to their cheeks and a puff to their eyes.

The next morning the ship sees the coast of Venezuela and reaches La Guairá when passengers depart on the day excursion to the capital Caracas. Passengers can choose between a thrilling ride in the *teleferico* to reach Mt Avila seventy metres above Caracas and the visit of the Museum housed in the historical residence of *Quinta Anauco.*

During the next day at sea, Mela takes the Hoover to vacuum all her cabins and alleyway thoroughly clean. She does her one to three o'clock pantry duty, before going to dance in a Sega show with Nicoleta and her roommate Marine. While dressing for the show Nicoleta tells Mela "I have to tell you something which will make you piss with laughing."

"Tell me what it is now."

"I cannot tell you now. I shall tell you when we go for dinner"

Being curious and never missing an opportunity to laugh Mela kept on pestering Nicoleta to tell her the joke until the latter had to pinch her hard signalling her that it was about Marine who was near them right now. The band formed by boys from the Mauritian crew, wearing straw hats and tight pants falling on the knees with, long sleeved striped shirts in pink, blue, orange and green were playing typical traditional Mauritian instruments, they wore a band of the same fabric as their shirt around the head. Yvon was playing the 'ravane' which was made of dried goat skin extended tightly on a wooden circle, Dario was shaking the maravane, a square box containing dried seeds and Gael was at the electric guitar. The girls were wearing large skirts below the navel with low cut blouses tied under the breasts, the Sega outfits were made of red fabric printed with bands of white tropical flowers, and they each had a big red plastic flower in the hair. The singer was the purser Eva who wore a white Sega costume, the Mauritian population was represented on this stage with African European and Asiatic faces. Mela had to wait to be back in the cabin to satisfy her curiosity about what Nicoleta wanted to tell her.

"Do you know that when I went back to my cabin the door was locked and as I was urging to piss I banged on the door angrily? Guess what I saw when she opened the door, she was nude except for her panties. What are you doing in eve's costume? I asked her perplexed. What do you think she replied?"

"She had been undressing to go in the shower when the banging on the door had made her think there was a fire or something." Mela replied

"She told me that she had removed her clothes as there was too much dust in the cabin and she did not want her clothes to get the dust while cleaning."

Mela almost choked on her food in a fit of laughter, other crew members having dinner had to look at them wondering what had taken to them again as those two were always laughing like mad.

The port of Barbados in Bridgetown is described as a little British town similar in its English country churches and Georgian mansions, its Trafalgar square and statue of Nelson but different in its glorious climate, pink and white beaches and warm crystal clear seas.

Mela would have loved to dive in those inviting warm waters in the new yellow bath suit bought at Curacao which fits her new slim body. By putting her on the strictest of diets, zwieback and tonic, the unremitting seasickness had slimmed her body by edging all the disgraceful bulges which used to protrude from her belly and backside. Unfortunately she would only finish doing the cabins at half past two and would be too tired to afford more than a quick tour in the port area to buy a T shirt and some postcards. The malaria prophylaxis implied the swallowing of two huge Chloroquine tablets once every week at the same time. Mela had taken her first dose on the previous Sunday and tomorrow would be time for the next pair. The effects of the previous week's pills were still bothering her with a ghastly stomach pain and dizziness, a feverish state and atrocious nausea. In spite of the litres of fruit juice and milk she engulfed as soon as the ship has anchored, her pains did not subside. On Sunday after morning duty she rushed to her cabin to try and lie down after having drunk this pair of those poisonous pills. Her pain became so intense that she was unable to take even a small nap. To make things worse they were sailing towards devil islands in the most devilish of Ocean routes where many a cruise ship had had to back off.

She went to bed to try and get some relief in sleep; she soon sank in a deep sleep. Bianca had gone ashore so she was all alone and quiet in the cabin. The sleep then slowly transformed into nightmares and she was struggling with horrible monsters in her sleep. She wanted to wake up and out of this terror but did not know how to do it. She thought of doing some brusque movement which would startle her out of sleep but found it impossible to budge, not a single muscle of her body seemed to respond to her will to move. She felt panic invading her when she realised that she had become completely paralysed. She had to call someone to help her but her lips stayed completely sealed together. She heard the door opening and Bianca coming inside the cabin she tried to call her friend but she was unable to do it. She stayed there desperate and impotent while hearing the sound of water running in the lavabo and the wardrobe door opening, in a few minutes Bianca would be gone for duty and she would be left all by herself in this helpless state.

Suddenly her bed curtains opened and a hand caught hold of her shoulders to wake her up.

"Look I brought you a vanilla ice cream cone from ashore, eat it right away before it melts."

Never before had she found a cone so delicious and a touch so sweet than after this drug induced nightmarish sleep.

Mrs D scolded the girls still loafing in the mess after seven.

"Do not lag behind girls, go and make the first sitting cabins quickly as the Captain has announced very rough seas tonight."

The Waldorf restaurant was almost deserted as the ship was wildly riding the waves shaking the ship's insides; the stabilizers were powerless in this angry sea. Most of the passengers had stayed in their cabins either to avoid throwing up the bile cocktails mixing in their stomachs or falling off as it was hard to keep one's balance on earth quaking grounds. Sea wolves and those on duty were the only persons to venture out of their cabins making it to the boat deck to watch the fascinating view of the waves crashing as high as thirty metres up. Some brave people had gone to dinner and the waiter Dario took orders from the unique table which was taken in his section. When he came back carrying the plates of food on the serving tray like some acrobat in a circus he found only one person left at the table. He was wondering if all of them had gone to the restrooms at once. Then he saw what had happened, the only person at the table had thrown up on the napkin and all the other diners had gone back to their cabins leaving off dinner for a calmer day.

Most of the cabins were unavailable for turn down as most of the passengers had turned down their bed themselves to lie down. Night duty was spent doing crockery inventory, a delicate and arduous exercise given the present circumstances. Only a few Bosemine tea were brought to the cabins before night duty was over.

Astor II was no exception to the numerous cruise ships unable to reach Devil Islands in French Guyana. Once more this island which once held a notorious French prison settlement stood up to its reputation. In spite of it being a peaceful place with coconut palms and Mangroves, it seems as if the devils hiding in its unexplored jungle territory are hovering over the ship pushing it back ferociously, blowing devilish winds to prevent any ship reaching its shore. The Captain decides to visit to cancel the visit to the Devil Islands and extend one more day and night at sea on the trajectory to Macapa in Brazil. The ship is cruising south leaving the waters of the North Atlantic Ocean to cross the Equator before entering the South Atlantic Ocean on its way to the Brazil shores.

While going out on the decks to see how the surroundings of the equator Nicoleta and Marine feel a torrid heat wave. According to old marine custom practical jokes can be played during the crossing of the equator on anyone happening to be on deck at this time. The two girls had only walked a few paces along the deserted decks when a hoard of sailors appeared from nowhere. Ignorant of that custom, Nicoleta and Marine innocently went to ask them about the surroundings. They were given no time to emit a sound as the jokers suddenly attacked armed with raw eggs, dry flour and buckets of water and ice cubes.

Their heads shampooed with raw eggs and flour, drenched from head to toe by iced water they rushed to the bathrooms.

Nicoleta was so angry that she went to the administration office to report this to Mr Mead.

"What kind of sailors are you, don't you know this is a sacred custom and every joke is allowed, you should have avoided going outside decks. There have been announcements the whole of yesterday warning people of that risk."

It was a long time since both Nicoleta and Marine had stopped heeding announcements, they only remember having heard the word equator mentioned several times but they had thought it was yet another excursion being advertised.

Chapter V

Amazing Amazon

On Tuesday the third of March, Astor reaches Macapa in Brazil along the Amazon River. It had already sailed one hundred miles along the longest and largest river on the planet, measuring six thousand and four hundred kilometres long and containing an island as big as Switzerland. The people living in Macapa are authentic red Indians with the costume of painted faces and bodies. They show typical long noses and semi closed Asiatic eyes and the yellow tint of their skin makes one understand why they call the white 'pale faces'. It is fascinating to watch this land and its people; it is like being into another time, another civilization. Zodiacs driven by the sailors transport the passengers and crew who are brave enough to venture from the ship out onto the river in this treacherous jungle. Most passengers prefer watching the scenery from the portholes of promenade deck or from their cabin. The view from the portholes is kept clear on the inside by the polishing of the glass panes from stewardesses and on the outside by the sailors. Mela holds her breath watching tiny children riding precarious little wooden boats alone on this large river. The little boys and girls looked like three or four years old, her anxiety is quickly dissipated seeing them expertly managing their little boats around the entrance to C deck to take all that passengers and crew give to them. She collects as much sweets and biscuits that she has in her cabin as well as some of the clothes she can give away and to offer the people in their little boats.

Those watching the scenery from the sundeck are drenched to the bones by a huge rain shower; with so much rainfall no wonder why this river is so big! Further along the Amazon is found a slightly more civilized place called Santarem but still without such sophistication as excursions and buses. In this place the yellow waters of the Amazon mix with the green waters of the Tapajos. The passengers visit the colourful open air market and watch the people and produce of that fascinating land. The heavy muddy waters of the Amazon enhance the discomfort of those prone to seasickness and Bianca has a hard time trying to get her cabin mate out of bed.

After the tenth time shaking and calling to no avail "Wake up Mela it's time, you will be late for duty."

Tired of calling and shaking she finally takes some cold water from the lavabo and throws in Mela's face to make her wake up. After a hearty breakfast of two fried eggs and tea Mela goes to her morning duty fascinated by the sight of this majestic nature around through the large portholes in outside cabins on A deck. That day while going for Lunch Nicoleta and Mela were looking forward to a good lunch of rice and lentils on the menu.

They had already taken their rice and when asking for some lentils were told there was not any more left.

"That's not possible, we have been starving so many days, unable to swallow a thing with seasickness or unable to eat food we could not stand and today when at long last, there is something we want you tell us there is no more for us. Come Mela, let's go to tell Mrs. D!" said Nicoleta fuming with rage.

Mrs. D brought them to see the personal and administration officer Mr Mead who was busy with some papers. He was a plump man with a large face and bored expression; he looked at them through his glasses with a disgusted grimace recognizing Nicoleta as a usual trouble maker.

"There are other things to eat apart lentils, I do not understand you people, you do not eat white sauce, no red sauce, no béchamel sauce, name the sauce and you do not eat it, what sauce do you eat?"

It was not easy to tell this arrogant man that red sauce made of sweet tomato puree was horrible to their tropical palates; they wanted good tomato rougaille with plenty of onions and garlic and ginger, thyme and chillies fried in plenty of oil, not tomato soup on boiled fish.

"It is not your home here and I am afraid if you want to keep your job you need to adapt to the food and eat what is served not being mere choosy than first class passengers!"

That day Mela ate one and a half apple for lunch and wept out her frustration.

On Tuesday when the ship reached Boca do Valeria Mrs. D and the Commodore Ivan Currie went along with the passengers and crew in the zodiac to see the awesome majesty of the Amazon jungle enclosing an unspoilt beach area. They sailed through the waters across little islets with birds and animals seeming out of this world like in some fantastic film.

Little boys and girls completely naked with only colourful paintings covering their bodies were fishing and catching large fishes with their hands or with simple bamboo rods. Men and women with only leaves across the genitals were moving around while giant brightly coloured Aras were flying around in splashes of red blue yellow and green feathers. They watched, fascinated, at little habitations on tiny islands the size of a little courtyard where a single hut stood with a one animal farm, to larger islands with a farm of goat and a few chicken. Little boats stood near each habitation as their means of locomotion.

The people were chewing a white root and spitting it into a large pan with another taro root to form a fresh drink and a sort of beer when fermented. They saw farmers fertilizing the soil by burning it for planting tapioca in the jungle. Plants and roots in every imaginable shapes and sizes, twists at all angles, plaits and huge leaves in all the shades of yellow and green in the most curious shapes populated this jungle. The passengers of the zodiac had all dressed in their rain coat to be protected against the dense mass of clouds which very often rose from the intense humidity to break into flooding rainfall. Millions of animals live along the river and in the jungle but the few visible ones were a real feast for the eyes, everyone kept a religious silence as if in prayer and contemplation over the greatness of this exuberant nature let wild. Little islands had their own population of huge white Egrets and other amazingly beautiful big colourful birds. They saw a capybara, the biggest rodent on the planet, a sort of brown rat the size of a cat, huge tarantulas, hairy spiders so big they could hap a bird in their web. Giant trees the height of skyscrapers rose up to the sky where squirrel monkeys climbed in the branches with piercing screams. All the noises of this jungle life mixed with the background thunder of the powerful Amazon buzz in symphony with the rushing noise of the river. Here nothing is wasted with a complete and elaborate food chain and echo system. Any fallen fruit or leaf is used to feed an insect, a bacteria or a mushroom, by digesting all the dead they act like microscopic actors in the huge cycle which starts and ends the life of the jungle by forming nitrogen and phosphorus used to fertilise the trees. The layer of fertile soil being so thin the roots not only nourish the trees but they also provide support to prevent erosion growing in open air and acting as support. Little brightly coloured mushrooms lay on the humus and bright and shiny scarabs as beautiful as small jewels decorate the green leaves.

Inside its water which floods each year from twelve to eighteen metres submerging an area as large as Austria, the Amazon River houses fascinating underwater creatures like the pink dolphin and the Anaconda, the greatest snake in the world and other fishes bigger than a man. The creatures big and small do as they can during the flood; they swim, run or get carried away. Thus fishes swim up trees and crabs wander along branches making Mela think of the song telling the story of the reunion of the little fish who loves a little bird.

A little fish and a little bird fell tenderly in love
But how does one do when one is up in the sky
But how does one do when one is down in water
What one needs to do is to pray
That huge rain carries the sky down to the water
What one needs to do is to pray
Those huge branches shoot up to carry the water
up to the sky

The Amazonian Iguanas are the biggest in the world reaching one metres eighty and weighing thirteen kilos. In case of danger they can leave the trees and hide in the river without moving or breathing. Millions of buzzing insects hovering above the zodiacs are trying to have a taste of the blood of the strange creatures in the zodiac, a completely new taste with the aroma of alcohol, insulin and also delicious young nice blood rich in haemoglobin. The white people in the zodiac like the commodore and Mrs. D have covered themselves in mosquito repellent while white and black Mauritians brave the mosquito jungle bare of any protection. The mosquitoes seem to be impervious to any cream and they gorge on the occupants of the zodiac who start to scratch adding to this jungle décor like some variety of clothed monkeys. The interlude in the zodiac has boosted the cruisers who return in high spirits, still carrying the atmosphere of this sanctuary as a sort of long lasting blessing.

On Friday while bringing breakfast to the Lassen couple on A forward cabin 210 Mela sees the real glory of the Amazon through the spacious cabin portholes. The outside décor can only be described in one word; green, green everywhere in the majestic vegetation reflecting in the huge river. She stays open mouthed admiring the beauty while the old couple also watch her eyes enlarging with wonder. Mr. Lassen then says "Mela, you know one little bird has knocked on the porthole and brought this envelope for you. 'She heartily thanked the passengers for whom she had cared for three months and put the envelope in her pocket together with the bank notes she had received as tips from other passengers.

Some passengers would leave the ship here on Saturday to be replaced in the cabins by a new lot of cruisers. The crew members are rewarded for their good service by handsome tips which boost them to put that extra effort required to prepare for the next embarkation. It is a festive atmosphere somewhat similar to the New Year's time at home in Mauritius when all is bright and polished waiting for the new year to come. This morning in the flurry of disembarkation nobody noticed that a stewardess was missing, fortunately at around nine when the senior stewardess was filling the duty form she found out that Annick had not reported to duty. Anna who went to find her found her fast asleep and told her to hurry up as there were lots to do.

The girls did not know whether to laugh or cry when they saw her arriving dressed in her jacket and tie, her face and hair done and wearing pantyhose and high heel shoes. She had lost her bearings and was talking incoherently; the ship's administration had to arrange for her departure from the ship. The work had to be divided with an additional cabin from her section given to each stewardess. One more cabin was not an easy task especially on such a day. After having done ten cabins with twenty berths and ten bathrooms, the extra duties of embarkation day have to be carried out, flowers, champagne and keys to be placed as well as all the necessary notices and cards provided along with the folders containing all relevant information about the ship and facilities on board, one more cabin was a burden, a heavy one indeed!

The French passengers in 310, the Costa couple are all flustered as they are missing one piece of luggage. The husband is a replica of the French comedian Louis de Funes even in his way of telling them "By this heat do you imagine what it is to have to wear this heavy winter pants!"

The wife, a short round and fat lady who has tears to her bright blue eyes because they have not got all their luggage, the stewardesses try to soothe her saying "Do not worry your luggage will come"

On this a panting utility steward appeared with a large suitcase which ended the anxiety of the Costas who thankfully closed their cabin door.

That night Mrs. D congratulated the cabin crew for their efforts, they had succeeded in cleaning all the cabins on time working eight hours nonstop. The pocket of her day uniform bulging with notes Mela carries her plastic bag filled with many things left for her by the passengers, shampoo, toothpaste shower gel, make up and perfume. She only carefully puts away the money in her wardrobe and leaves the plastic bag in the cabin before quickly getting ready in the embarkation uniform to go back upstairs to welcome the new passengers. The barmen have set a big table decked with a tablecloth printed with huge tropical flowers, the two big cocktail tanks in stainless steel glitter in the sunshine standing next to a fruit and flower fountain on each side. The Mauritian flag and coat of arms is found as background and passengers can have a seat under the big Astor umbrellas to enjoy their welcome cocktail. It is eleven at night when all the passengers are already settled in their cabins when finally the crew go down to some well earned rest in their cabins.

Comfortably installed on her bed, Mela opens the envelopes and counts the money she had received as tips. She cannot believe that she has received so many ten, twenty and fifty dollar notes, and the same in German marks and French Francs. She then opens the large envelope remitted by the Lassen couple who had stayed the whole maiden cruise of three months and she finds two one hundred dollar notes as well as a letter which brings tears to her eyes.

Dear Mela

> *My wife and I want you to know how very much we appreciated all you have done for us during our long passage from Southampton to Manaus. Your ever willing service, given with such good heart and personal charm has contributed so much to making this a happy and memorable cruise for both of us. We truly appreciate the delightful manner in which you have taken care of our every need.*
>
> *Please accept the enclosed gift as a token of our appreciation. We hope you will continue to enjoy your time on board the "Astor" until you return home with—hopefully—your pockets bulging with the reward, for all the hard work you have done.*

One day we hope you will find a good hardworking, loving husband and raise a family of sweet boys and girls. Then you and the world will be a happier place.

Once again many thanks for all you have done for us. We send you our very best wishes for your future happiness.

Yours Sincerely
Lawrence & Sibell lassen

After the fever of embarkation, the routine work takes over and while working at around ten Mela is summoned to Mrs. D office.

"Miss Mela what is this? I am hearing the passenger of cabin 304 has been calling the commodore at eleven at night to complain that you have sent her second teapot which had to be filled with hot water empty. You know that we are a five star hotel and yet you send a night tea to a passenger with the second teapot supposed to contain hot water desperately empty!"

Fortunately all the passengers were not like Mrs Plummer, the British lady of 304, there was the old German lady of 210 who was such a happy and joyful person who liked Mela and each time she saw her said "Hello Hello . . ." Her name was Mrs Beindorff but when referring to her the stewardesses called her "Hello Hello".

When they had gone to visit Manaus on their free time on Friday the stewardesses had been unable to find anywhere to change their dollars into the Manaus currency. This currency called 'Cruzados' was only available on the black market; they went to a backstreet where they met a little man with a rat face and dishevelled curly hair. He proposed to change their dollars for a very high rate, ten Cruzados more per dollar than the other money changers on the black market. He rapidly took their money and exchanged it for a stack of one hundred Cruzados notes, he then urged his clients to move away quickly telling them that the cops were coming. When they were in a calmer place and looked at the money they found that the man had put several one Cruzados notes between the one hundred Cruzados notes.

Mela had bought a nice yellow dress with a shining green frog printed down the front. "Hello Hello" had seen her in that dress and told her she wanted to have her photograph in that dress. After morning duty Mela went to her cabin to be photographed, Mrs Beindorff gave her the four dollars that the dress had cost as a gift. In her nice dress Mela went up to the sundeck to have one last glimpse of Manaus before leaving it perhaps forever. After yesterday's embarkation everyone was tired but there was the boat drill to be done and after night duty the senior stewardess ordered the cleaning of the large pantry refrigerator. That Sunday night passengers and crew slept soundly gently rocked by the waters of the Amazon River to wake up on Monday back in Boca do Valeria where new passengers could discover and old passengers and crew rediscover the primeval jungle paradise providing such an ever changing spectacle.

After one night sailing, the ship stops for six hours at a place where the Rio Tapajos River flood in the Amazon in a dramatic colour clash. She sails on to Santarem for a four hour stop to visit this little port populated by Indian traders in their shallow canoes loaded with goods for sale in the local market.

Mela and Bianca are relaxed on their berths talking about the wonderful Amazon adventure they are living. An announcement asking the Mauritian crew on the entertainment committee to meet in the female lounge on C deck can be heard over the loudspeakers. Commodore Ivan Currie was due to leave in the next port and the members of the committee had requested permission from new Captain Derek Kamp to prepare celebrations to commemorate, the day Mauritius Island gained its Independence from the British on the twelfth March 1968.

It was decided to organize a Mauritian night for the crew with Mauritian food and folklore. The girls would wear the costume to dance the Sega while the guys would play the music and sing. All through the meeting the heavy waves of the Amazon under the ship causes considerable discomfort to the participants who leave the meeting room to go up the decks in order to get the fresh air and see the view while the ship crosses the river upstream to Belem. As soon as they get the first gust of fresh air and feel a little bit better it starts to rain and they have to get back to the stifling oppressive atmosphere inside the ship.

On the twelfth of March they have reached Belem and another stewardess being sick, Mrs D sends Mela to help her. While working Mela is troubled by the hair on her forehead which repeatedly gets in her face and eye. It make her have to remove it from her sight when dusting, she has to let go of the bed sheet when she makes the bed because of it. While scrubbing the bathroom with soapy hands she has to rinse her hands to take the bloody hair away again. Then, exasperated when it lashes into her eye causing a sharp pain bringing tears, she leaves everything and goes in her cabin and grabs the piece of hair falling on her forehead and cuts it close on her brow. With all the time wasted on her hair she is late to finish doing the cabins and being on afternoon three to six o'clock tea duty, she has only twenty minutes to rest. Nicoleta wakes her up at two for taking her afternoon duty shift.

"Oh my God what happened to your hair has a rat been nibbling at it?"

When she hears that Mela has been playing the hairdresser, Nicoleta says "That's nice, now that we are to present the crew show you look like a rat eaten piece, come her let me see what I can do to save the face."

This afternoon she has the responsibility to collect provisions for the pantry and at the same time she needs to fetch ingredients for the Independence party from the provision master on C deck. The provision master is an Englishman named Ronneper and his assistant is a cheerful boy of Indian origin named Ravi who comes from the North part of Mauritius.

"Come on Mela put on a good face the day is almost over and I have nice things in store for you, moreover I have been instructed to provide you with all necessities for the Independence Day party."

"Ravi, you know I feel permanently nauseous, my head throbs and I feel so dead tired, I have had less than half hour rest since I woke up at six thirty this morning. I had additional cabins to clean with Annick gone, my afternoon duty is up to six and I have a half hour dinner break before night service which will end at nine and then it is not over there is the rehearsal for the Sega dance."

As usual Ravi cheers her up with his jokes and says "For once I have the ok to provide you with everything you ask for, come on let me tell you all that is available for the party."

Ravi packs the party provisions, packets of chips and snacks and bottles of drink and packs of beer as well as flour chick peas, herbs, condiments and oil for the preparations of Mauritian snacks called 'Samoosas' and 'Gato Pimas' which he helpfully offers to carry to the crew mess for her.

PART 2

CHAPTER VI

Death Angel at Fortaleza

Belem, the Gateway to the Amazon with its interesting botanical and zoological gardens and old town and fortress is built on a delta found eighty miles from the sea. Excursions take the passengers on a cruise to Guarjaru Bay for the exotic wildlife, game reserves and buffalo ranches on the island of Majoro in the Amazon delta.

Having volunteered to prepare Gato Pima, a Mauritian cake of Indian origin made of a paste of soaked chick peas mixed with herbs and chilli which is deep fried by little spoonfuls in boiling oil. She goes to prepare her ingredients after calling the girls to come and help decorate for the party. During the party Bianca's lover who was very friendly with Mela told her "I see you have been at the hairdresser, nice cut you have there."

But Nicoleta told him "You should have seen the massacre she did to her hair before I managed to salvage the disaster." and she told him and the others all about what Mela had done to her hair and they all burst out laughing Mela joining them as well.

The photograph was taking pictures of the party, people eating drinking laughing and dancing happily. The ship's captain Ivan Currie wore a circle made of paper decorations of the four colours of the Mauritian flag and from the group of persons on the picture Nicoleta was the only other person wearing the same decoration as the captain on the head. After their crew party, Nicoleta and Mela and the dancers and musicians moved to the pool deck to perform on the late night Sega show. On the occasion of the silver jubilee of the Independence of Mauritius, the Mauritian crew had put together a show to tell the history of their little Island. Most people on the ship had not even heard of this tiny island in the Indian Ocean, many thought it was Mauritania in Africa. The crew introduced their tiny Island in the Indian Ocean to the audience through a sketch where the crew of African origin dressed or rather undressed as slaves colouring their faces with black (for those who had lightened in the process of mixing with the French colons), Dario did not need to apply any black paint on his face and body as he had retained the pure African black colour. They walked on stage with chains on their feet threatened by the whip in the hands of the entertainment officer, a white boy having only taken the white genes of his French ancestors. They then broke their chains and danced to celebrate the abolition of slavery which had happened in Mauritius on the first of February 1835. Mela and Harmon, a waiter from the restaurant staff performed an Indian dance to show the arrival of the Indian immigrants, they acted like labourers doing the harvest of sugar cane. He wore a dhoti, piece of cloth wrapped around the waist and a turban. Mela was dressed like the traditional Indian coolie woman, she wore a large skirt and a choli, small blouse worn over the navel, covered her head with the shawl, plenty of glass bangles and a large red dot on her forehead. Moving to the rhythm of Indian music, Harmon with a big knife in his right hand played the part of a labourer cutting imaginary cane which Mela pretended to pick up. The audience warmly applauded the actors who were proud of their performance.

With all this activity Mela and Nicoleta did not have any time to taste the food prepared for on this special occasion in the crew mess. So far from the homeland every Mauritian felt the bond of a nation especially on such a day. It was only a pity that such solidarity is often spoilt by community differences which tend to take over the unity of the nation when back in the country.

As usual on days at sea Mela greets the passengers walking along her alleyway on their way to the restaurant for breakfast. The gentleman of cabin 200 managing a smile despite his stroke stops to chat, resting on his walking stick he tells her as he does each day when they meet "My sweet girl why do you work so much, each time I see you, you are busy washing vacuuming and cleaning or carrying, slow down, relax and take your time, do not tire yourself so much."

Mela usually just smile back and her friend Vania then tells her "What did I tell you, do as I do, you see how I do, I work and am relaxed at the same time, and I even take time for a smoke in between duty?"

This did nothing to relieve Mela's anxiety especially after the episode with the dreadful Mrs. Plummer. Nurse Dora had told Mela that Mrs Plummer had also been calling the Commodore to report all the staff working in her section, the waiter, the barman, the purser and even the nurse and doctor. She called the doctor to her cabin at midnight and once again at two in the morning and when for the third time she called, he politely told her that he would see her at eight on the next morning in the ships hospital on C deck. She told the Commodore that she had been on the point of dying but had been refused medical assistance. She was a hypochondriac and a whiner and gave the whole ship a difficult time in spite of being a perfectly physically healthy person who ate and drank heartily.

Nicoleta told her friend "Stop fretting over that old bitch can't you see she needs a dick to calm her, there are so many sailors wanting a woman to relieve themselves, the doctor ought to prescribe plenty of them to her. I swear that her fire will be put out and she will be more relaxed and leave us alone."

On March fourteen the ship reached Fortaleza in Brazil and Mela did not see the Gentleman of cabin 200 passing in the corridor. Since he embarked in Southampton, she had on each single day chatted with him in the the morning in spite of his difficulty in elocution due to his mouth and left side distorted by a stroke. The glories of Fortaleza were being chanted over the loudspeakers by the cruise bureau exhorting the passengers not to miss the waterfront built on an old prison and the local fishermen in their 'Jangadas', crude sailing rafts made of tree trunks and the embroidery and lace for sale.

Later in the morning, the Doctor and Commodore passed the corridor and Mela thought that Mrs. Plummer was probably once more on the verge of death after another hearty breakfast.

But as usual the angel of death had not taken away the wicked but the best, she learnt from Vania that Mr. Caine the passenger of cabin 200, her nice morning date had succumbed to an ultimate third stroke in the night. This shocking news made her immensely sad and she could not help the tears falling on her cheeks.

As the ship was in the middle of nowhere without any facility to dispose of the body, the Commodore was in a dilemma as to the sending back of the corpse. Mrs Caine who was completely in shock nevertheless managed to show him a letter left by the deceased. He had expressed his wish to be incinerated on the ship and his ashes thrown in the water around the ship. The body of Mr Caine was placed in the morgue on D deck until the cremation was conducted by the ship's Captain Derek Kamp on C deck. In the assistance were only some of the staff and passengers who knew him well surrounding his wife for a short prayer before his ashes were solemnly thrown in the Amazon as per his last will.

The next day at sea the seasickness started to make its way to delicate stomachs and many like Mela had to visit the hospital. She is unable to swallow the Dramamine seasickness tablets, so the doctor prescribes a suppository to find some relief from the turmoil in her guts. She herself did not understand if the tears running down her cheeks were on account of her misery at being so sick or an emotional pain for the loss of her dear Mr. Caine. Feeling no better, she goes back to the doctor in tears, he gives her more of the suppositories and she needs to lie in her berth and can only start on her cabins at nine thirty. At noon she is still lagging with six unmade cabins. Nicoleta who has come to drag her to lunch says "Hi there, your face is like a chicken's ass leave all this and come and have some lunch before you collapse, after we have had something on her stomach I shall help you, come I feel like my stomach has sunken in my back with hunger."

Nicoleta when back from lunch helps her friends to finish her work by doing a cabin for her. Mela is touched by this gesture of a real friend who has shared her pain as she had shared her laughs; a friend in need is a friend indeed.

Salvador de Bahia was discovered by the Italian explorer Amerigo Vespucci while he was exploring the coast of an unknown continent on a small ship he found this land on the first day of November 1501, on all saints day and named it San Salvador de Bahia saviour of all saints. In this country which was once the centre of the eighteenth century slave trade, the passengers could go by ferry to Itaparica Island and the mystical folklore and spectacular churches and forts or see the 'Copeira' and 'Candomible' local equivalent of Voodoo.

After a long nap from one o'clock to four thirty in the afternoon on the firmly anchored ship, Mela feels better and quickly finishes her night duty. Mrs D comes in the corridor and decides to inspect a few cabins. She finds Vania's shower curtains appalling and tells her that it was not the way she taught to maintain it, she had to take it off and wash at the next disembarkation but in the meantime she had to brush it and remove the grime which had collected at the bottom. As for Mela she was caught not having put any bathmat in one of her cabins and Mrs D found the mirror of her bathroom was not shiny enough. The lecture she got made her wince with shame and resentment for having been caught at fault.

That night the crew explored Salvador De Bahia visiting restaurants and night clubs. Miraculously healthy and hungry again Mela sampled the food at the Barrenda restaurant and shakes her body to the song 'Holiday It' of Madonna. She went with her friends to dance the night off in a disco. Ashore on firm ground, she is herself again and always hungry, after gulping down her own burger she eats some of the cheese burger that Nicoleta is still eating after ages as she is sipping more of the Bacardi coke than munching her burger. In between dances, she then also gulps down a piece of pizza found on the plate of her friend Yvon.

Astor leaves the west American coast to cross the South Atlantic Ocean over to the shores of West Africa. For six more days passengers and crew would be shaken in all their bones as the ship rides the South Atlantic waves on its way to Lome, a port of the African country Togo. The ship's hospital staff consisted of the German doctor Hoffmann, the German nurse Heidi who was tall, thin and white as a ghost, Mauritian nurse Dora whose small size and black skin contrasted with the whiteness of Heidi and beautiful British nurse Jane.

During the trip they are kept busy giving out hundreds of Dramamine tablets and plaster to the seasick. The incessant rocking of the ship intensifying as the ship picks up speed makes many people desperately sick despite the stabilizers. The captain accelerates the pace at night when most people are safely tucked up in their berths. Those who can afford stay in bed just stay inside their cabins not daring to try standing up; they only take ginger tea and zwieback.

For those who, like Mela, need to work, there is no other alternative than struggling to walk on the unsteady floors and carrying dozens of sickness bags in their pocket. Seasickness leaves one completely dazed and confused with spinning head and trembling legs, it produces hot flushes making one sweat profusely then giving way to cold spells raising goose pimples on the skin, the pullover is continually being pulled over the head to cover and uncover the cold or hot body. Mela carries her sickness bag in one pocket while in the other she keeps zwieback which she munches and throws up in a cycle. She cannot go near the mess as the smell of food makes her even sicker. The waves in the fore of the ship rise to the boat deck and in her cabin the portholes are attached by furious waves which splash thunderously against the thick and fortunately tough glass.

Passengers on their way to the public area waver in the corridors like drunkards; some enjoy this sensation while others are terrified of the rocking fearing for their lives.

The doctor gave Mela a plaster to stick behind her ear to try and fight seasickness because she could swallow nothing, as all she took was immediately thrown back with the bile.

On the third day at sea around eleven in the morning, Mrs. D tours the pantries to find out how her girls are coping with such devilish sea. She enters the cabin Mela was trying to clean while vomiting in her sickness bag.

"Hey you are green in the face, go to the aft and get some fresh air quick you will do the work later."

Struggling against the receding floor under her feet she holds to the rails and walks all the way to the aft and meets Nicoleta who is also going for fresh air. They stagger down the stairs holding on to each other up to the heavy door leading to the B aft deck, the wind rushes at them in great gusts almost throwing them off balance. They quickly rush to throw up in the sea holding on to the railings trying to expel their very guts with loud sounds coming from their throats. Staff from each section had also been sent by their superiors on the doctor's advice to get in the fresh air to relieve the sickness. When they had thrown up the heat caused by the seasickness slowly subsided, they felt the cool icy wind raising goose pimples on their bare arms and pulled on their sweaters. They were watching the rough sea in fascination when they heard someone swearing and weeping.

"Aye Mo, Aye Mo, I am going to die I want to go home I piss on this bloody work and ship hou hou hou!!!"

They looked to where the sound was coming from and saw a young Indo Mauritian boy; working in the bakery. He was thin like a pole and was throwing his guts crying as a baby. Nicoleta and Mela revived from the fresh air and relieved of the bile in their throats got into such fits of laughter that they had to go back inside to work. During their time on the ship each time they were sick and went on B aft for fresh air they could not stop laughing as Nicoleta aped the sick boy and the repeated the big rude words he had used.

Bianca had gone for her early gym and when she came back to wake Mela she found her crying with pain down on the floor. She was having terrible stomach cramps, was sweating and her hands were cold and clammy. Bianca massaged her tummy used a gown to tie her tummy. The Maloprim tablets were due to be taken the next day and it gave stomach pains to add to the chorus of her pains.

On the Sunday a nice Greek buffet was set in the mess for the crew and at last Mela had a nice dinner. The next day she even went to dance in the cabaret farewell show and her passengers on A forward, Mr. and Mrs. Piera came to congratulate them "I have to tell you how wonderful you all are, working so hard and still giving more to us with this wonderful show, we are proud of you."

While dressing behind the scene a song was playing which went

> *"Those were the days my friend we thought they'd never end we'd sing and dance forever end of day, we led the life we chose, we'd fight and never lose, those were the days oh yeah those were the days . . ."*

She thought how appropriate this song was, for in spite of all, this time given to her on this ship would be the best part of her life.

Early on Tuesday the twenty fourth the anchor was sank in Lome, port of the West African Togo. Being on tea duty Mela was only free from one to three o clock she went down the gangway in her day uniform up the waterfront in the port area where local people were selling wooden sculptures just like in Haiti. She purchased a cute series of tiny wooden elephants in various sizes, once more after a long time the Mauritian crew heard people who like them spoke the French dialect, the Creole. Togo is one of the most prosperous of the African countries being described like the land of small miracles. Like a precious stone she glitters by the side of the sapphire waters of the Benin gulf in occidental Africa along its six hundred and fifty kilometres proving that often small is best. She is in herself a miniature Africa with a wide variety of ethnic group rich in culture and diversity representing all of the best Africa can give. The coastline with its coconut palms is similar to the beaches of the South Pacific. Green mountain slopes and picturesque valleys and undulating hills and large plateaux cover the land going into deep savannah, habitat of many wild animals.

The cruise bureau has organized a visit to the main market in Togo where all the daily trade is carried out or the fetish market where products used in Togolese religion and traditional medicine are for sale. All sorts of strange items from bird's feathers to animal skulls are displayed. The sellers exhort tourists to buy something to protect them against evil. Most people get scared just looking at the stuffed animals' head with their fixed grin showing huge sharp fangs. Some hunter passengers take this unique opportunity to buy a ferocious animals' head to show off as their prize. Further along the streets of Lome is the rue des Arts where one can find all sorts of handicrafts, wooden statues and valuable souvenirs. There is also the handicraft village where artists demonstrate their skills in batik, wood sculpting, knitting, painting and various other skills to the fascinated visitor who feel compelled to bring back home a remembrance of the land and its people. The market of the fishing port is a sight indeed with coloured pirogues selling their catch to women fishmongers. Those who take the full day excursion can visit Agbodrafo, an Old Portuguese town named Porto Seguro during Portuguese colonial times. Sitting peacefully on the shores of Togo Lake, this part of the Slave Coast, nowadays still show vestiges of this painful past in monuments like the slave house 'Woold home' and the well of the chained. The visit to Togoville, centre of animist religious practices is done by bus route around the lake or by twenty minutes by Pirogue across the lake. Devotees from all over the country converge to study this religion; dwellings of its devotees have fetishes and wooden sculptures in front of their houses. In the afternoon after lunch the tour takes its passengers back through Aneho, first centre for German administration created by Gustav Nachtingall in 1889. The Ivory Coast is reached at Abidjan where colourful local markets in the districts of Treichville and Adjamo reveal the life of this beautiful land.

CHAPTER VII

From Banjul to Dakar

Malaria prophylaxis has awful side effects, Mela who has been taking those 'Maloprim' tablets feels terrible. Her stomach is in constant pain and nausea while she works in a state of stupor with dizzy head; moreover frightening nightmares have come to populate her sleep making her wake up in cold sweats, her heart pounding with fear.

"Mela, Mela, Mela . . . ." Vania was calling her colleague and finding her vacuuming the cabin carpet unable to hear with the noise of the Hoover. Vania entered the cabin and switched off the power to be heard and said "Come and see what this 'likisorma' passenger has done."

Mela followed her anxious of what she would be seeing, but there was only a paper in Vania's hand. Puzzled Mela looked blankly at her friend. Vania then started telling her the story "My passenger was feeling unwell so I got an order form to get soup from the galley. I had brought the order form to the passenger's cabin to fill in when I remembered having forgotten to ask which soups were available tonight. During the time I was away to the galley to enquire, the passenger had already filled in the form."

"What is the problem Vania, you fill it or the passenger fills it is the same, what's the difference?" Mela replied a bit annoyed at having been interrupted in her work "That's what I also thought when I brought the completed form to the galley after they had chosen the soup they wanted, the whole staff passed the form and roared with laughter making a fool of me, just look what is written on this form. I am so angry, if only I did check it before making a fool of myself in front of all those men in the galley!"

Mela took the form and her semi conscious state turned into full wakefulness when she read what was written on the form. In the space where they should have written the order for soup was from A forward pantry to Galley which is normally filled by the stewardess they had written *from* **Banjul** *to* **Dakar** the name of the next port of calls. She burst out laughing so loudly that Vania had to tell her to stop or the passengers who were in the forward inside cabin would hear her laughing and would know she was laughing at them as she had sent another form to be filled correctly.

On Sunday another party is given for enabling the crew to socialise and have a good time. Such parties were frequently organised to provide unwinding from the very hard work which spanned seven days a week without any day off during six long months.

Mela went to hide in another stewardess's cabin so that Nicoleta would not force her to come to the party. The good sleep had refreshed her and allowed her to work with renewed strength the next day in Banjul when she was on tea duty. She cleaned cabins, made up beds washed showers and polished furniture while listening about Banjul in Gambia over the loudspeakers. The cruise bureau described the itinerary of the day excursions Abuko nature reserve under nature protection since 1968 offered its rich wildlife. Boat tours were proposed to Gambia River to see deserted red cliffs which had been once covered in lush green vegetation where innumerable exotic birds used to nest.

A bright new day was shining on Dakar in Senegal as the Astor threw its anchor and Mela was determined to spend her time off wandering in the streets of this country often called the Gateway to Africa as it is found on the western most extremity of the continent. She had heard so much about the land of the black President and Poet Leopold Sedar Songhor who was married to a white French woman. Mela had read many of his poems in her school textbooks and was eager to see the home of this great man. Some passengers went on half day bus trip to visit the vivid colourful flower market, the Cathedral where the first bishop of Senegal had lived and the huge Mosque before visiting handicraft village of Sambedioune for taking back little pieces of Senegal. The bigger spenders took the eight hour tour to see the inside of Senegal. Huge Baobab trees the size of a hut could be seen with fruits hanging which monkeys climb to grab giving the tree the name of Monkey bread tree. They watched hills made from termites and Joal and the Marigots, houses built on silt.

They went to the island of Fadiouth, a natural island accessible by the coast before walking along an eight hundred metres long bridge and returning along the coastal road after a fabulous lunch in Nianung.

Mela and Bianca strolled along the streets of Dakar visiting shops and talking in French with the local people. They went into a small prêt-à-porter garment shop where she tried a black checked black and white skirt and a white embroidered blouse. The sales girl looked at her and said "Trop Jolie." (Too beautiful), which made her change into her new outfit to stroll around. She then ate pineapple dipped in chilli and salt paste till her tongue was burning from the hot chilli and the tears in her eyes was not only physical but also tears of joy to find a place just like home with such nice and welcoming people and such sweet little pineapple, so delicious with the chilli paste just like at home.

Another day and night was required riding the high seas to reach the fabulous Tenerife island in the North Atlantic Ocean, another day of rocking, swaying and vomiting for the seasick.

On the 1st of April when the announcement claims arrival in the Port of Tenerife Canary Islands some think it is an April fool's prank being played on them as no relief is felt as usual when the ship anchors. The arrival in the port is scheduled for six in the afternoon and the whole day is spent haunted by the waves of seasickness. As soon as the ship anchors and the gangway is placed, passengers hurry ashore to feel the firm ground but they still feel the rocking as if some balancing mechanism in their ears and head had prolonged the ship's motion. Some take the excursion in the modern buses to adventure through Santa Cruz to enjoy a hot barbecue and entertainment with folklore of the Canaries while others stroll around to shop in the tax free port.

The basket of hot rolls croissants and sugary Danish pastries that Mela brings down from the galley brings sudden tears in Nicoleta's eyes.

"What is the matter love, has someone been bullying you?" Mela asked her friend but the latter denied shaking her head letting tears fall on her cheeks. They were the first to arrive at work and they were alone in the pantry. Mela puts her arms around her friend and kissing her on the cheek "You have to tell me what has happened to make you shed those tears."

After a moment Nicoleta dries her eyes and tells Mela "Seeing this basket full of fresh bread that we so often throw away the next day as nobody eats it, makes me so sad. It makes me think of my little Ray who used to ask for more bread in the morning and my mother would refuse to give him more as we had only enough for one serving, half a hundred gram loaf each."

That evening strolling along the port of Tenerife Mela and her friends felt a wave of homesickness and they entered a telephone booth to try and phone Mauritius without success. At nine thirty at night they were seated in a cafe restaurant and having their very first Spanish delight called 'paella' They feasted on this yellow rice served in a black metal dish with huge chunks of delicious chicken and coloured pepperoni and grilled tomatoes with whole red crayfishes with their whiskers protruding from the plate. That wonderful savoury dish was so tasty that it faded the memory of the rough seas. They strolled around and waited outside the latest possible for allowing digestion before embarking. The next day at sea was as miserable as the other ones and Mela did not feel the strength to undo her long hair and bother to comb through this tangles. She just tied it in a bun and went to work. Most of the passengers slept late and went to have their breakfast after nine. That day Mela received more than three hundred dollars of tips from her passengers. She only could make nine cabins out of twelve as four passengers were either sick or tired and had stayed in bed.

The route to Morocco was choppy and she had to call the nurse for the sick passengers of cabins 304 and 308. She had to take a suppository for herself as the beast was already raging inside her throwing flames of heat in her face, weakening her legs and making her break in cold sweats. Waves of nausea engulfed her stomach over spilling into her ever ready sickness bag.

The port of Casablanca appeared through the porthole when the crew woke up on the Friday morning to a calm firmly anchored ship. Another blessed thirty three hours free of that horrible sea sickness. Shore excursion buses had pulled up in the pier before the ship and were awaiting the passengers to embark on the different excursions scheduled during the stay in Morocco. Announcements calling passengers to the scheduled excursions could be heard over the loud speakers. The officers kept on calling tour participants, to visit the Royal towns of Mo, to the seven hour tour to Rabat, to the capital of Morocco and one of the four Royal towns of the country with its many cultural and historical buildings. In Casablanca passengers would visit the Hassan tower and the mausoleum of King Mohammed five, the king's palace as well as the Oudaia-Kasbah and the roman ruins of Chellah. The thirteen hour tour reached the Royal town of Marrakech after a three hour bus trip to visit the tomb of Saadier, the impressive town wall and Badia palace situated at the foot of the high Atlas. Here in one of the most important centre of Moroccan trade the colourful lively vines confers its oriental atmosphere with its people, snake charmers and musicians and typical lunch was served in an Arab restaurant offering Moroccan specialities.

The overnight tour in Morocco brought its participants to a city tour through Casablanca and drive to Marrakech for lunch in the hotel where they would spend the night before driving to a city tour of Marrakech for seeing the Djema-el-Fna. Dinner is served in a typical Arab restaurant with local folklore, on the second day after breakfast at the hotel the passengers can either relax by the pool or prolong the visit to the town before leaving for the ship after lunch.

All those who wish to go ashore do find some time to see the port and surroundings of Casablanca. The women on board go to the drugstore to buy necessities like sanitary pads or tampons and their birth control pills. Mela and her colleague are pleased to meet the people of this country, friendly as her own people back home they also speak French and have similar features and skin colour. They spend at least twenty minutes chatting with the Moroccan dispenser who seems very keen to know about Mauritius this Island whose existence she ignored till then.

Passengers and crew shuttle from the ship to the lively commercial capital of Morocco admiring the wonderful displays of flowers along the wide streets lined with impressive buildings. In the souks laden with brassware, rugs leather goods and pottery, they enjoy bargaining with the locals for buying a beautiful rug or a nice brass souvenir.

That night the sea is choppy and Mela is held back after nine on evening duty. She has to call the nurse for the passengers of cabin 304, 308 and 316 who are seasick. She is also feeling ghastly as it was Sunday, the day for taking the dreadful Maloprim Malaria Prophylaxis tablets. Starting to feel the oncoming of seasickness, she asks for a suppository from Nurse Dora. When she finally reached the cabin for a much needed rest Bianca was already snoring in bed.

The Spanish shore of Malaga was seen at ten the next day where the ship anchored for sixteen hours to allow the passengers to discover the town of Malaga, Granada and Ronda.

Guarded by the old Moorish Gibralfaro Castle the port of Malaga is the birth place of flamenco where one can listen to genuine Malagueno singing while drinking local wine.

The half day tour drives through beautiful typical places in Andalusia to see the mountain village of Mijas and visit the bullfight arena before taking the coastal road along the Costa del Sol through the beloved holiday destination of Torremolinos back to the ship.

The full day tour to Granada crosses the Sierra Nevada for two hours to reach the famous centre for Moorish culture, to visit the Alhambra and the king's chapel and loaf through the gardens of Generalife. Ronda, one of the oldest Spanish towns is reached after a beautiful ride through the mountains of Andalusia. The visit of the old town and the bullfight arena precede lunch in the posh Reina Victoria Hotel.

During the stay in Malaga, Mela has to bring tea to one of her passenger who has to stay in bed due to his asthma. She takes advantage of the steady floor to vacuum the cabins and shampoo cabin A200 which is badly stained by traces of vomit and coffee. It is already quite late when she goes ashore to see Malaga, but the ship is not leaving until two in the morning and all the passengers and crew need to be on board only one hour before embarkation. It is almost ten at night when she and Nicoleta go down the gangway to view the town of Malaga. They still have a few hours before the ship sails but they are both so tired that they decide to spend less than one hour outside. Horse carriages were standing on the town centre; they negotiated with the horse carriage owner and agreed to pay twenty dollars for a small trip around the town. They sat in the carriage and took photographs and the man drove the horses across the street to the other side of the boulevard and in less than ten minutes was back in place. The man was signalling to them to step down but Mela was trying to tell him that they had hardly done any visit. The man got into such a fit of rage when she refused to get off and started to shout and vociferate in Spanish so violently that, terrified, they both hurriedly got off the carriage. Back in the crew bar Nicoleta was relating their misadventure to the others while demonstrating how the man had shouted and vociferated using his Spanish jargon and everybody was taken by fits of laughter. When the ship sailed at two in the morning for Mahon in the Island of Minorca, Mela and Nicoleta were in bed fast asleep as the next night at sea was party time. One of the sailors Serge was having his fortieth birthday party and all the crew was invited.

One of the passengers on A forward Mrs Court of cabin 204 had also her birthday and invites her friends Mrs. Biermann in 206 and Mrs Beindorf in 210. Mrs Beindorf also known as 'Hello Hello' fetches Mela from the pantry to celebrate. They drink a glass of champagne after cutting a small birthday cake brought from the bakery ashore. Mrs. Biermann offers Mela a wonderful black evening outfit bought in Morocco. It is this dress that she wears to go to the staff party where they all have a great time dancing and enjoying the nice food.

The island of Minorca in the Mediterranean appears on Tuesday morning, this place with its historical links to Britain is much unlike the other Balearic Islands. The magnificent harbour in the capital Port Mahon is a friendly, not touristic place agreeable to browse around. Megalithic Torralba d'En Salord is one of the sightseeing's of this spring green island where delicious lobsters can be ordered in the fishing village of Fornell. Like in most of ports which they get to visit they stop to taste local food, they order Russian salad and grilled liver in one of the port restaurants. While eating they talk to Englishman who also came for his lunch and they learn that he owns one of the big yacht anchored in Mahon. As in many of the ports in the world, the taste of the food would be the only remembrance of the place that they would take back. That day, during her tea duty Mela is harassed by the Passengers of cabins 208 and 304; they call several times for insignificant reasons. They phone to ask for a clean bathmat, five minutes later they call again this time asking for ice cubes then again for a pot of tea and more towels. The ship had sailed at four in the afternoon; they were getting bored waiting for dinner time. They passed the time amusing themselves by pestering the stewardess. The ship sails further north along the Mediterranean and reaches Ajaccio in Corsica on Wednesday the eighth of April for a fourteen hours stay in the birthplace of Napoleon. The Gorges of Prunelli museum can be visited on the half day tour by bus driving through the pine forests to see olive groves and vineyards, woods and waterfalls and the ancient village of Cauro. The full day tour, Calanques de Piana drives through the calm Maquis landscape to climb up to the North Empor discovering a view over the Sagone gulf and along the coast to the eighteenth century Greek village of Cargese. After stopping for lunch in the fishing village they return to Ajaccio via the gorges of Speluca over the Sevi Pass at one thousand one hundred and one metres of altitude.

CHAPTER VIII

Mediterranean Triangles

When Mela at last succeeds to talk with her family over the phone she asks he sister 'What day is it in Mauritius?"

"What's the matter with you; it is Wednesday like everywhere else in the world, do you think you are on another planet or what?" replies her laughing sister.

The food that is mostly missed by the Mauritians on the ship is the delicious small fishes caught in the wide lagoon around the island. Their insides removed they are washed and deep fried with salt and plenty of black pepper giving out an appetizing smell. Crispy and hot there are crunched whole under the teeth and eaten with the bones, head eyes and everything, in some spicy burning hot sauce with plenty of chilli. Fish served on the ship resembled chunks of white flesh in some hopelessly plain sauce smelling awful.

The ship had anchored in the French port of Nice where one could stroll along the Promenade des Anglais.

Most of the passengers were out on the various excursions to visit the South of France.

A half day excursion drove to the mountainous villages of Eze and Saint Jean Cap Ferrat across picturesque views of fourteenth Century villages with their partially cobbled way and steps. Another one crossed the provincial landscape to visit the middle age village of St Paul de Vence with its narrow lanes and old fortress while the last one took the beautiful cornice route to Princely Monte Carlo, where lived Prince Rainer, to see the luxury villas and hotels before visiting the casinos.

The only full day tour to Cannes and St Paul de Vence drove over the coastal road via Cap Antibes and Juan Les Pins to the famous Cannes to visit a perfumery and lunch in St Paul before seeing typical middle age villages.

That evening Mela and her friends went ashore by tender boat to have dinner in a restaurant on the waterfront. They all decided to order fish small fish like at home.

"Do you have small fish?"

"You want filet of fish?"

"No, what we want are small fishes that can be eaten whole."

"Yes, we do have this sort of fish, how to you want it, spicy in a curry sauce?"

The whole table ordered the fish and were salivating in anticipation to eat the head and bones in a nice spicy hot fish curry. When the meal arrived on their table they looked at each other puzzled. There was a plate with a yellow sauce but no fish to be seen, they called the waiter to ask him if the fish was to be brought after. He then took a serving spoon and showed them the myriads of fishes in the sauce. Not small fishes but tiny fishes that looked just like Cabots, the larvae from frogs that they used to see back home in dirty canals on rainy days. They had to pay ninety francs, the equivalent of five hundred Mauritian rupees, an enormous sum of money and none of them could eat even a spoonful of this dish. They simply could not bring themselves to eat those tiny creatures, it reminded them too much used waters in dirty canals on rainy days. The waiter was puzzled to see the dish of delicious bichique untouched. People from Reunion Island which is found at half an hour flight from Mauritius are crazy about this sort of fish a delicacy but for Mauritians it looks as repulsive as frog's larvae. That night when the ship left Nice at midnight, Nicoleta, Bianca and Mela and all those present at that famous dinner were still laughing their heads off at their misadventure. Tomorrow in Genoa would be the end of the fantastic sixty nine days maiden voyage, and many passengers who had taken the full cruise would leave the Astor.

Mrs Beindorf the old German lady known as 'Hello Hello' by the stewardesses said goodbye by embracing Mela bringing tears to her eyes. She told Mela that she would have lots of children on the next cruise. Stewardesses and waiters were generously rewarded and wished good seas ahead by happy and grateful passengers

The fourteen cabins in her section having been vacated on Friday, Mela had already done the stripping and cleaning and washing and polishing during the whole day until four thirty in the afternoon. During evening duty, as all her cabins were empty she stayed in the pantry to fold towels. On Saturday when the rest of the passengers were leaving, Mela was sent to help those who still had many cabins to clean.

Mela wearing her embarkation uniform, a white shirt with black bow tie, black skirt, panty hose and shoes and grey jacket with silver buttons goes outside on the rain drenched decks. She moved cautiously to avoid falling on the slippery deck to have her picture taken next to the Astor welcome board. It is wooden board with the orange Astor Life buoy, on the upper square is a Mauritian and ships company flag over the word 'ASTOR' is written the sailing information, the port the ship in anchored in, the time of sailing and the name of the next port of call.

Astor has anchored in Civitavecchia, the eternal city of Rome along the Mediterranean. Having lost her luggage, the passenger in 208 stays in bed feeling depressed. She is not able to go out to see the Eternal city or to participate in the exploration of the glories of this ancient Capital. The full day excursion offers a tour around this holy city to see the great monuments like the Coliseum, to visit the exclusive boutiques of via Veneto and the Spanish steps where the Romans used to see the world pass by. The fabulous treasures of the Vatican, like Michelangelo's ceiling in the Sistine chapel are to be viewed and a coin kept handy to throw in the Trevi fountain. After lunch in a typical Roman restaurant they continue to discover other seeing worth places like the Saint Peters square and the dome.

During the next two days the ship cruises south down the Mediterranean sea close to the volcanic island of Stromboli, further south through the straits of Messina between Italy and Sicily. The great cone on Stromboli still wreathed in smoke looks like a huge black ice cream cone with smoke coming out of its cream on top viewed from the ship's deck.

The Aegean islands dotted with picturesque villages make a tawny patchwork on the glittering blue of the sea, offering magnificent views from the decks for photos and videos. Mela has got lots of children in her section as the ship has embarked more than one hundred children and teenagers aboard in Genoa. She practises her German with two little German girls named Veronica and Fanny who spend lots of time talking to her while she works. During her time off she goes to play with them to the children's room on sundeck.

The passenger of 314 is an Irish man who gives a hard time to his wife with his abusive drinking. Mela regularly has to deliver orders of duty free liquor to his cabin. The woman has told Mela how worried she is about him as he is very sick and his children have paid this cruise for him as he had worked so hard in the coal mines in his young days.

The little girls Veronica and Fanny see the old man walking in the corridors in his pyjamas. They come giggling to the pantry to tell Mela about it.

"What can I do for you?" Mela asks him while bringing him back to his cabin.

His wife coming from the bathroom then told Mela that he had gone out while she was in the shower.

"You know what I want? I shall tell you what I want . . . ."

But before he had the time to express his wishes the woman told Mela.

"You can leave now I shall take care of him, do not worry."

When meeting couples who told her they were celebrating their wedding anniversary Mela used to ask for how many years they had been married. There had often been very old couples in their eighties like the Lassen couple who had been celebrating their diamond jubilee, sixty years of marriage during the maiden voyage. Asking the question to an Irish couple who seemed to be nearly ninety years old she was astounded when the lady replied "Three months only, in fact this is our honeymoon cruise."

She then explained "We used to be two couples and have been travelling together for years until five years ago each of our spouses died. We have decided to marry to keep each other company."

That evening a mass was celebrated in the conference centre on A deck and all the Catholics on board were immensely happy to attend mass after such a long time and be able to have holy communion during lent and the holy week.

Entertainment kindly offered by the entertainment staff followed in the Astoria lounge as gratitude for the crew's friendly service. Yvon, a waiter from Mauritius performed a dance on the famous singer Madonna's song called 'San Pedro'. He dressed as Madonna; his chorus girls were Mela, Mylene and Lizzy. Mela wore a yellow strapless gown that she had bought in Rhodes, the skirt made of three layers of material stitched by gold piping fell below the knees, and she had let her long hair loose. Nelly with her short haircut wore a satin skirt of old pink colour over strapless black top and black leggings. Her afro hair crowning her head, Liza had on a red strapless top with a balloon blue nuanced skirt. The three girls danced on their high heeled classic black shoes while singing along. The whole lounge applauded when Yvon removed his panties and threw it to the crowd aping Madonna in one of her concerts.

The magicians and dancers and the Polish band performed to the enthusiastic audience who applauded ardently. Then there was the famous singer Nita Doval, who sang in twenty eight languages and spoke fourteen languages. She sang tubes like '*don't cry for me Argentina*', songs of Edith Piaf like '*Rien de rien, Non, je ne regrette rien*' and a lot of other songs taken on in choir by the audience.

"You have been the most fantastic of my audiences since I am on this ship therefore it is my wish to thank you all for your care and friendliness. To you, each and every one of the staff, you who have been so kind to me and specially to Collen my personal waiter who has taught me some Creole words, I would like to express my warmest thanks and my appreciation of your kindness which has made my stay on this ship so memorable.

Please be lenient of my pronunciation as it is the first time I talk Creole in front of such an audience with one hundred and fifty pairs of Mauritian ears."

All the Mauritians strained his ears to listen and try to understand her message in Creole. She took the mike off the stand and shouted "***Bouss liki tou dimunn!***"

There was a roar of laughter which lasted for a good ten minutes with many Mauritians falling off their seats and holding their ribs in pain, tears of glee were running down their cheeks. Collen had taught her to say something as rude as 'All of you, go fuck yourselves' in the Creole language.

They sailed Northwards from Crete to stop in Rhodes where people could go ashore on excursions or simply stroll along to the friendly tavernas and fine beaches. The morning excursion was announced, it would drive along the east coast to visit the famous Acropolis. This reminded Mela of the song of Mireille Matthieu, a French singer of the seventies entitled *'Acropolis Adieu Adieu l'amour'* which her young sister used to sing.

The evening excursion went to Filerimos along the North west coast to see the middle age cloisters of Johanniter-Ritter and Antique Jalysos. Leaving Rhodes in the North, the ship follows a south easterly trajectory for another day at sea to cross over to the Port of Ashdod in Israel. It then moves in a northerly direction along the coast north to Haifa and finally draws a south-westerly line to reach Heraklion in Crete at the south of Rhodes. In its wake are formed two triangles meeting heads in the middle of the Mediterranean between Rhodes and Ashdod North to South and between Heraklion in Crete and Haifa east to west, the base of the eastern triangle being the route from Ashdod to Haifa in Israel and the base of the western triangle being the way from Rhodes to Heraklion.

One of the stewardesses, Paree has a cousin who had married a Greek met on Mauritius while she worked in the hotel where he had stayed. The couple had come to see their cousin and visit the ship. They had invited Paree and her friends to have dinner at their house in

Rhodes. Paree had invited Nicoleta with whom she used to drink beer and Bacardi rum in the crew bar and Nicoleta had invited her friend Mela. They all dress up to go for this dinner in Greece with the new pieces that they had bought in Casablanca; Mela wears a black outfit, black trousers and top embroidered with gold threads in the front while Paree and Nicoleta have put their sexy leather miniskirts and high heeled boots with beautiful glittering tops.

The ship is moving east one hour ahead in the time zone to Israel causing the clocks to be advanced by one hour. When the little alarm clock bought from the ship's boutique which each crew member keeps on the lamp above the berth mercilessly wakes them from a blissful sleep they feel like murdering it.

Astor has reached the Holy land of Israel and where loudspeakers direct the passengers to the excursion buses. Air conditioned luxury coaches would take people on excursions to old Jerusalem where the first stop is at Ashdod in the south Mediterranean. They would walk in the steps of the Lord Jesus himself, seeing and walking in places where Jesus was born and where he had preached and had died. This cruise would be the highlight of their lives for the group of two hundred Catholics Germans from Bavaria and the black forest, who had embarked on this Easter cruise to Holy land accompanied by two priests. Fifteen hours in Haifa was programmed for them to live in places straight from the bible during the tours. Italian French and English groups of passengers, families, clubs or friends and colleagues had met for living this lent and Easter of 1987 together; they would walk in the steps and places they had heard of each Sunday at mass.

Today it was time to change the linen in the cabins and the stewardesses were very busy with full ship. The ship had arrived at seven in the morning and was not to leave until ten at night. While the cruise bureau emitted incessant announcements calling passengers for the tours, Mela, who was looking through the portholes on A deck saw the passengers going to join their waiting buses. The tour drives to Jerusalem through the venerable western wall, Via Dolorosa, the dome of the rock and church of the Holy Sepulchre with lunch in Bethlehem before coming back to Ashdod through modern Jerusalem.

Mela would have given anything to also be able to see Jerusalem on holy Friday and but she had to wait for her duty to be over as she was on one to three o'clock duty. She hurriedly changed and joined a group to go to Jerusalem as soon as she was off duty. Exhausted after last night show and laugh and this morning's heavy chores she sank in a blissful sleep in the taxi on the one hour drive as from the harbour. Happy of this unbelievable chance they had to walk the Via Dolorosa on holy Friday, they thanked the lord for this marvel in their lives. On the return journey Mela was fully awake and filled her eyes with the magnificent views of Old Jerusalem while anxiously glancing at her watch, it was nearing six time to take evening duty. They managed in arriving on the ship at quarter past six and quickly getting in their uniforms and reach the pantry where they nibbled at some fruits and biscuits as they did not have time for dinner. Fortunately for Mela many of her rich passengers on A deck forward had gone on the three day tour. The passengers on the B deck took the full day tours keeping their rooms on Astor for the night; in the evenings there were much cleaning to be done in the bathrooms as most of the passengers had to wash off the dirt brought from the dusty roads.

The next two evenings would follow the same pattern as the excursions were to repeat themselves during three days. Those having taken the full three day excursion would be going to most places straight from the bible. On the first day the visit started with Masada by bus to the fort of King Herod who had asked the shepherds to go and enquire of the birth of the new leader of Israel in Bethlehem. The shepherds following the eastern star until it stood still over the place where they found the Lord and his mother the Holy Virgin Mary. They then fell down on their knees to worship him and opened their stores of treasures to offer him gifts of gold and frankincense and myrrh. They had gone back using another route carefully avoiding King Herod as they had received a warning in dream that Herod wanted to kill the baby.

After Masada the excursion continued to the Dead Sea of Galilee where the people could dive and enjoy the amazing sensation of floating in this sea so concentrated in salt that sinking is impossible in its waters. In Qumran they visit a cave which had been first discovered in 1947 and go to see the world's oldest town in Jericho. The first day would end by dinner and overnight in a hotel in Jerusalem, on the second day after breakfast the tour continues to the holy town of Jerusalem, the western wall, place of the temple and dome of the rock, Via Dolorosa and church of the Holy Sepulchre. After visiting an oriental bazaar the tour drives to Olberg and Gethsemane garden and stops for lunch in Bethlehem before ending with the visit

Christ birthplace, the church of the nativity. The third day brings the people to visit the town of Haifa and the Baha'i shrine in the Persian garden on over to the Panoramic roads to the old tower at the crossroad town of Akko. The tour then goes further North of Israel to Nazareth over Tiberia to the lake of Genezareth and return to Haifa over Tabgha and Capharnaum. This tour worth two hundred and seventy German marks around fourteen thousand rupees was the equivalent of about five months of an assistant cabin stewardess salary.

Easter Saturday was easy for Mela as most of her passengers were on the three day tour and the previous day cleaning had remained intact. She does some more polishing and vacuuming in the vacant cabins during morning duty. The ship is to stay during forty hours in Haifa allowing plenty of time to see around while waiting for the people gone on the three day excursion. Today Mela goes through to Nazareth and Galilee at leisure; she blesses the Lord for this wonder in her life and asks for health and courage in her prayers. She writes her secret wishes on a little paper that she squeezes in between the rocks of the venerable western wall, in between the rocks where thousands of people had stuffed a secret letter written to God.

On Easter Sunday the crew feasts on Easter dishes with Mauritian and oriental sauce, an oriental dish made of mutton meat marinated in yoghurt and oriental herbs and spices. Mela and her friends use up the energy spared by not having the passengers for two days by climbing up the steps in Haifa's uphill roads.

Easter Monday at sea, the passenger of cabin number 208 enters his cabin as Mela is changing the sheets. She makes a move to leave the cabin but he says "Never mind I shall not stay very long you can go on with your work."

While she changed the sheets he talked to her about the prospects of working in America and gives her a book as he learns she enjoys reading. In spite of the interesting conversation Mela has to say goodbye to get on with the many cabins she has to clean.

Tuesday morning after a peaceful day at sea the Astor said good morning to the port of Heraklion in Crete to stay for eleven hours. Passengers went out on the daytrips to visit Greece. The half day tour went to Knossos, visiting the elaborate palace of king Minos and the unique museum. In this museum where are displayed cultural objects from the Minos era and one can see the labyrinth where Theseus fought the bull headed Minotaur?

One of the full day excursions went to Phaestos to the south coast over Gortys and AghiaTriada to visit the second biggest palace of this historical island and to the fishing village of Matala to have a Greek lunch in a tavern on the beach. The other full day trip drove over Malia to the east coast along the famous windmills and picturesque Mirabelle bay to visit the oldest church of Crete and the harbour.

Nicoleta and Mela go out during their time off to see the museum where Mela bought a delicious little wooden sort of harp or guitar which played delicious notes of Greek music when a little key was turned. On the way back, they were eating oranges, the juice running down their chins when suddenly they stopped. In front of them, on the way towards the ship an aeroplane was passing over the ship while a passenger was filming the scene of the reunion of sea and air transport.

Katokolon is the Greek Island also known as Olympia the stadium where the first Olympic Games were held three thousand years back and where the Olympic flame is still lit every four years. The Astor reaches the port at ten in the morning and leaves at six in the evening allowing a five hour excursion bus to this historic place.

Mela while chatting with the young man, passenger of 210 who seems very keen to talk to her, tells him about that night's crew show when she will perform with the Sega show.

Near to the show time she looks for Nicoleta everywhere before going to get ready for the performance. She is anxious as she cannot find her friend and the time for the show is approaching. After going to look for her in the crew bar she comes back to the stewardess quarters without Nicoleta. She was about to give up the performance when Vania's cabin door opened and Nicoleta came out of it.

They hurriedly dressed and put the big plastic flower clip in their hair to go to join the band in the Astoria. The band was composed of the sailors John, Sylvio, Mario and Eddy and Pascale, Maureen and Clarita. The Astoria was full; the passengers in their evening suits were seated in the comfortable chairs waiting for the show to begin.

Eva the Mauritian purser and Laval the sailor sang in the microphone while the dancers swayed their hips on tiptoe and waved their large skirts moving in rhythm with the strong quick beat of the Sega. The passengers were fascinated by the dancers swinging their bodies, balancing on the tip of their toes while moving their hips in circular motions and lowering their bodies to the ground where they went down on their knees and bent their upper body backwards until their head lied flat on the floor with their hands describing rhythmic movements in the air above their head. Mela blushed when she saw the passenger of 208 come in front to take her picture.

Chapter IX

Turkish Delights

The Captain's cocktail party and farewell dinner occurs on the last night of every cruise, it is also the day when the crew are given their rewards by the passengers. Mela is very angry when her passenger of 304 tells her that he has left her fifty dollars with Vania. She knows it is useless to ask for her money as Vania had the bad reputation for pocketing tips belonging to others from credulous passengers and fiercely denying having done so.

When Nicoleta hears of this, she is outraged and says "I told you to be careful with that scoundrel, like a fat like a hen she masticates peanuts all day long as if she about to lay some giant egg. When I told you she cannot be trusted you did not believe me, it serves you right to be her victim. She claims to be vegetarian, I wonder why, as she is no Hindu to be vegetarian for religious reasons. People of her type would be more likely to be vegetarian, for doing some sort of black magic or voodoo. I cannot stand seeing her waste food in the mess, taking two eggs in spite of not eating the yolk and then throwing away the whites as well. I have experienced poverty having had only bread and water to feed my children on some days and I hate people wasting food like that."

Fortunately all passengers are not as stupid as the one in cabin 304 and Mela is comforted to receive her tips personally from all her other passengers. While she is cleaning the cabin of the young man in 208, he comes in and talks to her offering her some vitamin that he takes but Mela tells him that she is unable to even drink water when the sea is rough like tonight. He then confided in her saying that his sister is in cabin 206 and that he himself had been a waiter on board the cruise ship, the Canberra.

The young woman in twenty-six is the contrary of her brother as her cabin is a complete mess while his cabin is always neat and tidy. Clothes and shoes and make up litter her furniture and the bathroom is always wet and muddy with the various make up she uses. She is tiny and beautiful, fine featured and soft skinned while he is big with rough features, if he did not tell she would never had imagined them as relatives, even less as brother and sister. The passengers are saying their thanks and bidding farewell while the ship has docked in Venice, the famous Italian dream city which Mela only knew from books and films.

The disembarkation duties are so hectic that from eight in the morning to nine in the evening there is not even time to glance through the portholes. Tender boats shuttle to the mainland bringing departing passengers to catch their transport, bus, plane or train back home. It is also time for some members of the crew to go on leave the senior stewardess of A forward pantry sector,

Marion and that of boat deck, Martina are going as well as the Mauritian stewardesses Marine Ida, Anita and Vania. Mela has to hurry up as all those cabins have to be stripped bare and thoroughly washed, polished, vacuumed and made ready to welcome the next passengers with all the required amenities of a five star hotel room. Mela like many of her colleagues do not even bother to go down to the mess for meals, they just nibble at biscuits and drink milk from the pantry to be able to finish on time and get into their embarkation uniforms, jacket and tie, high heel shoes and make up to smile and welcome the arriving passengers at five in the afternoon.

With the noise of the vacuum cleaner and the water in the bathrooms Mela did not even hear the excursions to Venice being announced on the loud speakers. The half day city tour on foot over the bridges and lanes to Markus place to visit the beautiful Mosaic dome and the Dogues castle. On the full day tour which starts with the visit of Markus place and continues with a boat trip in the lagoon to Maurano Island with its world famous glass pockets on to the nice beaches of Venice, to end by visiting the Lido and the fascinating inner city.

That night a new German stewardess called Trudy and a girl from Mauritius called Francesca who lived near Mela's home had arrived. Francesca and Mela knew each other by sight having met before at church back home but they had never spoken to each other. Francesca felt reassured to find someone she knew so far away in the wide world. She had come to replace Vania and expressed her anxiety of not being able to handle the workload.

"Don't you worry, you have been used to work in a factory, and this work is easier and more agreeable by far, there is no supervisor behind your back to harass you. You only have to do your work as required and everything will work out fine. Your sector is next to mine, if you have any doubts you can call me, I shall be here to guide you."

During the first week Mela helped Francesca with her work and did not go off duty until all of her cabins were done. She got fresh news from back home and they gossiped about common acquaintances. Francesca told the other girls who had come in her batch how helpful and kind Mela was to her. Some of them did not have this luck and had a rough time with stewardesses who were offensive and surly to them. After night duty most of the crew, avid of news from homeland went to the crew bar but Mela having got her share of it went straight to her cabin, kicked off her high heels to get into bed. She is too worn out to do anything else than leaf through the numerous magazines and books left by the departing passengers.

The four girls who had come to replace the stewardesses gone on vacation had adjacent cabins and they all slept in one cabin, two on each berth. They were a happy lot Francesca and Nelly, Marina and Paton, they sang beautiful songs at night and Mela enjoyed listening to them while doing her laundry next to their cabins. Those were the happy days where like four sisters they did everything together and shared everything, one of them doing the laundry for all four.

"Don't you find it cute the way they are, doing everything together like real sisters?" Mela told Nicoleta

But Nicoleta knew better about people psychology and the strange mentality of the female human race said "I do not find it right living like that like sardines in a box without privacy. Did you not hear Mrs D when she said that we should keep our privacy as it would be the only thing that would be really ours here and that we should never allow friendship or whatever takes it away from us as it can make our life a hell once we lose it? Let me tell you the way they are living is not right, can you see both of us are we not friends and it is not for this that I have to live with you ? It does not look good and you will see nothing good is going to come out of that?"

Mela found this foursome so cute, they were trying to cheer up Nelly who did not stop crying, grieving for her fiancé that she had left back home.

Like the whole crew, Mela, had also been briefed on the dangers of fire which would be the only thing able to sink the ship. The Astor had been designed to float even if a catastrophe similar to that which had caused the sinking of the Titanic; a collision with a glacier broke it in two. The Chief security officer had stressed that the crew should be on the lookout for any fire and report anything suspect at once.

She was coming down to her cabin one afternoon after duty when her oversensitive nostrils caught a strong odour of burning. She went all around her living quarters, in the laundry and in every nook and cranny to find out where this odour was coming from. The smell was alarmingly strong but everything seemed perfectly normal around, she decided to report the case to the chief security officer, Mr Reed. Also known as 'the sheriff', he was a tall and lean Englishman with shaven head on a very stern face; he followed Mela and also started a thorough search to find the source of an eventual fire. As he too could not find anything, he started knocking on the cabin doors to check inside. He apologetically woke some people from their rest and politely asked them to check if anything was burning. No discrepancy was signalled until they reached the cabin of the foursome, the odour intensified as soon as their door was opened. In a very untidy cabin with clothes and shoes all over the place, the four girls were working on each other's hair, this strong burning smell emanated from hair straightening chemicals bountifully applied to four heads.

Mr. Reed shook his head at Mela "Tell me, miss, have you never been to a hairdresser and smelt the odour of hair straightening product?"

On the 25th was a day at sea before a series of daily waking up in a new port and a new land. On the twenty sixth the new passengers visit the Olympia on the slopes of the Olympus, birthplace of the Olympic Games with its trees columns and ancient temples of which the magnificent ruins of the temple of Zeus where once stood the statue of Phidas and the temple of Hera.

The next day in Athens, twenty four hours are available for seeing the famous Acropolis majestic monument to former glories offering a superb viewpoint above the modern city where the Archaeological museum is a feast to any History fanatic. The swarming alleyways of the Plaka allow souvenir hunters to bargain for best buys. The whole night is available to spend in the sparkling centre for the city's exciting night life. Two half day tours are proposed, one which travels by bus to Cap Sunion over the picturesque harbor along the coastal road. It goes to one of the wonders of the world, the famous Poseidon temple where passengers can enjoy either a sunrise or a sunset depending on the departure time of the tour and then see the Mormon temple. The other tour goes to Plakka the oldest part of Athens where is found the picturesque Labyrinth from antique ruins, to Byzantine churches and to enjoy typical Greek folklore in a Tavern.

The ship leaves Athens at eight in the morning on the twenty eighth, for one day and one night at sea to reach Istanbul in Turkey. Two full days and a couple of two day tours are available for the passengers to discover this fabulous place. The seven hours day tour goes to the Dolmabahche palace, unique summer residence of the Ottoman Sultan. Crossing over the Bosporus Bridge it goes to the Asian and Skutari part of the town past wooden houses for a Turkish tea before returning to Europe over the Bosporus Bridge to visit a silk tapestry factory. These are some of the most fabulous sights of the world and 'Turkish Delights' could have been an appropriate title for excursions in Turkey.

The full day bus trip to Hagia visits one of the biggest churches in the World with its huge cupola and lavish mosaics. The splendid awe inspiring Mosque of Suleiman, and the splendid blue Mosque loaded with treasures plunge the visitor in the calm and serenity of ancient times. After seeing the Topkapi once the sultans' harem and now a glittering museum, the pace accelerates and the day ends with the crowded bustling bazaar longing labyrinths and rooftops to bargain for splendid silverware and exquisite carpets.

One of the two day tours with overnight stay in Turkey goes over the Bosporus Bridge to Kartal where the bus crosses over to Yalova and resumes its drive to reach Bursa. The green Mosque with its twenty cupolas, once an advanced theological school nowadays an archaeological museum is seen after lunch. In the evening a sumptuous Turkish buffet in the hotel is followed by a fabulous Folklore show of oriental music and belly dancing.

The other two day excursion drives the passengers for a domestic flight from Istanbul airport which would bring them for to lunch in Kara. Kappadokien is then headed for to visit the Tokali, the black church and an Onyx factory. Dinner in the hotel is followed by a Folkloric dance from the Kappadokien region and a good night's rest. On the next day, sixth to tenth century towns carved in the cliffs are seen over in Kamala. This fascinating labyrinth of tunnels, caves, wine cellars and chapels was once hiding place for runaway Arabs. The passengers go back to their floating home the next day their bags and heads bulging with Turkish delights.

Astor leaves Istanbul on the thirtieth of April at midnight and reaches Canacale in Troy the next day at ten in the morning. During the forty hour stay in Istanbul the crew also have time to see the town and pack their cabins with Turkish delights, carpets silverware and souvenirs. Mela and her friends take the local bus to town to find shopping centres for famous Turkish leather and jewellery. They try to find their way by talking to people on the buses and are lucky to find friendly and helpful University students on the bus who speak some English. The huge displays of glittering gold and gemstones in the shops fascinate the eyes and the friendliness and helpfulness of the very nice people warms the heart. The temperature is about fifteen degrees and our tropical friends are freezing. They gratefully accept the tiny cups of steaming apple tea served to them in the shops. Mela buys two yellow leather suitcases, one very big and one small as her two nylon bags would not even be able to contain one tenth of her possessions.

They decide to meet their new Turkish friends again on the next day and try and find if they can arrange for them to visit the ship. At the security office they were told that any request for visitor's passes had to be done one week in advance. They promised their Turkish friends that the visit would be for next time the ship would returned there. On the bus they meet a new friend Angin who accompanies them to bargain for leather clothes. As usual Mela always has something in her bag to nibble at as it had become a habit to her to bring food along as it seemed that once her feet touched firm ground her stomach worms revolted and made her ravenous. She took out a big apple on the long bus ride but the Turkish students warned her it was Ramadan period and eating in public was prohibited. She quickly excused herself and put the apple in her bag, to calm her grumbling stomach she drank as many little cups of the steaming apple tea which the shop owners served to customers. In the shop Angin met one of her student friends, her name was Emine Aykut and she took Mela's address and gave her address so that they could be pen friends. Mela with the precious help of her new Turkish friends purchased a leather outfit with jacket and skirt. They helped her bargain for and purchase a pair of pearl earrings and an aquamarine gem set in a ring from the fabulous Jewel shops.

On Labour Day, the first of May a party was announced for the crew members in the female lounge. The mess room had a television set but the female crew could meet and watch television in an area next to the mess called the female lounge. The ship had anchored in the antique city of Troy where the half day tour had brought passengers to the ruins of the nine cities, the buried town and the museum. The full day program was a repetition of the morning excursion with lunch and the visit in the afternoon of Assos, once home to Aristotele and Paulus.

The party was running in the female lounge which was gaily decorated for Labour Day. Paper streamers and balloons had been hung on the walls and ceiling and snacks and drinks were displayed on a corner table. Some of the crew were dancing to the music while sipping their drinks or nibbling snacks. Mela was enjoying a chicken wing and noticed that Bianca was sitting quietly in a corner with a sad face. She went to enquire what was wrong and stayed a long time by her friend's side trying to figure out what had happened to make her so sad.

"What is the matter Bianca, why don't you eat something and enjoy the party?'

"I do not feel like partying, my heart is bleeding."

"Tell me what is the matter yesterday we were happy in the streets and shops of Istanbul, what has caused this sudden change of mood?"

"It is him, he is so jealous he has resented my going out yesterday and has been very cruel telling me that if I continue like this he will end our relationship."

Tears ran down her cheeks and she hastily wiped her eyes which were already red and swollen. The story between Bianca and her lover Hervey was really a soap opera with many dramatic times where they even came to physical violence. It seemed that Bianca attracted the sort of possessive, violent and paranoiac man; she had miraculously got the chance to escape her husband to meet with the same type of man so far away on the ocean.

The next morning the ship leaves the coast of Turkey for visiting a series of Greek isles, Tinos Mykonos and Delos on its way to Corfu on the Greek mainland.

Long ago when Greece was at the centre of the civilized world, some Aegean islands knew great power and prosperity. Amongst was Delos, hub of the Cyclades named after circle (kyklos) since they form a ring around the once sacred Delos. Today Mykonos is the most famous of the Greek islands, there are also the other islands, Tinos, Paros, Sifnos and Naxos, not forgetting Santorini, all linked and separated by Homer's 'wine dark' sea. They all seem to be much more brown than green and they all share the notorious north wind, the Meltemi and a haunting barren air conferring to them that particular atmosphere of long past with a relaxed and human pace of life.

During the seven hours halt in Tinos the gleaming white houses on hillsides terraced with vines and figs offers the taste of life on a typical Greek isle. The harbour itself is like a touristic village with cafes and shops and even though the crew do not have enough time for a proper visit, a couple of minutes during lunch time is enough for them to go down the gangway and stroll along the shops and cafes buying postcards or simply enjoying the leisurely atmosphere.

While cleaning her cabins on A deck Mela can watch the port through the ship's portholes. At two in the afternoon after duty she goes up the bridge deck with Nicoleta and stays for one hour to see Tinos fading in the distance as the ship reaches Mykonos. On those Greek Islets devoid of tour facilities only individual excursions are possible. Mela and her friends go out by the tender boats at night after duty to eat out and dance in the Disco at Mykonos.

On the next morning while Mela is preparing her early morning tea in the pantry the ship leaves Mykonos at seven to reach Delos at eight. The loudspeakers boast about the unique unforgettable atmosphere of Delos, the sacred isle of ancient Greece with its marble temples and two thousand year old houses and famous avenue of marble Lions, birthplace of the Sun God Apollo.

At two, while on her one to three o'clock shift Mela hears the announcements saying that the ship is leaving for Corfu on the Greek mainland. The song from Julio Iglesias *'Je n'ai pas changé'* comes to Mela's lips and she hums it all through the day and the night contaminating all those who hear her singing

> *'Je n'ai pas changé,*
> *Je suis toujours ce jeune homme étranger*
> *Qui t'écrivais des romances qui commençait par*
>   *je t'aime*
> *Et finissais par demain*
> *Je n'ai pas changé*
> *Je suis toujours ce garçon un peu fou*
> *Qui te parlait d'Amérique*
> *Mais n'étais pas assez riche*
> *Pour t'emmener a Corfou'*

The song told about the crazy young Spanish man who promised to bring his sweetheart to see America when he did not even have enough money to bring her to Corfu. Soon the whole Mauritian crew were humming this song in the pantries, in the restaurants, in the crew mess and even hummed by sailors on the decks, in the end the German and British crew had also started singing the song in their own accents.

The passengers resume their touring on the excursion buses, they visit town of Corfu, which unlike the other Greek islands is green and verdant on two half day tours discovering its arcaded streets, sunny beaches, and wooded headlands bearing similarities to Venice and the South of France.

Chapter X

Sailing the Devils

On the eve of disembarkation, Mela and Nicoleta go ashore for one hour to relax and unwind before the strenuous work the next day in Venice. As from Wednesday the fifth of May Astor starts its second series regular docking in Venice but the cabin crew, always taken up by the usual exhausting rituals of embarkation only get to see the place through the portholes from a distance. They are busy during the whole day stripping and cleaning to get cabins ready. They then wear their nice uniforms with bow tie, high heeled shoes and make up to welcome the next lot of cruisers. By the time they are done with the work, the ship is already sailing out of Venice.

This cruise to the eastern Mediterranean cruise went to the ports of Venice, Dubrovnik, Heraklion, Haifa, Port Said, Alexandria Valletta, and Malta passing through the Straits of Messina, the Isle of Lipari, Stromboli, Elba and ending in Genoa. Dubrovnik in Yugoslavia is reached at noon the next day after spending the night at sea. Here is the country of the seamstress, Elaine Matesa who is also the assistant Housekeeper; she proudly shows the Astor ship to her family. Another day at sea carries the cruisers over to the Greek island of Heraklion where day excursions drive to Knossos by bus. Passengers are brought to discover the intricate palace which was once the centre of the first civilization in Europe and where culture from three thousand years back is displayed in its archaeological museum.

The second biggest castle on this historical island is reached driving over to the south coast through Gortys and Agia Triada Phaestos. In the small fishing village of Matala passengers eat lunch in a typical Greek Tavern on the beach before moving to the east coast. Aghia Nikolaos reveals its beauties of archaeology and its windmills while the bus drives over to the Mirabella viewpoint and to see Crete's oldest church.

'Relax at sea' is the theme of days where the towering heights of the ship above the ocean floor cruises over the oceans at full speed. Passengers take advantage of those long idle hours at sea to explore and discover the amenities, and climb the decks to view the grandiose ocean unfolding before Lady Astor in millions of sparkling bubbles and sheets of mists which spray the decks giving a delicious salty tinge to the air.

Jerusalem is the next port of call, in this Holy land with sites straight from the bible, once more the Dome of the rock would be admired and prayers on pieces of paper would be stuffed in the Western wall. Fervent Catholics would solemnly walk the Via Dolorosa and remember the passion of Lord Jesus. While putting the next day's programme sent by the cruise office in the cabins, Francesca reads the excursion programme and tells Mela "Look how wonderful, the tour tomorrow is going to the garden of Gethsemane, the church of all Nations and the tomb of the Holy Virgin and also to Nazareth and the Tiberiades lake to Genezareth and visit Kapharnaum, birthplace of the apostle Simon Peter and also the third source of the Jordan river!"

Soon after their duty, the foursome consisting of Francesca and the three other friends Paton Nelly and Marina hurry to take a taxi for going to see these sacred places. Mela really needed a good rest so she decides to stay on her berth and enjoy her book. She has reached a very interesting and funny part of the book which made her laugh to tears.

After an early morning breakfast most passengers are on the decks to watch the ship entering Port Said, and catch a first glimpse of Egypt. One of the most exciting ports in the world, Port Said is where traditional feluccas and ocean going liners congregate at the entrance of the Suez Canal. Long tour buses are already aligned on the quay for the two excursions scheduled during these two days in Egypt. Cairo, Luxor and Alexandria are the tours which uncover the citadel, the Mohamed Ali Mosque and Egyptian museum, driving further on to Gizeh.

Mela reads the tour brochure in the passenger's cabin and learns about the contents of this fabulous excursion. 'Riding on camel backs in the dark night towards the huge lighted golden pyramids and Sphinx passengers travel in ancient times before a fabulous dinner and overnight stay. On the next day a short domestic flight brings them to Luxor to be driven on the west side of the Nile River to visit Thebes, the dead town and the Tal of the king and the tomb of Tut-ench-Amun, the coloss of Memnon. The temple of Karnak and Luxor is discovered after lunch at the Luxor, the flight back to Alexandria then returns them to the Astor. This tour costs eight hundred and thirty German Marks while the land tour costs only three hundred and fifty German marks. The latter also features a visit to the Mohamed Ali Mosque and Egyptian museum, driving further on to Gizeh, riding on camel backs to see the pyramids and the Sphinx and after dinner and overnight in the Hotel they visit the tomb of Memphis and the Alabaster Sphinx and the stepped Pyramids of Sakkara. After lunch they take the return trip to Alexandria by bus over the western roads.'

It is not even noon in Haifa and Mela has already finished doing her cabins. She wants to go out to have a swim at the beach but she cannot go out by herself. Her colleague Flossie who was always ready for a chat and never in a hurry to leave the pantry after duty is on one to three duty today. Mela liked when she stayed on when taking duty at three over from her. Mela would fuel the conversation by questions while she went on talking about her past life and her misfortunes, sometimes she stayed for more than one hour until almost four o'clock. Mela was glad to see the duty time fly by, but when it was Flossie's turn to take duty over from her she did not stay to talk but hurried away as fast as possible. Today for once she stays on to talk to or rather to listen to Flossie.

"Oh dear do you know what had happened to me last Sunday, at my boyfriend's on D deck?"

"No you never told me about that, go on with it"

"He was drunk and was violent he closed the door and was hitting me and as the music was playing loud nobody could hear my screams. I did not know what to do, and then I got an idea and wrote 'Help Me' on a piece of paper that I slipped under the door. A sailor passed by and called security that came to rescue me from him."

Mela was still smiling to herself when she went her cabin to change her bed linen and start tidying up. Flossie's stories were all so extraordinary that she sometimes asked herself if the girl did not invent all the things that she claimed to have happened to her.

She finally manages to form a group with three other girls, sharing a taxi; they drive to a beach for a swim in the icy cold sea. That night Juliette is celebrating her birthday and gives a little party for the stewardesses in the female lounge. They all share a happy moment eating dancing and chatting till almost midnight. They tell funny stories about the passengers and Mela makes everybody laugh with the story of the passenger who had written 'From Banjul to Dakar' on the order form. Francesca said "I had an old lady who came with a tattered suitcase which seemed to be at least one hundred years old and I said to myself, no way that the purse is going to feast with this passenger. But on her departure she gave hastily put a folded note in my hand, I was expecting around ten dollars; imagine my surprise o find a one hundred dollar note."

When some make a move to go to bed Nicoleta retains them "Come on stay on we are having such fun, do not worry for tomorrow's work, the overnight tours has left many cabins untouched we shall help those who still have passengers on."

The richer passengers and A deck and the upper decks almost always take part in those very expensive extended tours. This is a blessing for the stewardesses on A deck and the upper decks who get a nice rest. Blessings never come alone, the work which is already much lighter becomes even easier, the passenger of cabin 314, a very nice German lady calls Mela to tell her that only one bed needs to be done as she is alone, no need to manipulate the heavy couch to turn it into a bed.

The crew are allowed only a short time ashore as even with fewer passengers on board, the ship is only staying for seven hours in Port Said. The port area is like a small souk with people selling all sorts of things from textile to toys, from electronic equipment to jewellery. "Lacoste shirts for one dollar only Mam, take it for one dollar Sir." The Mauritians buy hundreds of fake Lacoste T shirts and numerous electronic gadgets; Mela finds a very amusing toy showing a bearded Father Christmas playing drums when the batteries are put on, for her young brother.

The ship leaves Port Said at three in the afternoon to reach the port of Alexandria the next day at seven in the morning. The two half day tours in Alexandria which cost only fifty five German Marks offer to visit of the town in bus to see the Pompeii Saul, the catacombs and Montazah Park with its impressive old tour museum. The tour continues then to drive past the Sidi Aboul Abbas El Moursi Mosque before returning to the Astor driving along the West coast. Driving between the desert and the middle sea they arrive to the monument dedicated to the African warriors of the Second World War where a Military museum displays many objects from this painful epoch. For the stay in Alexandria the famous French song of the eighty's by Claude Francois, comes to the lips of many.

> *Les sirenes du port d'Alexandrie chantent toujours*
> *la meme melodie*
> *Alexandrie Alexandra, Alexandrie ce soir tu*
> *danses dans mes bras*

Mela goes ashore with Nicoleta for a short time as they are both on duty and once more try riding on horseback; of course it is only the saddle on an old racer past its prime time. Nicoleta says in between her teeth "Do you think we will be thrown off after two minutes like last time?"

But this time the experience is not so awful like in Spain, expecting to stay for a very short time on horseback, they enjoy the short ride for the ten dollars which they pay for the trip. They laughed like mad while Nicoleta made funny comments about car models on the street. The ship crosses over to Malta Islet and the twenty four hours at sea makes Mela sick again, she vacuums the carpets with her sickness bags ready in her pockets and as soon as she feels the hot vomit coming up she puts the bag to her mouth and relieves herself, closes the bag and put it in the large garbage bag.

Astor tries to brave the hostile coasts and approach the Isle of Lipari and Stromboli to view its spectacular scenery of volcanic rock formations. The picturesque villages and local characters of this group of volcanic Virgin Islands found North of Sicily retain their privacy and remain hidden from foreign eyes. Like many other cruise ships before her, dangerous seas make it impossible for such a huge ship to venture out in the treacherous waters around those Islands who live up to their reputation for being Devil islands. The maneuvers taken to first trying to sail towards those islands, and then changing trajectory to head for the Island of Elba brings on another day of rough sea.

Tonight is crew show and Mela has to perform the Sega dance in the Main lounge. How she wishes that there is no crew show tonight, she only wants to lie down and rest as she is feeling so bad. Tonight's rehearsal cannot be skipped as the four girls have to practice the synchronized choreography doing the strenuous pose of lowering their upper body while sitting on the knees until their heads touch the ground next to the feet. She finally manages to gather enough courage go for the rehearsal during her day break. Forcing the bitter tonic water down to avoid dehydration she also keeps on munching the dry zwieback which she takes hours to chew and painfully swallow hurting her throat still sore from vomiting.

When she enters the cabin at past midnight after a much applauded show Bianca tells her "I see you feel better, you see we shall soon also get accustomed to the waves and become real sailors."

The port of Elba is more welcoming and the firm ground so much easier to walk on than the floor of the ship in the recent choppy seas. Napoleon Bonaparte has been exiled on this island found midway between the Italian mainland and the island of Corsica. Along the coast are revealed picturesque elaborate villas and the magnificent scenery of the Procchio bay on the Capraia Island. Mela goes to the beach with Lina, the girl with whom she went to the hotel in Antigua and two other stewardesses, they freeze while swimming in the sea water; afterwards they lie on the hot burning sand of the beach, the salt drying on their skin turns them all white. They go shopping and Mela buys a little

Elba doll as souvenir of this land. She showers with lavender shower gel which gently soothes her skin from the aggressions of the strong sea water; it is pure bliss to be able to still smell the marine air in one's nostrils while bathing.

The next day in Genoa is the end of another cruise; the stewardesses prepare all their tools for the disembarkation rituals. They busy themselves collecting sheets, pillow cases and stocking their cleaning buckets with all the cleaning stuff, having everything ready for tomorrow. This disembarkation day is at the same time the best and worst day of every cruise. A hectic day when as one has to work until heels are sore and hands blanched with water and detergents, most of them do not bother using gloves for cleaning as it hamper their movements and the work is done quicker without gloves. This day was also the day when the departing passengers would give them their tips and their pockets would be bulging with dollars. Francesca called that day the 'fett kabba" (the feast of the purse). "Why it is the feast of the purse?" Mela asked. Francesca explained "When I was working in the textile factory in Mauritius the end of each fortnight we would get our pay and the girls used to say "Today the purses are in feast!"

The last week of May would be the last cruise; the last fortnight of hard work for Mela before going back home to a well deserved one month holidays.

On Thursday the twenty first of May the ship is due to Porto Cervo in Sardinia, where is found the Costa Smeralda, playground of jet setters and Millionaires. However rough seas make it impossible to enter the port for viewing the rugged beauty of this coastline with its towering cliffs enclosing tiny bags of white sand lapped by the emerald green sea. In its place the ship goes to the island of Elba where Mela and her friends, who are free from one to six in the afternoon, again share a taxi to the beach. The feeling of the burning hot sand incites her to plunge head first in the water; with this burning sun she expects the sea water to be warm. She plunges head first in the sea and she gets a shock by the freezing cold water which numbs her head. She rushes out to friction her freezing head with a towel and warm up on the warm sand but very soon she sees white scales forming on her skin.

"Look at you, just like a salted seal drying in the sun, I bet that a fair amount of salt can be scraped from you just now. Let's go back you need to wash it off with a warm bath of lavender otherwise your skin will be bruised and irritated by the salt." Nicoleta told her.

Naples appears on the twenty second of May and the vivid blue waters in the bay fringes with fascinating islands like Capri and Ischia. Along the way to the spectacular Amalfi drive are the ancient wonders of Pompeii preserved by the eruption of the Vesuvius volcano.

After duty the stewardesses go to the bazaar to shop, they buy beautiful fine Italian pyjamas and clothing and snake skin shoes. Passengers have joined the excursions to the municipal square with wonderful flower gardens where they can find the flower calendar representing each day, date and month tagged with the name of a flower. There is also an excursion to see the Carlo opera, the king's palace and the Archaeological museum with materials from Pompeii and Herculaneum sites.

Another tour brings the passengers to Pompeii by bus to stroll and shop along residential streets which have souvenir shops. On the bricks of the street walls can be seen old inscriptions back from the time when the city was sunk in the lava and ashes of the volcano. Passengers have a typical Neapolitan lunch in the middle age village of Amalfi before rejoining the ship. The boat trip over the bay to Capri provides visit to the wonderful lights in the blue caves and the Villa Axel Munthes in Anacapri belonging to the famous author of "The house of San Michele".

Towering Mountains guarding the straits of Messina, this is in Sicily where the ship docks on the next day. Historic buildings stand at the foot of the majestic Mount Etna where, not far from the fashionable resort of Taormina is the destination of the excursions. The tour drives past the Cathedral to Messina where is found the famous Astronomical clock in the church of Christo. Further on in Taormina through the Calabriens Mountains they continue to the Monte Tauro terrace overlooking the Greek amphitheater and finish the tour with a shopping binge in the town.

"Oh, have a look, how beautiful!" exclaims Mela while strolling in the port area.

Little white stone statues, reproductions of famous sculptures by Michelangelo like the Venus de Milo displayed by the roadside were on sale at twenty dollars for three. She purchases a set of three of those world famous sculptures.

The ship continues its incursions in the Mediterranean waters to the island of Malta.

Some of the passengers explore the town on foot to the Barracca garden overlooking the old town and the two natural harbors of La Vallettas. In the Johannes cathedral and the palace wonderful paintings and a large collection of cones fascinate the visitor.

Those having chosen the bus trip see the world's third largest thorn in Mosta and experience an enchanting contrast to the hustle bustle and friendliness of this sunny island inside the silent city of Medina. They drive to the only three Neolithic temples, the oldest foundations of prehistoric life from the ice age in Ghar Dalam in Tarxien.

A few more days and Nicoleta and Mela and other crew members, their pockets bulging with the rewards of their hard work, would at last go to spend a well earned one a half month holiday with their family. It is a big headache to pack as airplane voyage only allows thirty kilos of luggage; they need to arrange with friends to keep some of their heavy stuff on board during their absence.

They simply roam about in front of the ship as they do not have time to see the town; at least they would be able to say that they had been on the Island of Malta!

The ship docks in Sfax in Tunisia on the following morning, tender boats cross over to the land for discovering this coast fringing the Sahara, with camel trains plodding through the shimmering heat haze to reach the oasis of Gabes. Here one can catch a glimpse of paradise in the desert; green palms providing shadow and rest while bright red glazing pomegranates, fat and sweet yellow dates and large yellow bananas to quench the desert thirst are a feast to the eyes.

The shore excursion office calls the passengers to join the excursions buses on the pier. The excursions drive to Sousse, with its well known swimming beach and its historical sightseeing to the Ribat cisterns and the Catacombs through Monastir, where was born its President called Bourgiba. Another lively Arab city full of oriental mystery is Tunis which reveals its fortress, mosques and bazaars along with the distinctly French air of its broad boulevards and exclusive villas standing in front of the limpid lagoon. Some passengers spend the day lazing on the beach at Hammamet while others prefer to go for seeing handmade carpets in desert villages.

When tender boats are needed to reach the shore, the ship has to put in place a series of dispositions and logistics which take quite a lot of time to transfer all the passengers ashore. On that day, Mela still struggling to finish cleaning her fourteen cabins, only watches the shore through the portholes, like in Venice. She really feels too weary to even venture out on the sundeck to see the town from afar.

The ship leaves Tunis at ten in the evening to navigate during two nights and one day over to Mahon in Minorca. The sea is rough and after all those days spent anchored in the Port the rolling is felt by many passengers and crew who start getting this hateful sensation of nausea, cold sweats and headache. Mela who wanted to start preparing her luggage has to abandon her cabin and go to the fitness centre on C deck where she hopes the larger space would make her feel better. The sickness accentuates and she finally gets into bed exhausted from throwing up the sour and bitter bile continuously rising in her throat. Hoping to combat the sickness she tries to swallow a Dramamine tablet but a heave of nausea sends the whole tablet to rejoin the contents of her stomach in the sickness bag before it has time to produce any effect.

Everyone is relieved to find the ship docked in Minorca at seven in the morning on Thursday morning. Most of the passengers in her sector had spent that time of rough seas away from their cabins, in the larger spaces of the public rooms to avoid the shaking which would have made them sick. The cabins having remained tidy and clean there was not much to do apart from cleaning the bathrooms.

Mela and Bianca were ready before noon, in a nice little restaurant they chose their lunch from a selection of attractive dishes, salads and seafood like at home.

This tranquil island with its narrow country lanes reminds one of rural England and its remote rocky coves with superb beaches. Passengers have taken excursions to visit this vast natural harbour which once housed Nelson's fleet and where the villa in which he stayed can still be seen. They visit the beach of Punta Prima and the fishing village of Binibeca, the historical monuments from Moorish, Spanish and British times and eat in the factory domain of the well known Menor Gins.

On Mahon, the second largest Balearic Island passengers are brought to the archaeological museum, the megalithic altar and the old light house. They proceed to see the fabrication of handicrafts, shoes and jewels which they can buy as souvenir.

After her one to three o'clock duty Mela grabs some quiet sleep, free of creaking doors and drawers which open spontaneously on their own with the roll in rough seas. She wakes up at five and resumes her packing up.

The next day the ship docks Ajaccio in Corsica, birthplace of Napoleon, a jewel set in a wild landscape of jagged pearls, olive groves and vineyards, woods and waterfalls. Mela being on duty is unable to go out here. She however learns about the beauties of the land by the announcement done by the shore excursion office.

"First call for passengers to the city tour, drive to the picturesque villages through pine forests and the idyllic village of Cauro the birthplace of the freedom fighter Sampiero Corso, the gorges of Prunelli and picturesque and beautiful landscapes.'

'Last call for the Calanques de Piana tour to tour, drive north of Empor to discover the view over the Golf of Sagone, over along the coast to the eighteenth century village of Greek origin named Cargese with its old Greek church and further on to the fantastic Calanques red cliffs.'

Early on Saturday thirtieth of May 1987, the ship docks in the town of Nice in France, also known as the Queen of the Riviera, Nice is very pleasant with fashionable boutiques, renowned 'Promenade des Anglais' and beaches famous throughout the world. Various tours are scheduled to visit this very fashionable South part of France. The tours bring its passengers over to Saint Jean Cap Ferrat along the coast and over a set of steps to see the fourteenth century picturesque mountain village. It goes further on to Saint Paul de Vence driving through provincial landscapes, middle age villages with old fortresses and streets. Half day excursions go to Monte Carlo, seat of the Monegast kingdom of Prince Rainer, husband of late actress Grace Kelly who perished in a car accident. Passengers can visit the world famous gambling casinos of Monte Carlo and the luxury villas and hotels belonging to the Prince. The full day excursion drives along the coastal roads via Cap Antibes and Juan les Pins towards

Cannes where it stops for allowing the people to stroll along the flowered boulevard of 'La Croisette', perfume manufacture can then be watched in its factory.

Tonight is her last night aboard the Astor and tomorrow when the ship arrives in Genoa she would leave the ship to go back home. Mela and her friends wear their Sunday outfits to go by tender boat to Nice.

PART 3

Chapter XI

Crisp Summer Fjords at Geiranger and Sogne

Time has come for Mela and the other crew members to leave the ship for their half yearly vacations. Most of them have spent the whole day cleaning up their section; the new passengers would arrive at the same time as their replacement, so they are the ones who need to get all the cabins ready for embarkation. After this last duty, they rapidly prepare themselves and struggle to carry their tons of luggage into the lifts down to the shore.

As soon as they step outside, the usual feeling of intense fatigue and depression after the heavy work done for disembarkation and embarkation seem to have vanished. As the car leaves the pier Mela and her friends exhale loudly feeling an intense sensation of well being. It was as if their stress was concentrated in a huge spiral tied to the ship which was magically loosened as the car moved further away.

After the small ship's cabins they find the large luxury rooms of the hotel in Genoa wonderfully spacious. They are the hotel guests tonight, somebody has done the beds for them and they will dine in style at the restaurant. Friendly Italian waiters chat with them in Italian and even though they do not understand a word the communication nevertheless passes by signs. Two waiters stand either side of Mela kissing her cheeks while Nicoleta takes a picture. After a little tour of the town they go to sleep as they need to get up early next morning for the flight from Genoa to Paris. They decide to tour Genoa by night in a cab but the speedometer is moving at such a pace and the thousands of Italian liras displayed make them ask the driver to bring them back. Anyway the intense fatigue of the day's work is being felt, their aching bones requesting the rest of a good night sleep. At five in the morning Mela is woken up from her deep sleep by the sound of knocking on the door to her room "Hurry up we need to get the flight to Paris and the bus is coming in a few minutes!"

At seven o'clock they board a small Air France plane to flight terminal one at Charles de Gaulle airport. The flight takes only one hour but they need to transit in the Paris airport as their next flight to Amsterdam is not until another twelve hours. They try killing time roaming about trying to find something worth buying in the Paris duty free shops. Mela buys a perfume and at lunchtime, they go for their prepaid meal in the airport canteen. In Amsterdam they would take the connection to the airport of Nairobi in Kenya on the African continent. While trying to find the gate called satellite three they get confused in a labyrinth of corridors and gates until they realise they are completely off track.

One of them asks the way at one of the desks and learns that the flight is embarking in fifteen minutes. The way to satellite three seems so long; down this corridor, up those stairs, to the left down those stairs, to the right again. Panting, the Mauritians heavily laden with hand luggage weighing more than fifteen kilos follow the airport officer, and fortunately manage to reach the embarkation door of the flight to Amsterdam five minutes before closing.

There are eight more hours to wait in Amsterdam as their connecting flight to Nairobi has been delayed. The town of Amsterdam, which in most movies seen by Mela is the centre for crime and smuggling circles, is terribly boring to her sitting in the airport lounge for endless hours on. Time seems to stand still while they wander aimlessly through the airport hall, taking little naps on the sofas. Once again they check what is on sale at the duty free shops and Mela buys her brother a scientific calculator while Nicoleta buys perfume and chocolate. They eat lunch then try to pass the time watching the people departing on the other flights. They start a cycle of little naps each time in a different place on seats vacated by departing passengers alternating with short walks. As the hours pass the boredom increases until they have lost all interest in the airport hall and sulkily wait on until finally the time comes to board the flight to Nairobi. It is almost nine at night when they finally arrive in Nairobi to take the final flight to Mauritius. The last meal is already long forgotten and grumbling stomachs remind them of their prepaid meal. The airport representatives ask for payment for the meal, but the prepaid vouchers clearly state that the meal has already been paid for. Anger adding to their hunger the

Mauritian travellers start heating up and demand their rights. The manager is called and after a lengthy debate the Mauritians are requested to follow a man upstairs to the restaurant where the prepaid meal was finally to be served. They carry their heavy bags up five flights of stairs to the restaurant but their hunger already considerably reduced by the attitude of the Kenyans, vanished completely when the meal was brought by reluctant waiters. At the sight of the first course, a sort dirty lukewarm liquid served in chipped enamel bowls, nobody wanted to eat anymore and all the food remain untouched on the table.

They embark on empty, grumbling stomachs on Air Madagascar to Moroni in Comoros Island. Misfortune continues following the crew and this time they are deprived of many of the video clips they were carrying. According to the customs officers they are too indecent for viewing, Hector gets blue in the face when his film is confiscated, and tells his friends "The rogues saying the dancing is too indecent to be viewed, as if I bought it for them to view, the bastards I'm sure they take it for themselves it, they simply find these Madonna clips too nice to let go."

From Comoros, they take a short flight to Antananarivo from where the last flight would bring them to their final destination, Mauritius.

The time back home is spent happily with loved ones, facilitated by the carefree holiday time and precious money to realise many little dreams. Nicoleta and Bianca take their children to shop for necessities and make arrangements for the keeping of the children while they would be away.

Mela is really happy of her slim body sculpted by seasickness and vomit and is enchanted by the innumerable little small blessings like being able to offer gifts to her family. She visits her newly married cousins and goes to a restaurant and to dance in a nightclub. She eats all her favourite food like green leafy vegetables, Chou Chou, aubergine and salted fish ad sweet potatoes. She participates in an anti drug campaign with her cousins and friends and watch a play on drug abuse.

Her attempt to play Mrs. D and get the house cleaned lamentably fails as her brothers and sister are not at all willing to play the part of cabin stewardess. She tries to tidy up her things and collect all her old school copybooks which have taken years of dust and make a big fire. To celebrate her twenty fourth birthday at home, the family share a delicious chicken briani and cut a sweet potato pudding as birthday cake.

While Mela and her friends are enjoying their holidays with their family in Mauritius Lady Astor makes her way to the Mediterranean sun of Spain Portugal and North Africa. This early summer cruise discovers Majorca and glorious Costa del Sol, Casablanca and Lisbon. On the second of June at eight in the morning, Astor arrives in Palma, in Majorca with its majestic Cathedral rising above the expensive yachts lining the waterfront.

The cruisers have almost twelve hours to start celebrating summer in this fantastic historic city. Here on the fine beach resort only a few miles away from the harbour is found supreme nightlife.

The four friends sharing the same cabin fully enjoy the discovery of new lands where the handsome tips they earn enable them to buy so many nice things "Look at the daily programme Fran, do you think we shall be able to do some interesting shopping in the North African capital on Wednesday?"

"We won't be able to experience the atmosphere of oriental mystery at the Kasbah and alleyways zigzagging down to the sea like the passengers but we should definitely be able to play souvenir hunters. And that would be possible only on the condition if those old cats in my section de give some handsome tips." Replied Francesca to Paton

On Friday the Port of Malaga in Spain is in view, a day for the cruisers to enjoy Costa del Sol's flower decked houses and lovely bars and its Moorish castles and modern casinos. Passengers can take excursions along the coast to Torremolinos or Marbella either on the beach or over the mountains to visit the Andalucía cities of Granada and Cordoba.

Our foursome with their boyfriends goes out this night to see the Flamenco nightlife in glamorous Spanish bars. The girls pay the entrances as the boys being only utility stewards do not earn any tips. They dress up and go out to wine and dine spending most of the money they have collected till then.

"Let's drink to this wonderful cruise and this night out in this bar where we celebrate the firm ground and our eternal friendship."

They have emptied several bottles of expensive wine over a delicious dinner started with tapas and ending with paella. When they get back on the ship that night, the discussion continues till early morning when they finally go to bed. The two utility brothers Clayton and Sylvio share a cabin together so they bring their girls

Paton and Marina while Nelly goes to sleep with Joe in his cabin and Francesca has to sleep alone.

Saying farewell to Flamenco nightlife the ship sails on towards the rock of Gibraltar, Britain's fortress found at the entrance of the Mediterranean which displays numerous fascinating sights from the Second World War. From here, those who are nostalgic of the charm of Spain can still cross over to visit magnificent Seville and the sherry country round Jerez.

Early on Sunday morning, Astor docks in the bustling port of Casablanca and the crew gets ready to go out in this reputed town of cheap shopping and friendly people and more interestingly familiar French language. Haunting images of Humphrey Bogart and the music of 'As Time Goes By' welcomes the passengers who get down the gangway. One can wander in the timeless narrow streets of the old quarter, the Medina and the Mallah amongst an intriguing mixture of old Moorish, colonial French and modern Arab architecture in this city and bargain with street sellers and local craftsmen. The more adventurous and wealthy would take the trip along the coast to the Imperial City of Rabat or up into the mountains of romantic Marrakesh. The week unfolds into new lands and on Monday the ship reaches Lisbon, the elegant Portuguese Capital built on seven hills overlooking the river Tagus and its great suspension bridge. The bus excursion travels along the city's tree lines avenues to the major sights like the Tower of Belem and the Monument of the discoveries. Further on one can see the Royal place at Sintra and the fashionable resort of Estoril.

More memorable evenings happen when nights fall with the *fado*, nightlife of the Alfama and Baixa districts but and as there has not been any disembarkation and fett kabba as yet the musketeers cannot afford another glamorous night out.

Passengers sleep the few hours of the fado night and wake up to a late breakfast at sea until the ship reaches Vigo. Once the home port for Spanish Galleons, Vigo is nowadays a pleasant fishing port where the four girls visit the prestigious twelfth century churches, they would say their payers in the churches of Bayonna and Castillo de Monte Real and the historic shrine at Santiago de Compostella.

During the following days at sea, the foursome spends their time off doing each other's hairs and nails and face while singing popular tubes at the top of their voices. Fortunately the adjacent cabins where the occupants wanted to rest in peace were not disturbed as the sound was camouflaged by the sound of the engines and waves. Days at sea are normally the time that the administration officers and the housekeeper went round the crew cabins while the crew were at work to check the cleanliness.

"What's that souk" Exclaimed Mr Mead the administration officer when opening cabin 217.

The beds were devoid of the mattress which was found on the floor, there was no space for walking except over the mattresses which were littered with items of clothing, mainly soiled feminine underwear and discarded cosmetic articles. Dirty plates, cups and glasses stood all over the little table, the lavabo and the empty beds; four of each showing that there were four occupants and that had often had their meals in there. He opened the bathroom door to find no shower curtain and shower walls turned yellow from lack of care. They entered the adjacent cabin to find the same state of chaos. Mrs D became red in the face with shame as it was the section of the stewardesses. She consulted her list and found it to be Francesca and Paton's cabin next to that of Marina and Nelly. Mr Mead wrote a red card and left it over the door. Since the beginning of the Astor, never before had they seen such a dirty cabin, it had been clearly stipulated in the rules that cabin should be kept tidy and clean with details of the cleanings to be done regularly.

The four girls were called to a meeting in the administrator's office in the presence of Mrs D. They were given a warning for not abiding by the rules and deprived of any time ashore for a whole month until they had proved their discipline to the authority.

More seaward days carried the ship over to Guernsey, while the foursome split up into two some, thoroughly cleaning their cabins and sleeping in their own cabins at night.

Guernsey, the most picturesque of the Channel Islands enchants the visitor with its sheer cliffs and hidden coves, wooded slopes and charming little ports like historic St. Peter.

Astor leaves the English port of Dover and cruises over to the German port of Hamburg, one of Europe's oldest ports, now an attractive modern city offering leisure shopping in traffic free precincts and arcades. During the thirty three hours there, the excursion office proposes the city tour to see the large Alster Lake, the spacious parks, tree Line Avenue and canals and after nightfall the evening can be spent in the bright lights of the Reeperbahn area with all sorts of entertainment namely the world famous sex shops.

The prohibition to go ashore being on the four girls, their boyfriends go out alone to the hot Reeperbahn quarter where are found the world famous sex shops. The girls are crossed when they understand that the boys are going out in spite of the ban imposed on them.

Paton was particularly angry that her boyfriend Clayton had not even informed her that he was to go out; in fact he did not even bother to come to see her during the last days.

As for Nelly the warning had awakened her up to the fact that her job was at sake and she had come here to get enough money to at last be able to have her family with her childhood sweetheart, the fiancé whom she had left back home with so much tear and sorrow. She took the firm decision to end her relationship with Joe. The poor boy had fallen in love with her and he could not understand why all of a sudden she had fallen out of love for him. As she refused to speak to him, he tried to ask Francesca to talk her into getting back to him.

Joe and Francesca kept the habit of taking a drink in the crew bar; she tried to cheer him up. When trying to talk to Nelly she had been told "I would kindly ask you to mind your own business and leave me alone, if you want to continue talking to me please avoid this subject, if you are unable then just stop talking to me and I mean it."

Of the entire fjord cruises available in the year 1987 Astor offered one with the most splendid Itinerary. Travelling from famous Sogne and Geiranger Fjords by way of the awesome Svartissen Glacier winding in and out of spectacular fjords with their sheer cliffs, plunging waterfalls, soaring peaks and deep, still mirror bright waters; it provides a succession of breathtaking sights up to the climax of the North Cap in the strange light of the midnight sun.

Esther the tour excursion officer walks out of the ship her radio telephone in hand to coordinate the departure of the tours. She liaises with the local agent to make sure all the buses are ready with the guides in the respective languages. During this cruise, her duty brings her for quite a long time on the embarkation deck she gets to talk a lot with the chief security officer Mr. Reed.

Joe has finally understood that no progress was made on the attempt to get Nelly to speak to him again. Francesca was always there to have a chat with him talking about the places he visited ashore where she was banned for the moment.

"What marvels did you discover today my friend, tell me yours then I shall tell you mine?"

Joe looks at Francesca over his jug of beer and says "Marvel, my foot, it is so expensive out there that I could not even buy myself a beer I only tasted the soft ice cream offered by the boss who was ashore with us."

"I myself did not go ashore as you well know being actually imprisoned on the Astor but my passenger told me all about the tours they went on. I of course did some probing but they were all very eager to share their experience with me. Specially after learning that being on special duty I was tied on the ship. I did not of course reveal the real reason to them; you imagine what they would have thought a cabin stewardess punished for having a chaotic cabin, good bye my tips."

"I would be glad to know about the tours but just let me get us some more beer."

"Mrs Ford of 415 told me that after cruising up the dramatic and beautiful Sogne Fjord to land at Vik they went over the mountains to lunch at Voss and drive via Stalheim to rejoin the ship at Gudvangen. The old French gentleman in cabin 423, Mr. Minier took the six and a half hour excursion because it would bring him sweet remembrance of another stay here with his now deceased wife. He went past the Hove stone church where they had been together to Hoperstad church from the twelfth century with its decorated roofs of Drachenkoplen. He walked along steep roads to Morkdalen dark valley and ate lunch in a hotel found on the slope of a gorge with a view over the waterfalls before driving on to Gudvangen. The couple in 429 went on a half day tour From Gudvangen to see the wonderful three hundred metres high Kjelfoss waterfalls. They drove through the valley past traditional farmhouses over to see the imposing mountain life with view over more waterfalls. They stopped in Stalheim hotel where coffee was served with a breathtaking view over the Norwegian mountain life."

"Ok do not worry I shall pay one of the next overnight tours for you dear and that with my credit card, the gold one at that." Joe joked

Molde Romsdalfjord, the city of Roses is where is rendered the Astor in mid June. The four girls who cannot go ashore are consoled by the high prices of Norway which would not anyway have allowed them to buy anything. Instead they spend their time off on the sun deck looking at the ship gliding through the awe inspiring beauty of the fjords. While in the passenger areas and cleaning cabins they can hear the details of the tour proposed to passengers. 'Drive to the viewpoint of Varden to see the majestic setting of the eighty seven snow-capped peaks of the Romsdal-Alpen, visit the Romsdal museum with its typical houses of the Viking era and watch a traditional dance to end with the visit of the Molde church.'

Here passengers are invited to leave the ship in one port to rejoin it one port further on in Andalsnes. Francesca once more get the details of this overland tour by the French gentlemen of cabin 423. It is much clearer to her to understand in French than when told about it in English.

"We crossed Romsdalsfjord to Vestnes and drove over the Orskog hills to Orskohfjellet for lunch, then, along Storfjord to Valldal right into the remnants of the Viking civilization. We then went further on up to eight hundred and fifty metres to Trollstigheimen along Trollstig road with a view over mountains and peaks. We took to Europe's steepest road to rejoin the Astor in Andalsnes after driving to Horgheimseidet along the Troll wall. I did not take the half day bus tour as I had already been here with my beloved wife on a cruise and we did this tour. It is also very nice and goes through beautiful Romsdal, surrounded by giant mountain peaks like the Romdalshorn and the Hexenzinnen. I remember how happy she had been to see the magnificent scenery of the thrilling Mardall falls which is Europe's highest falls. The brightly painted houses clinging to the slopes of rugged mountain sides shows Norway at her most charming at the summer resort of Andalsnes. We had had coffee and cakes in this beautiful mountain setting."

On the twenty first of June Astor anchors in Honningsvaag, land of the midnight sun. Mrs. D calls the foursome in her office. "I know it has been very hard on you not going ashore for the last weeks and you must find it particularly hard to be missing the highlight of this cruise. The behaviour you had was a very serious breach to the rules and I myself have been having bad marks for that, we can do nothing for the ban but once more I would exhort you to keep to discipline. The ship will come here again in the next cruises and I want to make sure that you make it then. Can I count on you for that my girls?"

The tour buses embark the passengers to cruise further on to the Nord cap plateau, Europe's northernmost point with its one thousand feet cliffs comparable to the Cape Horn or Cape of Good Hope. Here one can watch one of nature's greatest wonder, the sun still shining over the great Arctic Ocean at midnight.

The next day, Odile the Mauritian purser accompanies the half day tour to the Capital of the North, Tromso, which is a charming old city on a forest covered island. This jewel art town with modern commercial buildings and wooden houses of the nineteenth century is often called the Paris of the North. The two months of uninterrupted sunshine here is some sort of compensation for the terribly harsh winter, the sun does not sleep, giving life to trees and flowers. The tour drives through the centre town bringing tourists to visit the museum with its collection of costumes and accessories typical of Lapland; it is here is that is found the world's most Northern University. The purser, who is the tour escort of the day, takes pictures of the meteorological station and Northern observatory and kneels in the Eismeer Cathedral with its mightiest forces architecture for a silent prayer. She then marvels with her passengers at the bird's view of the place with cable car ascent as the tour ends.

On the twenty third of June passengers have about five hours to see the third largest glacier in Norway called Svartissen by taking a refreshing walk of about one and a half miles from the port. Esther and Mr Reed go to have their meals together and they find joy in each other's company, she was amazed to find that despite his severe look and shaved head he was so nice and amusing. She finds herself impatient to go on to excursion duty as it would mean lots of time with Mr. Reed.

Seven hours is spent in Trondheim, one of the oldest Norwegian cities founded in the year nine hundred and ninety seven on the twenty fourth. The nurses are the ones who are to accompany the bus tours today, Heidi and Dora board the buses filled by passengers. They have the chance to see the eighteenth century Stiftsgaerden; they then visit the largest wooden building in Scandinavia. In the historic places and buildings, the prices are so high that they cannot afford to buy anything. There are wonderful objects displayed in the arts and craft centres but they are so expensive that only very few passengers purchase something.

"Heidi, don't you find it nice to be away from the ship and the sick in this marvellous landscape." Dora said while taking pictures of the Sveresli viewpoint with its panoramic view over the town and its surroundings. Heidi responded by that tight smile of hers, she was a dedicated nurse and seemed to be happy only in when caring for the sick. Dora who was a very dark skinned short Mauritian girl with her ready laugh was a contrast to Heidi. The German girl's anxious face was as if carved from the medical emergencies she'd had to attend as a nurse, her angular features framed by sparse very pale blond hair that she tied in a head band, her long thin body and ashen white complexion seemed to be at its place only in a medical setting. The museum in the town of Sverresborg shows the architecture and buildings typical of Lappland since the time of mud brick houses to more recent times. The excursion ends with the visit of Nidaros-Dorns, one of Scandinavian's most beautiful churches.

That night Mr. Reed invited Esther for a drink in the crew bar. She was very excited at the prospect of spending her free time with him; she carefully chose a nice green muslin blouse to wear under her jacket with the tight sexy black skirt. The bar was very crowded, it seemed that whole crew had come tonight; they went to sit at a small corner table. Some of Mr. Reed's friends said hello with a wink to demonstrate that had noticed his luck tonight and Esther blushed.

CHAPTER XII

Romance and surprise in Russia

On the twenty fifth, the ship anchors for only one hour in Hellesylt to disembark passengers taking the overland tour of soaring mountains, it is the shortest stay of the cruise. The tour would drive to the site of plunging waterfalls and dazzling glaciers and rally the ship in the afternoon at Geiranger. Armed with her radio telephone, Esther goes down the gangway for supervising the shore excursions departures. She tenderly kisses Mr. Reed on his cheeks when meeting him at his security post.

The passengers who have boarded the bus in Hellesylt have been intently listening to the explanations of the local tour guide. As they drive past, he shows them the Hellesylt waterfalls and he brings them further on to see the deepest European lake, the Honningsdale with a depth of six hundred meters. Before driving on along the Nor fjord to see the village of Hijelle with its famous Viking past, a refreshment is served in Grodaasthen, the bus then zigzags on to see the Bulde waterfalls. After lunch more waterfalls are to be seen while driving on to one thousand and five hundred metres high peak of Dalsnibba where there is a panoramic view on snow capped mountains.

Meanwhile the ship continues round to Geiranger where the half day panoramic tour will depart, and where passengers who left at Hellesylt for the overland tour would come back on the ship. Today it is the turn of another Mauritian purser and the British nurse Jane to accompany the tours. It is as if tour escorts are chosen black and white, after the pair of white Heidi and black Dora. Rosy the Mauritian purser is of African origin and has dark skin while the British nurse Jane is Snow White herself. Comfortably seated on the bus, they admire the scenery through the Flydal valley, driving round hairpin bends to the summit of Mount Dalsnibba. At the top they stop for a breathtaking view over Bergen and its neighbourhood with waterfalls lakes and fjords while having coffee and cakes in the Djupvasshyta.

On the twenty sixth the ship reaches Bergen for a stay of twelve hours in the Capital of Fjord land. The second engineer Gregory Princeton had an accident in the engine room when his head bumped against a protruding iron bar and had to be brought to the hospital. When hearing the announcement in the staff mess for the two excursions scheduled here, Jane could not help herself wishing she was out, breathing the crisp summer fjords icy pure air. Being on duty today she breathed the antiseptic odour of the ship's hospital. She is caring for the young officer who winces with pain as she dressed the deep cut in his brow that she had assisted Nurse Heidi to stitch. He holds on to her hands a little more than required and she blushes while getting on with the dressing. She asks him to come two days later for a dressing change.

The white Mauritian pursers Kristy-Anne and Laure and sports officer Fabrice are escorting the tours. They had all been waiting their turn to enjoy the free excursion in exchange for assisting the passengers although there was also a local tour guide. Kristy-Anne escorts the half day tour going past Hakonshalle to see the Rosencrantz tower going past fascinating mountain chalets. The fish market reminds her of their family beach house where her rich Franco Mauritian family spend the holidays during winter. She used to go with their Indian cook to choose fish at the market when she was a little girl. They see the Town Park and posh residential areas. They see old Bergen's traditional white-painted houses on their way to visit the house and grave of the famous composer Edvard Grieg. The tour ends by the visit of the eight hundred year old wooden Stave church, and one of the best aquarium in Europe.

Laure escorts the full day tour which is a longer version one which continues in the afternoon for lunch and more sightseeing. The local guide provides explanations as they drive along the Sorfjords streets and stop at the biggest windmill of the land in Vaksdalthrough. They see deep gorges before halting for a typical Norwegian lunch in Voss. In the middle aged church which they reach after crossing lush vegetation Laure is happy to sit down in the religious silence and open her heart to God. She is allowed three wishes when entering a church for the first time and she thanks God for this wonder in her life which had arrived just before her future wedding. She then used up all three wishes on prayers for safety for all on this voyage, success in her marriage and plenty of healthy kids. While the bus climbs up to the viewpoint to the Skervett waterfalls, the people who are heavy with the plenteous lunch and tired from getting on and off the bus and from all the walking to the viewpoints, start to doze off. The guide himself takes a little rest switching off the mike to let the people catnap while they drive down the valley. Up along Gavinsky he gently wakes everyone up to watch the opening up into the Hardangrfjords, and shows them fine orchards up steep slopes. The Steindal waterfalls are in view a few minutes later and they stop for pictures before moving on to Gullbotn onto Bergen's skier's paradise. Back on the ship, Laure eager to tell the other pursers about all she had seen, quickly changes into her evening uniform and grabs a quick dinner before taking her duty art reception. On the twenty eighth at dawn the ship reaches the British Port of Edinburgh in Scotland, where this cruise ends and passengers disembark by tender boats. Jane sees Gregory coming in the hospital as soon as the ship has anchored. She is pleased to see him but tells him "It is tomorrow that you have to come you can rest today, I shall keep the torture for tomorrow."

But he came nearer to her and said "You know what torture is to me, it is to be away from you, I would be happy to be tortured by your sweet hands. Would you come with me for lunch ashore?"

Jane accepts the invitation as she is free in the afternoon, they go out to Edinburgh where he hires a car and they drive along the famous princess Street for lunch in a posh restaurant. When they go past Sir Walter Scott Monument they see the tour bus on its way. Passengers go to visit the castles and Saint Giles cathedral and Holyrood house before stopping for a couple of hours for shopping, there is no escort from the ship on this tour as there are only a few passengers taking part in it.

"What are you looking at?"

"It's the people from the ship on this tour bus, thanks God there is no escort or they would have talked about us."

"So what, they will have to talk about us anyway, I am not going to leave your side and they will be bound to see us together sooner or later?"

Jane was pleased to hear this as she had also fallen deeply in love with Gregory and sincerely hoped that they continue life side by side. She was only a bit worried that things did not turn out right and because of that she preferred to be sure before breaking the news.

Jane personally dressed the engineer's wound in his cabin where they spend most of their free time together.

The passengers have embarked on Cruise number 008 to the Baltic capitals. While listening to announcements by the cruise bureau over the loudspeakers, the girls who are still unable to go ashore feel an intense glum and a strong desire to walk on firm ground. They bitterly resent not having been more careful and thus earning this harsh punishment. They would miss the pleasure of summer sunshine cruising with the attractions of seven countries and five capital cities of the Baltic as described by the voice of the shore excursion manager, Karin telling the passengers all about this exciting trip.

"Ladies and gentlemen, on this cruise you will have the opportunity to appreciate the distinctive national character, sights and cultural appeal of each one of the following seven Baltic capitals. Leningrad, winter capital of the Tsars is the highlight of this cruise and running close are the white princesses, the cities of Stockholm, Helsinki and Copenhagen and last but not least is the city of Gdansk or Gdynia in Poland from where we shall cross over to Kiel Canal, cradle of the Astor."

Summoned to Mrs D's office, the punished girls were anxious to know what other calamity had come upon them. They worried about lots of little details which could cost them yet another ban ashore. They were afraid that the forgotten cup or the full ashtray from yesterday had been found in their cabin during spot check.

"I am pleased to inform you that after the past weeks and regular spot checks to your cabin it has been decided by management and this after forceful persuasion from Mrs. D's reports on your work that the ban has been removed and you are to go ashore again as from the next port in this cruise."

They are so happy that tears come to their eyes while the housekeeper embraces each of them telling them to enjoy the shore again. The four girls have lost the habit of cohabitation and their friendship has slowly changed to indifference. Francesca and Nelly are barely on speaking terms since the episode of the harsh words exchanged, moreover Nelly did not like her friend being on speaking terms with her ex boyfriend.

As for Marina and Paton they still share many times together and this sharing is bothering Paton who finds her boyfriend Clayton much too close to Marina.

The first excursion for them in Kiel is very different to the previous ones as foursome, each one goes separately. Nelly stays aboard to save her money while Francesca waits for Joe to go out in town. The tours go to visit the charming old hanseatic town of Lubeck and other picturesque towns nestled in the meadows, hills and lakes of Schleswig-Holstein. Sylvio wanted to take Marina out but she said she was on duty and Clayton told Paton to go out with the other girls as he had to replace a colleague.

The French passenger from cabin 423 Mr Minier comes back from the half day excursion and stops by the pantry where Francesca is on one to three o'clock duty. As usual, he tries to keep her updated.

"Do you know that this ancient town of Gdansk has been Prussian and Russian before becoming Polish? The Historical Municipal museum is a very good place to see that remnants of its past but just by walking down the of Gdynia roads you can see the blend of Gothic, Baroque and Renaissance buildings."

Francesca politely listens praying that he does not go on and on as usual, she would be going ashore with Joe at three thirty and she wanted to have time to prepare herself in order to look her best.

Today the tour escorts on the full day tour are Mr Reed and Esther the newly formed couple of the Astor. They can be seen hand in hand ashore and they wait for each other in the officer's mess to have their meals together. While visiting the beach town of Zoppot, they walk bare feet in the sand holding hands like teenagers.

Mr Reed takes pictures of a laughing Esther with a view over the vast beach. They then move on to the eastwards village of Oliwa where she tenderly lays her head on his shoulder while enjoying an organ concert in the cathedral. The town of Stockholm in Sweden, the city on Water, also called 'Venice of the North', is reached two days later. The town's elegant modern designed buildings and its stores of merchandise sharply contrasts with Gamla Stan, the old city, with its royal palace and narrow streets populated with boutiques and restaurants. Water trips are available here to go to the famous amusement park of Skansen, the Zoo and the nearby Wasa museum.

The escorts seen from the cabins where Mela is working on A deck look like red and white spots. They are wearing bright red polo shirts and white trousers to accompany passengers as the cruise bureau announces the departure of the different excursions. The half day trip circulates through narrow streets to see Stockholm's oldest cathedral and on to Fjaligatan viewpoint for a photo stop before driving on over the harbour to visit the Municipal museum in town.

The full day excursion is escorted by Kristy Anne and the ship's photographer Billy Drake in whose arms she had danced several tender slows in the Astoria lounge the night before. After a short bus drive, they stop in the seventeenth century Drottingholm Palace, residence of the Royal family; he takes pictures of passengers in the various nice spots while they visit the whole castle, the gardens and Chinese pavilion. While the local tour guide is giving explanations about the Swedish residential quarter during the drive back,

Kristy Anne and Billy are absorbed in an intimate private tête-à-tête.

Astor leaves Sweden and heads for Finland where various tours have been organised to discover this fantastic land. Finland with its country like atmosphere and its parks, forests, lakes and shorelines has a famous reputation for design architecture. This can be seen in its stunning modern buildings and striking statues, while charming old manor houses stand as witness to its glorious past. Heidi escorts the half day tour uncovering the elegance of its spacious Capital Helsinki, to see the Dome and University grounds and the Sibelius monument in its Park. After visiting the cliffs to go back to the ship driving through the magnificent garden town of Tapiola, she is relieved to get back to her patients and doctor. Carolina the British dancer who is a part time art student escorts the longer, five hour excursion. She works as a dancer in seasonal tours to finance her fine arts studies. She has carefully collected all the documentation she could find about this place in order to be fully immersed in the surroundings. While the bus drives north among the wonderful landscape to Ainola she looks once more at the notes taken from her late reading on the previous night. She is delighted to see the house and tomb of the Finnish composer Jean Sibelius and the workshop of the Famous Finnish painter Pekka Halonen and the town of the Architects situated upon a cliff hill.

Marina's boyfriend Sylvio has gone ashore with his friends as she was again on duty. Paton once more had to go with friends as Clayton told her that he had to stay on board near the toilet as he was suffering from acute diarrhoea. As soon as everyone was safely ashore,

Marina who had been hiding in the passenger toilets stealthily went back to her cabin to make sure that Paton was gone. The day uniform roughly thrown over the sofa and her master keys lying on the table showed that Paton had hurried ashore after morning duty. Marina hurried to D deck where an impatient Clayton was pacing the cabin floor. As soon as she opened the door she threw herself in his arms and they kissed passionately. They had been waiting for this moment for so long, even though they had tried to resist the attraction which drew each to the other like a powerful magnet. Clayton did not want to hurt his little brother even if he noticed that Marina did not really mean a lot to him. As for Paton it was a long time since he had become bored with her, he had realised that they had come together as a result of loneliness to comfort each other. It was with Marina that he had discovered real love; he was happy when she was aroud and wished to always be with her. They had been thrown together when she came to see his brother in their cabin and on occasions when the two others were absent, their love had taken over. It was since several weeks that they had been playing hide and seek trying to get a stolen kiss, a few stolen moments which caused their desire for each other to swell. They fell into each other's arms unable to let go of each other, they peeled away their clothes and went into the shower closing the bathroom door.

Aline, today's tour escort is enjoying her tour to Porvoo a typical village dating from 1346, she relaxes in her seat admiring magnificent landscapes commented by the local guide. They stop to visit the middle age cathedral and the town museum before enjoying a sumptuous lunch in a luxury hotel which was the former residence of the Russian Tsar. Leningrad, an exquisitely beautiful city that occupies a host of islands at the mouth of the river Neva, is still closer to the spirit of the tsar. Marina and Clayton have decided to try and go ashore without letting the other pair know, they want to spend the night together in the Russian capital. Marina will linger in her cabins pretending to be taken up by late passengers while Clayton would pretend having gone out with his friends. They wait till about two hours after the night duty is over, giving time to all the stewardesses to be out of the way before meeting on the gangway. Marina had asked Clayton to tell the truth to Paton. She said that once he did this she could also tell Sylvio that she was in love with his brother. Clayton hesitated at first unable to find courage to say it, when at last he gathered the strength to reveal the truth it was Marina who, fearing the consequences, prevented him from talking.

Carolina is again escorting the full day eight hours tour to visit places which would be very useful to her studies. The excellent Russian guide brings them to the heart of Russia to see the baroque palaces and awesome Peter and Paul fortress.

"Ladies and gentlemen, you are actually on the famous cruiser Aurora where the Russian revolution began."

Even more spectacular attractions found in the magnificent winter palace impress the visitors who then eat a typical delicious Russian lunch before going on to the Hermitage where is found over two million of the world's greatest art treasures. It would need days to really appreciate all but she is nevertheless over the moon to have at least the opportunity to admire wonders like works of Rembrandt, Van Dyk, Tizian, Raffael and Rubens.

Marina and Clayton walk along Leningrad's Avenues holding on snugly to each other freely exhibiting their love. They stop in a bar and order some drinks, they want to try real Russian vodka. They drink to their love kissing passionately, oblivious to the Russians who anyway do not show any interest in them.

"Clay, it's nearly one, we need to make a move, sailing is at three and we need to be on board before two."

"I know love, yes I think we ought to make a move otherwise we will become drunk and fall asleep here while the ship leaves for Latvia."

They have one last iced vodka and another Russian kiss before moving on to return on board their floating home. Marina goes to C deck to her cabin which she shares with Paton and when she finds it still empty, assumes the other girl has slept in Clayton's cabin on D deck.

"I want you to stay with me tonight, after all this vodka I would simply not be able to make it to bed alone and, do not tell me to pretend with Sylvio once more, no way it's you that I love and I prohibit you to go and sleep in that bed downstairs where she is lying."

Clayton who was only waiting for her to ask replies "I will never again allow you away from me, I shall sleep here and as from tomorrow we shall reveal our love to everybody no matter what they think of it."

When the ship sails at three in the morning, most of the people on board are fast asleep except of course those still on duty, like the navigating staff and sailors.

Paton who went ashore with her friends went to sleep in Clayton's cabin to wait for him coming back from ashore. She did not see Marina's things around but could hear Sylvio snoring in the upper berth. When she heard the usual announcement for visitors to leave the ship one hour prior to sailing, it worried her not to see Clayton coming back and was afraid he'd been left ashore. She put on her dressing gown and hurried up to her cabin on C deck. She opened the door not noticing that Marina's bed curtain was drawn. She thought Marina was sleeping in Sylvio's bed, then she heard his voice telling her his love and passion for her, she froze unable to believe her ears.

Like a fury she ripped the bed curtain to catch the naked lovers unaware. She took hold of Marina and started beating her and pulling her hair. Clayton tried to hold her hands but she was so infuriated that she lashed at him scratching his face with her long sharp fingernails. The screams emitted by Marina and the voice of Paton screaming abuse woke up all the nearby cabins. Vani and Juliette came rushing from the adjacent cabins to separate the fighters and try and calm the fury.

"Calm down Paton, if the security finds you having a fight it will be direct return home, is it this that you want?"

Juliette took Paton to her cabin while Vani stayed on to hear the lovers explain what had happened. Vani told Paton about the decision taken by Marina and Clayton to be with each other. Paton started to sob heavily while Juliette tried to console her "I know what you must be going through, believe me, I have gone through it and I would advise you not to put your job and your health at stake. You must be strong and understand that the best thing is to stay away from Marina and Clayton. If your anger gets out of control and the management get to know about it then there will be trouble for you as you are the one who attacked them."

Vani offered to move in with Marina while Paton would move in with Juliette, to avoid confrontation between the rivals. Paton gratefully accepted and Juliette and Vani talked to Clayton and Marina into not taking this matter any further. Vani went down to Clayton's cabin to bring Paton's things back. The following day at sea was spent in a solemn atmosphere with Marina and Paton carefully avoiding each other. Fortunately they did not work on the same deck so while at work, so it was not too hard to keep them apart. Paton spent most of her time in the cabin with Juliette and Vani who also joined to chat when Clayton came to see Marina in her cabin. Marina and Clayton were at last free to see each other without having to hide as Sylvio had also been informed of the situation. When the ship reached Latvia, they went out ashore hand in hand, thankful that their secret had been at last brought out in the open.

Romanesque Gothic Medieval Latvia is a lively country speckled with Islands lakes and rivers. A tour goes to its Capital, Riga driving along crooked streets in the labyrinth of this intriguing town.

Denmark is the last of the Northern princesses to be visited as the Astor anchors in its capital Copenhagen. Here the cruise bureau proposes a wonderful castle tour to Amalienborg and Christiansborg Palaces, stopping at the open air museum in Lyngby before going further to Elsinore where are found three more castles bearing typical Danish names like Hamlet, Frederiksborg and Fredensborg.

One of the other famous attractions of Denmark is the 'Little Mermaid', statue of a mermaid sitting on a rock which is also the typical souvenir of this land sold in tourist shops. The Tivoli Amusement Park provides fascinating rides which the crew try. They alternate screams with laughs and sobs during terrifying rides while trying each of the type of sensation offered. They start in the fun slide, and then go for a tour in the sling around, and in spite of the quite expensive prices they are unable to resist the Carousel, Topspins, Tagada and screaming swing. It is only when they have used up all their money that they reluctantly stopped sampling the frightful rides.

Transiting through the Kiel Canal, after saying goodbye to the white northern princesses, Astor crosses over to reach the exciting modern city of Hamburg in the daylight. More pleasures are in store for the sailors and crew members who wait for nightfall to stroll towards the famous Reeperbahn area. They spend the whole night enjoying its sex shops and erotic entertainment; many of the men get to live the wonderful dream of loving a blue eyed blonde by paying one of the call girls on the streets.

CHAPTER XIII

Magnificent Magdalena

While the ship was leaving Denmark on Friday Mela and her colleagues were leaving Mauritius for a series of flights and transits towards Hamburg.

Early on Saturday morning they reached the hotel and had the whole week end to enjoy the hotel life in Hamburg waiting for the arrival of the ship. They walk around, window shopping in the numerous Turkish shops where the shop owners speak only Turkish and German. Unable to find adequate German words for asking the cost of a beautiful cutlery set, Mela tries to talk in French, Nicoleta and Bianca also try to help with French words. A deep voice then asks the question for them and translates in French the German answer of the shopkeeper. They see the owner of the deep voice behind them, a big black African man "Hello ladies, it is so nice to be able to speak French, may I ask from where you are?"

Bianca immediately answers "Pleased to meet you, we are from Mauritius and you?"

"Then we are almost neighbours, I'm from Togo, Mauritanians and Togolese meet in Germany, that's very good!"

"No we are not from Mauritania in Africa but from the island Mauritius which can also be considered part of Africa"

"We are not part of Africa we are an independent land, why do you say we are Africans, we are Mauritians" Nicoleta tells Mela in Creole and in a low voice.

"I am Bianca and let me introduce you to Nicoleta and Mela; can we know your name?"

"Sorry, the joy of meeting French speakers made me forget politeness, my name is Robert Mansard de Souza and I am from Lome in Togo, I live in Hamburg since seventeen years."

As this would be the last free Saturday until their next holidays in six months the cabin stewardesses made the most of that day. The Togolese invited them for coffee in his apartment; they were to get glad to visit a resident of this huge town. It felt so much better than to only see the interior of a place as nameless as a hotel

Bianca was under the charm of Robert and told her friends "Hey girls do you want to go out to dance in Hamburg tonight?"

"Of course we would die for going out to dance in Hamburg!" Mela and Nicoleta replied together

"Robert is certainly going to bring us dancing aren't you Rob?"

"Well, euh yes we could certainly do that . . . ."

"At what time do we need to be ready and where shall we go dancing?" Mela asked.

"I shall be back from work at around ten this evening, come to meet me here and we shall go then."

The girls went back to the hotel happily making plans for tonight's party. They started probing the suitcases to find the best outfit for dancing the night away in Hamburg's finest nightclub.

"You better get some sleep during the afternoon to be able to stand the night away without collapsing!" Bianca told her friends.

Mela buys a few things from the supermarket to send home in a parcel box by the post. She feels funny with acute tummy ache, she tells her friends "I don't think I shall be able to go out tonight, I won't even be able to take a bath in this condition, I really don't feel like dressing up to go out."

"Do not think we will allow you to stay back, we shall make you feel better, I have pills which work wonders, take two now and if the pain persist, you'll have another two in three hours." Nicoleta says

Bianca goes to the hotel reception and orders hot mint tea and a hot water bottle and pampers Mela "There, I am sure you will feel better by the time we are to leave, Robert will not come back from work until around ten."

When Mela answered their knock at eight o'clock sharp she smelt the fragrance as Nicoleta and Bianca, with faces carefully made up appeared on their high heel shoes wearing their best attire. Still suffering awful cramps in the stomach, she felt much more like lying down than going anywhere. She did not however want to mar her friends' joy and did a big effort to take a bath and dress up.

They went for dinner in the hotel's dining room; there was a sort of sour tomato soup and some sort of boiled fish on the menu. As none of them could eat a second spoonful from that plate, they went back to their room to pack some Indian food brought from home, octopus vindaloo and Dholl puri and set out for Robert de Souza's apartment.

The Togolese man was in the shower when they rang the door and it took some minutes for him to open. He let them into the living room while he went to fetch drinks and the girls opened up their food packets which they all shared happily.

"What is it, it's delicious, is it your home cooking?" Robert asked between mouthfuls of the food. They washed down the meal with tea and apple juice which was only what he had in the house not having had time to shop for more sophisticated drinks.

The night was wearing away and the girls were becoming impatient to get going but Robert kept on doing small talk. "What is the religion practised by Mauritians, is it Islam or Buddhism?"

"In Mauritius we have all religions brought by the population who came from diverse parts of the world. We have Hinduism Islam Buddhism, and Christianity."

"Do you practise any religion yourself?"

"Of course we do we are fervent Catholics, and to which religion do you belong?"

"I am a Catholic too, but here I only practise secretly in my heart because it is costly to be a member of any religion."

"Why is it costly, do you not give what you want and is not what you give kept secret?"

"No, it is not like that here in Germany, you need to declare your religion and your money is automatically debited from your account, you see that is why I prefer to pray in my heart without having to open up my pockets."

Mela cannot contain herself and burst out laughing which outrages her friends, but Robert joins in the hilarity until the four of them are all happily laughing. The clock was saying well past ten o'clock by this time and the cosmetics on the girl's faces was beginning to fade. Nicoleta and Mela kept on signalling to Bianca that time was running and they wanted to go out at last. Finally Bianca told Robert that if they were to go out it would be better for them not to go out too late as they would have to join the ship the next day.

They set out in the streets of Hamburg all excited to go and dance the night away. They climbed in a beautiful bus to the train station where for the first time they took a train which brought them to the centre town. Proud to be escorted by a powerful handsome man, they were fascinated with the lively atmosphere in the hot quarters of Hamburg. "Look at Bianca, she's like a hen in front of a cock she looks as if she's about to lay an egg!" Nicoleta told Mela who as usual burst out laughing. Bianca asked Robert if the nightclub was still far away as it was already more than forty minutes that they were walking in town.

"I am so sorry but I completely forgot to get money from the bank and I'm afraid would not be able to pay you any entrance into the nightclub. We shall do it next time you are in town, for tonight we can take a stroll and enjoy the warm evening air."

The girls were so disappointed but they made a good face and said "Yes certainly we shall do it next time anyway it's already so late, we can visit the town for this time."

They wandered around the Reeperbahn area famous for its sex shops; when they saw nude women in the shops show cases. They were puzzled at first as normally models are in showcases to show dresses for sale, then they understood that the women for the men to window shop. They walked along the streets where sex workers armed with all their weapons of sexy clothes and extreme make up balanced on terribly steep shoes to earn their living. The dresses were designed to reveal all the parts of the female anatomy which clothes were supposed to conceal.

Robert escorted them all the way back to the hotel, they took the last bus to the train station and it was past midnight when they reached the hotel. The prince charming had brought Cinderella's back home after the ball except that this time they had missed the ball itself!

When they reached their rooms Nicoleta said "Hey Bianca we have really danced tonight haven't, we are near to collapse.

The next morning was time to resume work and Mela was delighted to see her beloved Astor in Hamburg Harbour. As soon as they had been given their living quarters and uniforms they started right away to work as it was a disembarkation day for the first of a new series of cruises arriving and departing in Hamburg. Mela took the cleaning pail and Mr Hoover the vacuum cleaner over from Cecile who was a stewardess going on holiday and resumed her duty.

That night there is a barbecue on C deck and they were kept updated on the events during their absence. In spite of being exhausted, it was not until about one thirty that Mela could go to bed. There was such a lot of gossip to catch up with; while sharing the goodies from home with those who were missing so much the Mauritian food she learned about the breaking up of the four girls' clan and the events having lead to it.

Astor departs at four in the afternoon on Tuesday fourteenth leaving Leith in Edinburgh from the firth of forth and turns almost due north for cruising for almost three whole days towards the fjords. The strong waves of the North Sea roll the ships floor causing many people to become sick. Mela who had been off the sea for over a month started getting her hot flushes one moment and feeling so cold that goose pimples appeared on her arms. She felt so drowsy that she found it hard to simply stand and keep her balance. She was feeling so bad, her face had gone all green and it was hard to work, it was as if she was in a nightmare doing all the efforts to get moving but with strong resistance from she did not know where hampering her movements. Then she received the visit of an angel in the form of Francesca who noticed how pale and sick Mela was looking. During all the days at sea she finished her work and came to help Mela doing her cabins. She also provided a most miraculous remedy to take Mela out of her lethargy and made her laugh by telling her things about people from their village. Francesca told her gossip about people from the church at home who were only blank faces to her. While talking to Mela one day she suddenly burst out laughing. Mela was puzzled and asked her the reason for her hilarity.

"If you could see the transformation on your face when I am relating those things to you, your face lightens up and your mouth is ajar while you listen with interest and forget all about your sickness."

Mela also laughed with her and agreed that listening to gossip was indeed a very good remedy for seasickness as if by focusing her attention on something, the state of lethargy which the sea sickness induced in her was dissipated

The ship left Edinburgh heading North past Sea oil rigs and the Shetland Isles towards the Arctic Circle. During the long summer days, from the twelfth to the twenty-seventh of July passengers and crew would have the rare opportunity to venture into Arctic waters for a two day visit to the barren but spectacularly beautiful landscapes of Spitzbergen. This land found in the remote northern part of the planet was inhabited by a few thousand Russians and Norwegians and many more seals and reindeers and millions of seabirds. The cruise would then come back on its own trail via North Cape for a cliff view of the midnight sun.

The loudspeakers inform passengers about their whereabouts and the voice of Karin the Shore excursion manager resound in the corridors in four languages.

"Ladies and Gentlemen, we are about half way to the perpetual summer daylight of Spitzbergen. This remote and empty Arctic sea can reveal wonderful surprises, so keep your cameras handy, you might see whales, porpoises, seals and other marine life. Also with the increasing incidence of ice there can be many species of seabirds to be seen alongside brilliant icebergs gleaming as diamonds in the sun.

All through the next four painful days at sea, Mela is tortured by both sea and home sickness. The magnificent sight of glaciers and fjords makes her feel slightly better, the ships sailors having left their rope ladders and paint brushes to play water taxi men and bring passengers by the shuttle zodiac to Magdalena fjord. Running five miles East-West into the mountains the magnificent Magdalena fjords meet the two hundred and eighty feet ice wall of Waggonwaybren Glacier, one mile wide and ringed by three thousand feet peaks. Throughout the summer, icebergs are calved into the fjord, the North side is green with abundant plant life, bright alpine flowers and alive with birds. A large colony of little Auk surrounds the pyramid shaped Alkekongen Mountain. The sunless south side of the fjord shows slopes rising bleakly clothed in permanent frost and deep shadows relieved only by icefalls and glaciers. The Hanging glacier on this side juts out precariously above and once and again sheds giant ice cubes into the waters with fearsome crashes. Sun and ice, light and shade, life and desolation it is how all visitors remember Magdalena fjords.

While they get on the shuttle into the crisp cold outside air which bites into the skin, Mela and her friends almost forget the cold at the magnificent sight of spectacular Longyearbyen situated on a branch of Isfjord. Surrounded by the breathtaking scenery made up of beautiful peaks, glaciers, streams and rocky wilderness this town of Spitzbergen is home to reindeers, seals and arctic birdlife who share the place with about one thousand residents. A Governor administers this land whose inhabitants are occupied in fishing and coal mining.

"Don't you agree with me that this place should be named Black and White" Nicoleta tells her friends

"Why . . . ?" Asked a puzzled Mela

"Open up your eyes dear can't you see it; it's black and white in front of you!"

While Mela is still looking far away towards the mountains, Bianca tells her "Don't send your eyes so far, just look in front"

Alongside the twin piers and small boats in the harbour black mounds of coal form a sharp contrast with the background of snow covered mountains.

The fascinating landscape of the frozen Arctic Ocean lit by the eerie light of the midnight sun on the far horizon is the sight promised by the cruise bureau to passengers taking the tour in Honningsvaag. This town situated at mainland Europe's most northerly point is where the Astor anchors for reaching the land of the midnight sun. The tour extends to another charming capital of the north, Tromso, where the panorama of this forest-clad island can be viewed from a cable car, before the bus goes to visit its Marine aquarium and polar museum.

The Mauritians have met to share the delicacies brought from home by their colleagues, shrimp chutney and hot tamarind jam. Marion the German senior stewardess in Mela's pantry accepts to taste a spoonful of the food spiced with enough chilli to set the mouth of the habitual chilli eater on fire. Marion had never before tasted chilli in her life, as soon as the paste hits her taste buds; she flushes to a purple colour and starts coughing. Her worried colleagues then have to use a towel to scrape the taste from her tongue and make her drink milk to cool her inflamed mouth.

The overland tour scheduled in Hellesylt on the twenty third of July is announced as packed with startling sightseeing such as sparkling waterfalls cascading down sheer cliff faces of the Geiranger fjords, appropriately known as the most beautiful of all fjords. The enjoyment of a spectacular cruise upon the crystal waters of the same fjords is on the other hand promised to those who choose to stay on board.

CHAPTER XIV

Fire on the Iceberg

Hellesylt waterfall is the first place where tour bus stops; it then crosses the road past Honningdal Lake, which is Europe's deepest lake with a depth of six hundred metres. The tour continues after refreshment in Grodaas, past the dazzling Nordfjord glaciers to the famous Vikings Hill cemetery in the village of Hijelle. It then drives on along serpentine roads for a photo stop at the Buldre waterfalls, after lunch many more lakes come in sight while driving into the mountains to the Dalsnibba peak. Up on the peak, expressions like 'Out of this world', 'What Magnificence', 'Real Wonder' can be heard from groups of passengers who are astounded by the magnificent panoramic view extending over the Gletsher snow covered mountains, and the Geiranger fjords. The return trip via the narrow mirror like fjords and wild luxuriant forests in Flydal to rejoin the ship in Geiranger is also a delight to the senses.

The following days are spent at sea while the ship sails back south towards Scotland to Hamburg. On such occasions when the ship stays for several consecutive days at sea, a staff party is organised for the crew. They can thus unwind their stress from the hard work by having a drink and moving their body to the rhythm of music.

Mela is happy to see her ex passengers who come to visit in Hamburg; she meets Frau Elna Konig Jambor who brings her a beautiful pink purse with a couple of German Mark notes. Frau Elna was from Rumania but had married a German and had lived in Germany the last forty five years.

The Togolese met in Hamburg had been invited by the cabin stewardesses, to visit the ship. He had arrived at the gangway and an announcement was made for Mela, Nicoleta and Bianca to meet the visitor. Neither Nicoleta nor Bianca wanted to play hostess, they did not want to run the risk of getting into trouble with their boyfriend on the ship.

"That's not nice from you; he was so nice to us in Hamburg."

Bianca said "Sorry, but I remember only drinking tea and waiting a whole night to only have a walk in town, you know how jealous Hervey is, do you want me getting into trouble?"

Nicoleta told Mela "If you found that he was so nice then you do the touring, I am absent; I met a blond, blue eyed German steward at the doctor's party. There is no way I shall risk losing my chance by being seen with Mr Robert Mansard de Souza."

Mela therefore took the early duty in Hamburg and was free at ten thirty to show to guide her Togolese friend through her ship. She made up a story about her two other friends having had duty and apologized for their absence.

"They are so sad not to be able to meet you but they unfortunately did not get time off and are unable to meet you. They send their greetings and want you to know that they have a very good remembrance of you."

Mela was all alone in her cabin as her previous roommate had disembarked in Hamburg to go home on her holidays. Suddenly there is a loud knock on the door, although she was happy to see Nicoleta she pretended to still be angry at her for having been left alone with the task of showing the ship to their mutual friend. Nicoleta embraces her and says "Come on stop sulking, today I am sleeping in your cabin, I have juicy news about my blond blue eyed guy. Mela is all ears as her friend relates her love affair with her German lover and they both lie in the same bed talking until they fall asleep. Nicoleta soon finds herself kicked out of the narrow bed onto the floor as Mela is moving so much about, kicking around in her sleep. She finally goes into the upper berth to finish the night more peacefully.

During disembarkation on the next day, feeling very hungry they decide to take a quick pause to grab some lunch in the mess at noon. The whole crew seems to have come for lunch at the same time and the cutlery rack is empty.

"I am very hungry and also in a hurry, I think that I shall eat with my fingers." Mela says.

"Don't you dare do such a thing in public do you think you are in your house, just wait and see?"

Nicoleta then grabs a pair of dirty forks from the dishwasher rack which she quickly cleaned using hot water from the lavabo.

In the evening after a delicious dinner of chicken Mela is invited by Francesca to have a treat, green mangoes with hot salt and chilli. She eats the Mauritian delicacy to her heart's delight until her tongue is on fire and her eyes and nose are running.

Her new cabin mate had finally arrived, she was nice and helpful and even more cheerful than Bianca. It was so nice to have company again, she felt so miserable alone in that cabin with no one to talk to.

When the ship leaves Leith in Scotland on her northwards journey to the land of Ices the movement upstream shakes the ship; drawers and doors emit strange fearsome noises and open by themselves, as if by invisible hands. The continuous shaking make stomachs and heads revolve; people start getting green in the face and soon become constantly sick and throw up sour and bitter bile. Sometimes the vomit lands in an adequate handy sickness bag or the icy steel handrails of the ships balconies other times it sprinkles or showers less appropriate surfaces like dining tables or pillows or the poor person who happens to be on its trajectory. On such days Mela has to carry her stock of sickness bags, she always forget to order those from the provision master but her friends always make sure to order enough sickness bags for the 'Vomito', as they nick named her.

The departure of the ship at five in the evening for two days at sea towards Reykjavik, capital of Iceland holds promises of nice sleep as the clocks are put one hour back each night. Having used up about ten sickness bags before finishing duty Mela only wishes to go to bed. She has no intention of going out tonight even though it had been announced that the party organized on D deck by the sailors was going to be really good.

Nicoleta does not agree to let Mela go to sleep in such a sea. "Do you intend throwing out your guts inside the cabin, have not heard the announcement? Wind force is seven, do you think lying down will help? You know that the only thing that can help is a nice gust of icy fresh air. So you please wear something warm and come with us, I am definitely not leaving you out here alone. There is no way that I shall miss such a party babysitting you when there are so much nice drinks available there, we shall bring the baby to the party."

As they move down to the depth of the ship on D-deck in where the shaking is even more intense, they virtually reel trying to keep their balance holding on to rails and walls. At one point Mela has to empty her already empty stomach into her vomit bag. As soon as icy wind rushes in from the opening of the outside door whipping fresh marine air onto their faces she feels better. A few moments later she experiences intense well being as the seasickness abates and she even starts dancing to the beat of her favourite songs: *New York, One night in Bangkok, Tokyo, You're my heart you're my soul.* They all hold shoulders and dance to the music of the song '*We are the World*' while the ships decks seem to withdraw under their feet as it moves they fall over screaming and laughing to tears. The furious ocean waves roar making the music and screams of laughter barely audible. Mela even manages to eat several pieces of acid mangoes with salted red and green chilli. The crew was dancing with tears running down their cheeks and mucus down the nose, hanging out the tongues set on fire by the chilli. The party was well timed as work would only start at eight on the next day; it would in fact be at nine as time goes one hour back when travelling west, this meant a nice sweet blissful sleep. Moving westwards retards the clocks by one or two hours depending on the distance covered and the ship's speed. Wonders of this spectacular adventure cruise unfold during the long days of the Arctic summer. The scenery uncovers the magnificent frozen beauty of unspoilt islands of the North extending from the very small unknown Shetland and Faeroes Islands to whole wide world's largest island Greenland. Gigantic icebergs and astounding glaciers side by side with massive mountains lit by the eerie light of the midnight sun are the highlights of this cruise. Lucky people who get the chance of catching a glimpse of the white fluffy polar bears would cherish this memory for their whole life. This sanctuary so far up north is home to many other rare animals such as alert arctic foxes, mighty musk ox, shrewd snowy owls and majestic sea eagles. This old town of traditional timber found around the busy harbour is also a bustling modern city with all facilities of a capital city. The cruise bureau offers excursions to visit its botanical gardens, national museum and art gallery. The wealth of natural phenomena spread along Iceland's volcanic landscapes is tremendous. They range from bubbling geysers to volcanoes amongst spectacular waterfalls and mountains. Carolina is as usual part of a cultural tour; it is the visit of the folk museum on the outskirts of the Arboer city where historic homes are preserved intact. Kristy Ann and Margaret follow the tours to the spectacular golden waterfall of Gullfoss, the lava arena of Thingvelliris, the site of the ancient Viking parliament and the greenhouse village of Hveragerdi heated by natural hot springs.

More fortunate passengers take a helicopter hovering over the lava fields for a bird eye's view of Reykaner peninsula, the new volcanic island of Surtsey. The helicopter flies above Thingvelliris overlooking magnificent coastal glaciers and hovers inland to see the Hekla volcano.

The Greenland adventure is lived in a mixture of bliss and misery by Mela who is still not yet accustomed to the rolling of the ship. The spectacular frozen beauty of the landscape seen through the large glass portholes while she cleans the passenger's cabins simply take her breath away and makes her so happy. The terrible rolling of the ship moving through icy frozen waters brings her to a state of intense misery. She has to stock her uniform pocket with several sickness bags as she needs to throw up almost every ten minutes the bitter bile which such seas always produce in her stomach.

Mela and her friends have joined self defence classes given by the Jamaican cook in order to exercise their body muscles numbed by the continuous dancing of the ship under their feet.

The southernmost tip of Greenland, Cape Farewell appears at early hours of the morning in daylight. The light prevents Mela and many other people from sleeping as it is indeed bothering for somebody used to sleep in complete obscurity. The cruise bureau announces that the ship will be passing this spectacular site at four in the morning. On hearing that, Mela tells Nicoleta "I must see this place even if I need to get up at three o'clock to go on deck!"

But the ship was almost in Godthab and Cape Farewell had already said farewell hours back by the time she woke up. A visit of Godthab museum found in a 1747 built house is proposed to the Astor's passengers as part of the excursion in this land. The eight thousand inhabitants of Greenland's largest town live in tiny settlements of picturesque colour washed wooden houses on the Godthab fjord's steep mountains.

The town of Umanak situated well above the Arctic Circle in the middle of the wild white Arctic scenery is Astor's most northerly port of call which is reached after a couple of days at sea. At Disko bay in Jakobsavn great glaciers break from the Ice fjord as they meet the sea. The fleet of fantastic shaped icebergs thus launched display an array of colours from turquoise to mauve as the light changes. A grand barbecue on deck allows passengers to enjoy the frozen landscape around the warmth of the grill. Delicious heat waves from the fire make the bitter cold more bearable while sizzling pieces of chicken, beef, pork and fish are served straight from the grill.

Narssaq, major settlement of Old Norse ruins and interesting museum and pottery is reached after two days sailing. Land of sea eagles, seals and whales Narssaq has its own rare animal skins fur factory enabling visitors to bring back memorable souvenirs of this remote land.

Sitting on the bus to the beautiful Dyrness valley and up to Kvanefjeldet Mountain, Laure religiously admires stunning views of the long fjords with their numerous icebergs and the inland ice sliding down the mountains to the sea.

Four long days of abysmal misery with terribly choppy seas follow the breathtaking views of Narssaq as the Astor moves on an east trajectory towards the faraway Thorshavn.

Mela is desperately sick and uses dozens of sickness bags while working, fortunately her guardian angel Francesca is by her side. She helps her friend with her work and tries to lessen her agony of nausea and headache. One minute she is overwhelmed by spells of hot flushes alternating with cold which makes her body hair stand erect and goose pimples rise on her arms but Francesca manages by her stories from home, to bring at times a thin smile on her miserable face.

Thorshavn Faroe Islands is a small group of eighteen islands made up of steep cliffs and soft green hillsides, haven for numerous seabirds and place of surviving medieval culture with language legends, folk songs and dances. Unique Faroese sweaters made from local sheep's wool are a good buy during the visit to the original cultural centre of Kirkjubour. The cruise ends by Lerwick in the Shetland, northernmost of the British Isles settled by Norsemen since the ninth century and where many prehistoric sites can still be seen. Lodberries which are loading piers built out over the harbour can be seen in this picturesque harbour bustling with fishing boats and interesting old merchant houses.

The summer cruise continues with a tremendous combination of scenic splendour and historic cities on the innermost shores of the Baltic and the highlands. Here in Lapland the Lapps still live their nomadic life, they herd reindeers dressed in their distinctive and brightly coloured clothes.

The new passengers embarked in Leith Scotland have the possibility to see the Dundee Law extinct volcano crater with it panoramic view. In this village is found the famous Glamis castle surrounded by the majestic Grampians Mountains. Rosemary escorts the tour to visit the since1372 royal residence which was the showplace of Shakespeare's Macbeth. The castle is the childhood home of Elizabeth Bowes-Lyon later to become the Queen mother. Esther and Dora are escorting the tour to Edinburgh which drives past the Forth road through typical Scottish landscapes over royal miles to the St Giles cathedral, the commercial Princess street and the University. They enjoy breathtaking views passing Loch Earn, famous for its trout farms, through the wooded valley of Strathyre to Callander. After lunch at Loch Venachar they move further on to Loch Katrine for a little walk before seeing the picturesque village of Aberfoyle past the Stirling Castle.

The ship leaves Dundee at dusk on the sixteenth of August and crosses the sea for two nights and a day to reach the Port of Hamburg in the North of Germany on Tuesday eighteenth at eight in the morning. One of the great and historic ports of Europe, Hamburg is now largely rebuilt in a spacious attractively laid out modern city with tree lines avenues and extensive covered shopping precincts. The great Alster Lake is situated in the middle of the city where hundreds of bridges parks, botanical gardens and canals offer beautiful sightseeing by day. After the night falls it is the waking up of the famous Reeperbahn district near the docks with all manner of entertainment such as beerhalls, discos, cabarets and nightclubs. The Hansa theatre, one of Germany's last remaining music halls is also open for the evening. The cruise continues along the Kiel Canal which connects the North Sea with the Baltic from Brunsbuttel to Holtenau.

During the couple of days along the Kiel canal Mela remembers the bus trip taken on her very first day in Germany after landing at Hamburg Airport to the harbour of Kiel where the Astor had been a brand new ship waiting to be prepared for her maiden voyage. Since this January day during one of the coldest winters with temperatures of minus twenty seven degrees centigrade, they had crossed so many oceans covering thousands of nautical miles. In these last nine months there had been innumerable ports visited, thousands of passengers exchanged and maybe as many vomit bags used!

The modern city of Stockholm in Sweden known as the Venice of the North, occupies a string of islands where Lake Mallaren meets the Baltic. The delightful old town of Gamla Stan in this beautiful modern city reveals wonderfully preserved old buildings along each bend of its narrow, cobbled streets. One can spend time in its busy boutique and shops or visit the Royal palace overlooking the harbour and the thirteenth century Storkyrkan and Riddarholm Churches. Another way to visit the city is by pleasure cruising around among the islands in little boats. Today it is Nurse Jane's turn to go on tour and her sweetheart the second engineer Gregory Princeton who is half-heartedly going on his vacation comes to say his farewell on the pier. She is happy to be going out of the ship as she would have been so miserable when he had gone. On that day they were to visit Carolina Redviva and the Cathedral; in the well known Uppsala University's Library is found a famous Silver Bible. After a typical Swedish lunch they go to a place called Sigtuna which had been Sweden's capital in the year 1000.

Lulea Lapland is an archipelago of three hundred islands where Lapp camps and museum of local arts and crafts at Jokkmok as well as beautifully decorated village houses in the old Gammelstad can be visited. Here in Sweden's most northerly course at Boden one can even enjoy a game of Golf.

The next port of call is Mariehamm, main port of a large group of Finnish islands. Their strategic position in the middle of the Baltic between Sweden and Finland have made them change hands more than once during the wars of the last seven centuries. Margaret and Esther are escorts on the tour to the fortress of Bonarsund and Casteholm, in these ruins witness of the Port's wartimes, a Scandinavian lunch is served before proceeding to visit the historic Aland museum and western harbour of these nowadays peaceful holiday Islands. They see the four Mast ship called Pommend, souvenir of ancient navigation and romantic sailing boats. Margaret brings the French passengers who wish to shop to the colourful market place with plenty of handicrafts, a delight to shoppers. Esther accompanies the Germans over on the island of Seurasaari where all types of buildings from all over the country are gathered in an open air museum.

Other escorts, other passengers but same bus tours are scheduled in the next ports. Helsinki, the capital of Finland renowned for its modern design and architecture reveals is splendid old and new buildings set in spacious of parks and woodlands. Famous sons of Finland are honoured during the excursions; the studio of famous painter Pekka Halonen and effectively equipped workshop of the architect Saarinen are visited on a cliff hill.

Russian influence can already be felt in Helsinki's typical little town of Porvoo founded in the year 1346. Its middle age cathedral, its museum and the residence of the Finnish Dichters Runeberg all make one think of Russia, lunch is served in the ancient residence of the Russian Tsars converted into a luxury hotel.

The town of Leningrad in Russia is a jewel where shine several precious stones in various forms; the glorious winter palace, fabulous art collections of the Hermitage museum, baroque and pastel coloured palaces, Peter and Paul fortress and the famous cruiser Aurora which fired the first shot that started the Russian revolution. Mela has some time off during the day and goes ashore delighted to see the town and new people but her ready smile freezes when met by the cold hateful stares from the people in the squares. How she misses the warmth of Africans and the familiarity of Americans!

While discussing Russia, Hector, a blue black Mauritian utility boy very adequately voices the opinion of most coloured people who went ashore by saying "The people here seem to be reluctant to greet blacks; I think they fear we stain them with our black colour!"

The return via the Kiel Canal to the famous town of Hamburg with its attractive Reeperbahn quarter is longed for by the male crew members. They cannot wait to enjoy the glamorous sex life for which most of them are willing to pay the very high price. To hold a blue eyed blonde in his arms is a dream a fantasy for many a Mauritian man, imagine such a dream come true! Heads full of the intoxication of their nights on the Reeperbahn many crew members are refreshed having melted their fatigue and weariness in the arms of the delicious creatures on high heels.

Nicoleta was in a fury, she had not found her German boyfriend in his cabin and wondered if he was with another woman. She went out on the decks to cool off when she saw someone trying to climb on the ship's rail.

"Hey what are you doing, come down at once, and are you out of your head?" She pulled at the man who was trying to throw himself in the sea.

The man started to weep and she patted his shoulder "Tell me what it that has caused you is to such a desperate act, you can talk to me maybe I can help you find a solution to your problem."

The man then confided in her and revealed that after a few sexual intercourses with prostitutes in the Reeperbahn, he had started having trouble with his penis which was now really in a bad way giving off purulent discharge. He was desperate, sure he had caught his death and no cure was possible. Nicoleta brought him to see Nurse Heidi who examined him and reassured him that this was a common aliment that would be soon cured by powerful antibiotics prescribed by the ship's doctor.

"What is happening on this ship, death seems to be watching out for lives to take; I heard that Hedley drank poison after a fight with Gisela last night. Fortunately she called the doctor and he managed to pump it out of him on time." Juliette was relating the events to her friends in the pantry. Hedley was a very handsome entertainer who was going out with Gisela who was a very beautiful German waitress. He had been flirting with a woman passenger of about forty who was happy to have such an attractive young male in her bed. He loved Gisela and was sure that she would never come to know of his little adventure.

He knocked on her cabin door and as the door opened he rushed to take her in his arms. "You better take all your things and get out of my sight I never wish to see you again, bastard." She yelled at him in tears. "What's the matter with you darling, what did I do, tell me?' "I told you to get out; I do not want another word with you in my life!" She had packed all the gifts he had given to her and all his belongings found in her cabin in a bag which she threw at him. He started crying and begging but she remained adamant kicking him out of her cabin and of her life. He refused to go and sat down on the sofa waiting for her to calm down. "You may sit here if you wish but I am dead to you, I was since you cheated on me with that old woman. Good night to you, as for me I have found a new date and I am on my way." She had gone to cry her heart out on deck and came back to her cabin at dawn to find Hedley unconscious on the sofa, her empty bottle of nail polish remover next to him.

September and autumn in the northern hemisphere is the time for a real voyage of discovery into waters rarely visited by luxury cruise ships. Astor follows the path to the Polar Route to discover the spectacular unspoilt scenery of Iceland over to Labrador's rugged frontier settlements, its pine trees and log cabins and wood smoke, to cruise further on up the great St. Lawrence Seaway to Montreal. The ship sails from Leith on the first of September crossing the icy waters to Reykjavik on the south west coast of Iceland after four long days and nights of choppy seas. The passengers and crew, relieved to have at last reached firm land, all hurry ashore to the world's most northerly capital. Laura and Aline escort the morning tour buses cross the lava fields to the south of the island. It was Dora's turn to escort the tour but the barman David, her boyfriend had been scalded by the water of his inhalation apparatus. He had had a nasty bout of sinusitis causing him unbearable headache, he had placed a few drops camphor oil in boiling water in a basin and had covered his head over it with a heavy towel for trying to unblock his sinus by inhaling the camphor vapour. The ship had viciously jumped sending the scalding water to his face, fortunately his girlfriend Dora the nurse was in his cabin and gave him first aid care. Instead of driving to the fishing village of Grindavik, on along Bird cliffs to Krisuvik to sulfur fields, bubbling geysers and spouting hot springs she had to tend to the burnt face of her boyfriend. Kristy Ann and Margaret go on the afternoon tour when their colleagues are back to the front desk. They drive to Thingvellir and Hveragerdt along the island's biggest lake and typical landscapes to see the former seat of Viking's parliament. Rosemary and Heidi visit the natural hot water sources used in the Greenhouse Industry in Reykir on the full day excursion. After admiring the fantastic Gulfoss waterfalls tumbling down from a height of thirty seven meters into deep gorges the tour ends with the visit to the former seat of Viking's parliament in Thingvellir. As soon as she is done with her work Mela, who has as usual been suffering from seasickness, carries her piece of bread in her bag and hurries ashore. The calm and cool of the place seems to erase all her fatigue and pain and she wonders if the people here ever get heated or angry. In such silence, coolness and calm the rage virus which so often infects us human, specially, her people down in the heat of the tropics must simply be exterminated. She had gone to bed at around quarter to two after her little trip ashore for a nice peaceful nap until evening duty at six. She was sinking in a delicious slumber when she heard knocking on her door. She ignored the call hoping the person would go back but the knocks intensified, she still did not budge and kept her eyes tightly closed. Suddenly the door opened, a hand was on her shoulder calling her name and shaking her to wake up. She opened her eyes to find Bianca's boyfriend Hervey next to her bed.

"Get out of here quick, there is fire on the ship and in a few minutes the insulated steel bulkheads will close for containing any fire and maybe the whole section will be deprived of oxygen!" Hervey reminded her to take her life jacket and they made their way to the fire exits, they went through the doors shortly before the massive insulated steel bulkheads roared as they automatically slid on to imprison the cabins inside. They went to the assembly point on C deck to wait anxiously for further instructions. Apart from the closing of the insulated steel bulkheads all seemed quite as usual. They waited there for three long hours, Juliette and many others had started to cry, nobody was able to give them the least information about the fire. They were all thinking of the freezing arctic waters and of their families but nobody dared to say a word, they were paralyzed by fear. Mela thanked God for having left her cabin unlocked, if it had been locked, Hervey when not hearing any response to his calling would have had left thinking it was empty. Once the insulated steel bulkheads closed in order to contain the fire and prevent it from spreading to other parts of the ship, she would have been left alone in the section on fire, suffocating in the oxygen deprived cabin. The crowd started to thin out as everyone moved away, lost in her thoughts she had not heeded the security's officer who had come to tell them that the danger was over and it was safe again for them to get back to the cabins. The stock of matches in the store room had spontaneously ignited causing a mild fire. The situation had been brought back under control and they went back to their warm cozy beds instead of into the freezing sea.

CHAPTER **XV**

Crazy Canada

As usual time passes by slowly during the following days at sea; Mela spends her free time between her self-defense classes and the swimming pool on C deck. Many young crew members attended the Karate classes given by the Jamaican cook at nine thirty in the night; most of his pupils are among the cabin stewards who have finished duty at this time while restaurant and entertainment staff is busy with dinner service and night shows. The young and less young are all very glad to stretch their bodies in other ways than dusting and making beds. They enjoy these twice weekly karate classes which give them some sort of entertainment and exercise and improve their state of mind.

"I am really very glad to get to know all of you who come from different countries. I do sincerely hope that you benefit from the time spent here. Tonight we are going to start our classes but first, I have a few recommendations for you."

He listed all the benefits of practicing and insisted that this skill is to be used only for self defense and never for violence. He was a handsome, well built man in his thirties and the girls could not help themselves admiring his virility and the wonderful tone of his voice while he tells them about his family with three children back home. The young girls and less young women look at him while he speaks and in some hearts and minds romances start to shape. How nice it would be to be loved by such a man, oh God let me have even a night with him was what Brigitte the British waitress was thinking while Gabriela, the German purser was already viewing herself in his arms. They only get to feel his brief touch during a brief instant when he demonstrates a karate pose as he is faithful and very much in love with his lucky wife. On Wednesdays the fitness centre and swimming pool on C deck is open to the crew after nine in the evening. Some of the stewardesses delight in the modern fitness machines and heated pool for a couple of hours after night duty. Even if the chlorinated water of the swimming pool irritates her skin and eyes Mela enjoys the sense of well being that a good swim instills in her. Sun and sea water on the Mauritian beaches used to burn her skin and redden her eyes but she always enjoyed the same elation after a long swim. It did not bother her to pay the price with a ruined complexion.

In the afternoon of the eighth of September the ship reaches the first landfall in the New World, Goose bay which lies at the head of long narrow inlet cutting deep into the heart of a dramatic wilderness of soaring mountains and vast forests hardly touched by man's hands. Carolina finds priceless material for her research while escorting the tour to discover the Indian's village of 'Che Chan Che'. She takes plenty of pictures of its exposition of local handicrafts and delights in the traditional country music played in a village by the Hamilton River.

Another sea day and the Astor reach Corner Brook in Newfoundland, wild as it was when the Vikings discovered it a thousand years back with its countless long, deep inlets pock marking the coast; it reveals a superb panoramic view of the Bay of Islands at the Cook's monument. This large and jagged island nested next to a spectacular fjord where mountains hide narrow lakes and tumbling streams is today a lively modern city.

On the way to Canada, Gregory the second engineer makes a satellite phone call to talk to his sweetheart. The radio officer makes an announcement over the ship's sound system and everybody hears 'Miss Jane Randall is immediately requested on bridge deck for a satellite communication'. Satellite calls they are treated as top priority because of their frightfully expensive cost. She hurries to the bridge deck blushing with pleasure, proud to be the object of such care. Hearing this Mela tells Nicoleta "How terribly romantic, he must really be in love to spend so much to talk to her for a couple of minutes!"

This Sunday in Canada's port of Montreal is unlike other Sundays which are usually barely noticed during the ships daily routine. Conversations about this dream city fill the crew mess with information and speculations creating an unusually joyful atmosphere while the crew talk about the long stay ahead in this wonderful city. They are planning to make the most of this unique life opportunity and see as much as possible of this dream city in their free time.

"Man, sixty four hours in Montreal, the world's second largest French speaking city. Can you imagine the fun, the shops the nightlife the city, this will really be top."

The perspective of hearing familiar French after so many months of the strange guttural German, the singing Italian and rapid English is pleasant to the Mauritian crew who could not wait to hear some more french on the roads. Passengers take bus tours to visit the old eighteenth century town to the Jacques Cartier place and the Notre Dame Catholic Church driving up along the large boulevards in the modern centre town on to the Mount Royal Park and over to the mountain top. Laure who escorts this tour once more expresses the customary three wishes while she sits and prays in a the Notre Dame Catholic Church. Eva the purser who is also a singer escorts the tour on Saint Helen Island to the spectacular sight of ships being raised in the middle of the St Lorenz current in the Lambert channel.

Kristy Ann and Nurse Jane see picturesque views of little villages through the colour symphony of the Indian summer on the drive to Laurentian Mountains, the tour continues by a boat trip over to Lac des Sables.

David's face burns have healed and he has gone back to work in the bar, Dora can now again go out on tours. She is excited to escort the tour to Niagara Falls; this excursion goes by plane from Montreal to Hamilton to reach the falls after one hour on the bus.

With its million gallons of water falling in a huge and thunderous spray, the Niagara Falls attract millions of visitors spellbound by this spectacular natural phenomenon. After lunch in a panoramic restaurant the tour party spend the afternoon at leisure before the return flight to Montreal.

Mela and her friends also want to make the most of this wonderful city and decide to go out dancing in the nightclubs. After night chores they all dress up in their finest attire to go out; as they step down the gangway their expensive perfume momentarily fills the ships entrance before being lost in the overpowering marine smell of the port. That night they visit three different nightclubs, they start the night dancing at the 'September', continue in the 'Shipteme' and finish the night in the 'Winston Churchill'. Intoxicated with the atmosphere and the music Mela, Nicoleta and Bianca are invaded with a sensation of intense happiness. They dance to the rhythm of the music of the famous Diva Whitney Houston's song 'I want to dance with somebody' singing at the top of their voices.

A young man asks Mela for a dance with him "You are a fine dancer, where are you from in Montreal?" he enquires. They had to come very close to be heard over the loud music.

"I do not live in Montreal I am from the Astor, the cruise ship which arrived here yesterday. I am from Mauritius and you?"

"I'm Faizal from Pakistan I'm a chef in a hotel here since five years. Mauritius, it seems that I have heard about this beautiful island in the Indian Ocean, and I see it has very beautiful girls. Let me introduce you to my friend Arjoon who works in the same hotel."

The night goes on with so much fun, nice people, terrific music and delicious cocktails for a perfect evening. Suddenly Mela sees a crowd on the dance floor surrounding a man who is drunk and is fighting with some other men. Mela and her friends recognize a Mauritian waiter named Gokhool as the protagonist of the fight. He drunk and staggering on his feet he was challenging two sturdy blacks to fight. The men who were also drunk were about to give him a good thrashing when Mela and her friends interfered and pulled him out. They were asking for a taxi to take him away when Faizal kindly offered to bring them back to the ship in his car. Mela told her friends "I thought that I had left my drinking cousins back in Mauritius and for once could enjoy myself in peace but no, it seems one has followed me all the way to Montreal!" They all climb in Faizal's big Mercedes back to the ship thanking him for his precious help.

The next day the rounds to the nightclubs are resumed after work and the girls pray that this time there will be no Gokhool to spoil their fun. They form a little group and walk over from the ship towards the chic quarter of St Catherine where they dance the night away to the delicious music. The ship leaves the port of Montreal at eight on the morning of the sixteenth September and sails to reach the eighteenth century walled city Quebec at six that same evening. Strolling leisurely along the broad walk overlooking the harbour with its street musicians and fine restaurants, eager dancers in search of nightclubs again go out on the narrow streets after quickly finishing their night duty. They finally choose the nice music of the Brandy and Dagobert nightclubs along the way to stop and dance for a couple of hours.

Seats on both the night tours in Quebec are filled after only two announcements from the cruise bureau. Canadian Folkloric show and festive dinner in the renaissance style castle 'Chateau de Frontenac', overlooking the lighted sea of Quebec is on tonight's program. Passengers are driven through the historic old town via the Place Royale to reach the citadel which military walls delimit Quebec and the St Lorenz.

Another tour drives past picturesque landscapes to see the Cathedral and statue of St Anne de Beaupre. Kristy Ann who escorts this tour admires the wonderful mosaics portraying the saint's life in the Cathedral before moving to the Montmorency waterfalls where hanging fogs fall out about ninety metres in the air.

The next morning still groggy from the late night Mela wakes up and happily does her cabins as she has no day duty. "Stop dragging your feet come on finish with your cabins before noon so that we can take the lunch break to go out early" Nicoleta told Mela

"But how about lunch I'm hungry already and it's only a quarter to eleven!"

"Don't start with your being hungry, we shall grab something on the street don't think I shall have lunch here on this ship which I have seen for so many hundred hours while it is possible to eat out in a town like Montreal!"

Intoxicated with this Canadian summer they stroll happily along the nice shopping galleries of the town. They stop at a Spanish snack for crisp salad and Canadian toast which Mela finds delicious; she exclaims "This is simply marvellous!"

"And you were dying to eat Astor's lousy lunch for the thousandth time, you fool!"

It was pure bliss doing window shopping until something tantalising brought them through the door. They happily spent much of their hard earned money on clothing and shoes, putting more weight to their already bulging and overstuffed suitcases.

The ship will anchor for ten hours in the next port of St John in Newfoundland where Marconi had sent the first Trans Atlantic wireless message from Signal hill.

Those who still have time and money would be able to see the thoroughfare, sample the numerous Irish flavoured pubs aligned on Water Street, North America's oldest street. Mela and Nicoleta are not spared the usual nightmare during the two more next days at sea. While Nicoleta tries to drown the seasickness in Bacardi rum, Mela fights with it in her bed trying to sink in her book and forget the nauseous sensations.

The silence in cabin 711 was only interrupted by the quiet snores of the occupants sleeping peacefully. Mela was awakened by the sound of water running in the lavabo.

"Hey wake up you have tea duty just like me today isn't it?"

"What's the time, is it already 3 o'clock?"

"It is quarter to three but by the time you shower and get ready it will be almost time to go."

"I shall get up at three; I shall shower tonight after self defence classes."

At quarter past three the two cabin stewardesses leave their cabin and take the crew stairs to go up for their tea duty. Marina who was on one to three thirty duty had thoroughly cleaned the pantry tidying the mess done during cabins cleaning in the morning. The metal surface of the fridge and cupboards were shining like a mirror and the floor was still wet and shiny from polish applied to it. She was waiting outside holding the garbage in three bags, one for biodegradables, a second for plastics and a third with glass in it. On her way down she is going to carry those down to C deck to have the biodegradables burnt in the incinerator while the recyclables would be set apart to be sent ashore in the next environment friendly land.

"Could you please wait a few minutes before entering the pantry as the polish needs to dry a little more before you can walk on it?"

The rolling of the sea is being felt and Mela has to answer several calls to serve tea with Dramamine tablets for passengers who are feeling seasick. She is herself not feeling well and those three hours of duty seem endless while attending to the incessant ringing of the phone. When asked for a bucket of ice and champagne glasses in cabin 318, she thinks the passengers want to celebrate something but they tell her that they are simply taking champagne as medication for seasickness. She goes to the laundry to fetch clean bed linen and towels, while she stacks them up neatly on the linen shelves, the phone rings once more.

"A forward pantry good afternoon Mela speaking"

"Mela could you please come on D deck there is someone who wants to meet you"

"But I am on duty and cannot leave the pantry"

"It will not take long please come."

Mela decides to ignore this request which comes most probably from the utility stewards wanting to fool around. At dinner she tells this to Nicoleta who says "Never ever listen to such requests those rogues could lay a trap for you and may rape you, next time they call just call me and I shall deal with them!"

Tonight the self defence class is particularly hard and John the Jamaican cook makes the girls pant and sweat with his tough training. When the class is over, they still feel full of energy and do not feel sleepy although the watches indicate past ten o'clock at night.

Nicoleta declares "I am going for a stroll on the sundeck, cannot sleep right now."

"I shall take a shower and join you in some minutes I want to enjoy the view over the sea and the stars." Mela says

When she reaches the sun deck she finds Nicoleta lying on the long sun chair eating grapes and pears. She remembers their early days of seasickness when they almost only ate fruits at night up on the deck in the fresh air to avoid seasickness. Now after almost nine months of navigation they are more adapted to marine life and the fruits they are eating are a dessert to the big plate of delicious fried rice they had had at the crew mess for dinner.

Bianca who has also joined them comments "If we did not have so much work and self-defence exercises we would have become so fat."

On days where there is no self defence classes they play volley ball and ping pong on the sports deck. They then sink comfortably in the deck chairs till very late in the night watching the stars sprinkled sky while the ship breaks the dark waves at full speed.

The days at sea pass by with the boring routine of such days; everyone is longing to see firm land again. Suddenly the air seems to have chilled; the navy uniform cardigans are taken out of wardrobes as the freezing temperatures start to be felt, one shiver in the cabins and the temperature has to be raised. The experienced sailors say that there are cold countries nearby which cause this drastic fall of mercury. One can no longer talk the usual stroll on the decks which are swept with a continuous freezing draught.

On Wednesday the twenty third of September at seven o'clock in the morning, the sudden chill of the air is explained when it is announced that the ship has reached Narssaq in Greenland. Passengers are getting ready to go out on the excursion to this former Viking settlement to discover Greenland's stunning beauty and wildlife, its geological places of interest in Kvanefjeldet. Mela is tempted to stop and listen as the tour itineraries are revealed over the loud speakers, but then decides to go on with her work in order to have more time ashore. Odile the purser is going down the gangway to escort the tour to Kvanefeld which would allow her to see typical landscapes of Greenland as the bus mounts onto the Dyrness valley. Up the Kvanefjeldet mountain spectacular views of fjords and icebergs enchants the whole bus. Stunned by the beauty ahead they watch and listen in religious silence to the local tour guide "we are on our way to visit the Viking ruins in Dyrness where are found the Tugtupit rare stones."

The sight of passengers' happy faces while crossing C deck with snowflakes all over them coming from ashore accentuate Mela's crave for outside air. She has to wait until after one in the afternoon to go bathing in the icy air, drinking mouthfuls of this wonderful cold snow. The sailors adroitly avoid the huge ice chunks of floating icebergs using iron spikes tied to long wooden rods while the shuttle boat makes its way to Narssaq. High with the oxygen laden air everyone watches open mouthed not daring to pollute this sanctuary even with the slightest sound.

Juliette, Nelly and Maryssa are as fascinated as her and they play with the snow trying to make a little snow man while walking along the snow covered roads. In town they buy a couple of souvenirs some postcards of this remote land and Mela buys a hair clip as if to pin this place to her hair. They play in the snow making a small snowman which the mischievous Nicoleta turns into a snowwoman by adding two balls of ice as breasts and taking Mela's scarf to tie around its neck.

"Hello let me introduce you to Mela the snow woman." When they get back to the ship around five thirty hurrying to get ready for dinner and night duty, wet from snowflakes with faces glowing from the freezing air they are still giggling with glee.

Dora had only a few minutes to spare but decided to get quickly onto the shuttle for a quick look ashore. While hurrying onto the shuttle boat she missed a step and fell right out of the boat tumbling seven metres down in the freezing arctic sea. A sailor immediately ripped out a life buoy and threw it to her. Everybody on the boat was watching in awe as she struggled to catch the life saver and hold on to it while the sailors pulled her up, her black complexion had turned ashen grey with cold and fear. She bravely went back for changing her wet and icy clothes and put on her uniform to take duty.

Four days and a night at sea are needed before reaching the next port of Dundee in Scotland. Time advances as the ship moves in the earlier time zones bringing on the reverse of the wheel of fortune; rough seas, less much needed sleep and added to it Mela is feeling her period pains like distant thunder menacing to rack her body with pain. She realises that she has no sanitary pads and rushes to buy some from the ships boutiques which open as soon as the port seals are removed.

From Thursday twenty fourth to Monday twenty eighth of September, time halts as the ship crosses over to Great Britain the clocks are advanced one hour almost daily and while in Narssaq they were waking up at eight in the morning, the waking up has been advanced by four hours by the time they reach Dundee. The self defense classes are forgotten and everyone who needs to wake up early rushes into bed as soon as night duty is over at nine. The alarm clock which goes at three thirty in the morning drags one from a blissful sleep into the harsh reality of the moving ship, cabins to make, changing linen and hovering and cleaning soiled bathrooms. Mela is still seeing the reverse of the coin of the nice days in Montreal Quebec and Narssaq, in the strenuous work required by the disembarkation day at Dundee in Scotland. The severe stomach cramps are persisting and she thanks heaven that there are very few new passengers in her sector. She feels really awful and each effort aggravates her cramps. It is fortunate that this cruise no special requests have been made for any of her cabins. She can take her time and work slowly not needing to provide the extra effort that special requests would have demanded by needing incessant coming and going for fetching the required material. Fortunately many of the passengers are arriving in the next ports allowing her precious rest and giving the time to the cramps to subside. Once more Nicoleta had juicy news for her friend Mela "I need to tell you something which I saw and shocked even me."

"Something to shock you, then it must be grand come on get out with it."

"I told you tonight, not now, go on with your work; I do not want the whole pantry guessing what I told you right now. You know, from that stupid expression on your face."

That night the two girls went to the sun deck where Nicoleta related her adventure while going to her cabin's bathroom. She had gone to bed one night after gulping down several pints of beer in the crew bar. The beer had filled her bladder and she had groped her way half asleep to the bathroom. She opened the door to a stark naked white ass, still drunk; she tried to focus on the image until she realized it was Andreas, the German cook urinating in their toilet.

"What was he doing in your bathroom at this hour of the night?"

"Can't you imagine you fool, he had been sleeping in that slut's cabin or rather on her belly? He did not even bother to close the door; I got the fright of my life."

Chapter XVI

Indian Ocean Whale

Astor cruises back east towards the sunshine, allowing the crew to again enjoy Lisbon, Portugal's charming capital. Mela and Nicoleta remember their first visit there where they had ordered the famous pizza which they were eager to taste. The piece of hard bread with black olives brought to them had a strange unpleasant taste. They could not stand the smell of the herbs used in it and after the first bite itself they had to leave all of it.

"Hey Mela don't you wish to try another pizza dear?"

"No thank you I have my bread and butter and two large apples in my handbag, no thanks a lot!

"You will always remain the same old hag carrying food in her bag, you will never change your country girl ways"

"But I am no country girl I live in the capital city of Mauritius if you please!" Mela protested "It does not look as if you are from any city with your habits of

217

dressing and walking everywhere as if you were in your room!"

They strolled around and Mela bought herself a pair of Spanish dancer figurines, the man with his suit and hat and the woman in traditional red and black lace dress to bring back home to remind her forever of her encounter with Portugal. The ship stays for twenty hours in this port giving ample time to the visitors to explore the older Alfama district and new Lisbon with its superb views across the Tagus from the elegant squares. Carolyn has taken the escort to Hieronymus cloister and the Rossio place which shows the Estufa Fria, cool greenhouse with its wonderful plants. They are driven through the town quarters past the Queluz Royal palace on their way to Sintra where is found the summer residence of the Portuguese kings and the tour continues along the fabulous beaches at Estoril and Cascais.

The arrival to the south of Europe brings on an air of fiesta and it seems the air is already under the influence of the hot land of Africa which is now quite near. The ship lets itself into North Africa in the port of Casablanca where it is due for a thirty two hours stay. One is taken over by the atmosphere in this modern city where high white buildings rub shoulders with bustling souks and the old unchanged Medina. While new passengers discover the historic splendors of Morocco, the crew looks forward to meet the warm people and chat in French while purchasing the innumerable articles of clothing electronic gadgets, fake jewelry, music records in the shops, strolling along endless streets of crowded souks. The happy warmth of Africa enters through the skin to heat bones and radiate the heart and soul with a holy joy. The passengers are out of their cabins since early morning and the stewardesses are done with their morning duty well before twelve. This is the reason which allows Mela and her friends to be also on the streets of Casablanca for a typical Moroccan couscous lunch. In the town pharmacy where they stop for some sanitary pads which cost four times less than on the ship, they chat with the sales girl. Her friendliness as she speaks to them in French, reminds Mela of the girls of Muslim faith in Mauritius. The same style of clothing just showing her religion and the same friendliness like her Mauritian sisters in faith, she has such a ready smile and the way she talks to them is as if they have met one of their long lost cousins. The long stay in Casablanca has enabled passengers and crew members go out to shop on the streets and buy all the variety of things for sale in the souks. The streets offer all sorts of articles, from 'Lacoste' T shirts at a dollar each, also wonderful fake jewels and watches, leather outfits and jackets, audio cassettes, and an infinite variety of clothing and decoration, which certainly has burdened the ship with a few hundred kilos more. Mela cannot resist wonderful fresh red roses and she buys a dozen to bring for her cabin mate who is on duty and would not be able to go out during the day. Juliette on seeing the roses exclaims "Oh it's so wonderful, how did you know I love roses, and I simply adore those red ones, thank you so much love."

The passengers seem to have all gone out of the ship to the three excursions scheduled in Morocco. Esther is escorting the half day tour and through the old Medina to the cornice on the beach. Driving along with streets strewn with numerous thin Minarets to the Justice palace the passengers are brought to visit the Notre dame de Lourdes church and for shopping in the buzzing souks and bazaars. Kristy-Anne has been luckier and got the whole day tour to Rabat. She is fascinated by the Royal Moroccan town of Rabat, its palace, Kasbah and museum. More sightseeing is provided by the Roman ruins of Chelan, the Hassan tour and the mausoleum of King Mohammed V.

Those who wish to enter further on into Morocco book the one and a half day tour to Marrakesh, one of the most romantic places in all North Africa. Laure is on this tour going at the heart of Marrakesh, the Djemaa square from where visitors walk through the souks along reed covered alleys and further on to see the fabulous Badia palace and the Koutoubia mosque. The day ends after visiting the tomb of the Saadien princes, with dinner and overnight in this royal historical city. The trip continues on the next day going along the colossal walls of the town to visit olive groves.

The ship leaves Casablanca to reach Malaga the capital of the Costa del Sol after seventeen hours at sea. Mela and Nicoleta decide to skip the ship lunch as they are not on duty and try some Spanish paella in Malaga after visiting the famous cathedral. They walk around trying to locate the Cathedral by its roof from afar. After what seems like hours of walking, they finally reach the building.

"Where is the entrance, I can see only a wall, I think we took the wrong direction, the entrance is on the other side, we should have taken the opposite direction to reach the front."

"I am already almost fainting with hunger and there is no way I am going to walk all this way again, let's go and find our paella."

Unfortunately by the time they reached the town again, lunch time was over with all the Paella already consumed.

"This delicious Malaga paella vanishes as soon as it is done." said the restaurant waiter

"Look at this grilled fish it looks like delicious Rouget, I want to try." said Mela

They ordered the dish of grilled Rouget fish, which they ate with their fingers like at home enjoying the head and fins as well, licking their fingers with delight. Her mouth full of tender white fish Mela says "That's what I call fish, delightfully fresh and tasty!"

After the bountiful lunch, they are wandering along the streets doing some window shopping when it suddenly starts to rain. They walk leisurely in the warm rain letting it soak them while they wash their sticky fishy hands in it.

Mahon in the second largest of the Balearic Islands, in Minorca the same nice warmth of sunshine and food are again here to give joy and happiness. People in warm climate seem to have similar eating habits, as the climate gets warmer the food also increases in flavor and gets hotter and spicier. Food here in these Mediterranean islands is so nice that Bianca and Mela decide to eat out as much as possible. During their lunch pause from eleven to eleven thirty they go down the gangway in the nearby snack bars to sample a baby octopus salad with plenty of herbs and hot chili. They buy another two portions of the paella on the menu of the day for eating at three o clock after their duty.

The rugged scenic beauty of Corsica at Ajaccio reveals itself along the Mediterranean playground of the Costa del Sol before reaching Genoa for a change of passengers. It is already the month of October when the ship reaches Guernsey. It is the second largest of the French accented British Channel islands with spectacular rugged cliffs, nice little hidden coves and quaint little harbors. The island tour which goes to Jerbourg is escorted by the Sino Mauritian purser, Margaret. It drives to a view point over the islands Herrn, Sark and Jethou before driving to the west coast. Passing along wonderful landscapes of old strawberry farms it stops to visit the smallest church in the world which had been built by one priest only.

Another party is announced for tonight on C deck, a red party where each crew is invited to dress in red and white. Gone are the bleak cold days at sea in the cold with advancing clocks, the time has come to party and enjoy the daily change in yet another prettier little island bursting with sunshine and happy smiles. The outside joy has reached inside the ship inflaming it with the fiesta, on C deck square all has been made ready for a huge party and, the music blasts while the crew, dressed in red dances the night away. Mela and Nicoleta both dance with everyone on the floor and move their body to the rhythm of jazz and jerk and discos music. By one at night he doctor comes in with his suite of nurses and invite everybody to a party on the next day. Everyone applauds and sing 'It's Party time'.

On Sunday in Ajaccio Corsica people have gone out early and all cabins are already done by twelve. Cecilia who has also finished her work asks Mela to go out in town with her.

"Would you like to come out with me, it's still early; we could do some shopping as there seems to be nice things here."

They seem to have come into a deserted town, there is no one in sight and all shops are closed "Is it a haunted town or what? Are all the people dead? I cannot see a cat outside, what is happening?"

"I have no idea but I do not intend to roam about on the roads in this heat looking at closed shops, let's go back. We can have a sleep and be fresh for the doctor's party tonight."

While talking about their misadventure in the deserted streets at the party, they learn that people in Sicily have siesta between noon and three every working day. Everything is then closed while they have a midday nap.

Vani's French passengers of the maiden voyage Mr. and Mrs. Costa have joined the ship in Genoa for another short cruise; they greet Mela whom they know from the maiden voyage as their cabin was then next to her sector. The stewardesses dressed in their embarkation uniform are ready at their stations to welcome new cruisers. They had been standing restlessly during one hour with nobody in view not even the utility stewards who usually preceded the passengers with the luggage. The housekeeper informed them that, the flight bringing the bulk of the passengers having been delayed, they could go off duty.

Many of them then get down to the nearby café looking for some Italian delight, they opt for the specialty, a type of Italian milkshake brimming with ice cream topped with pink milk cream called 'Bibite Frappé'. Nicoleta as usual does not miss the chance to emit a naughty comment "Even 'Bibite' is on sale here and cold ones too, go ahead and make your choice girls!" The word 'Bibite' was used for penis in their Creole language.

"How do you find this 'Bibite' Mela?" This makes them splatter the milkshake which they were trying to drink all over while they choke with laughter under the amused eyes of the Italian barman.

There are two more days at sea to rally Heraklion in Crete where the ship halts from seven in the morning to three in the afternoon allowing for a half day excursion to visit the magnificent Palace of king Minos in Knossos and the ancient Greek site of Phaistos.

Most of the passengers enroll on the famous Cairo-Suez trip through the Suez Canal to Port-Said in Egypt when the cruise bureau announces it for the next stop in Port-Said. For this wonderful trip through the desert to the pyramids of Gizeh, the choice of tour escort has had to be done by lottery draw as each and every one of the escort staff wanted to accompany this almost four hundred German marks worth trip. Karin, the shore excursion manager is herself taking part to this trip while Esther will take over her post in the absence. Karin is happy to at last get off for two days out in the town of Cairo for a typical Arab dinner and overnight at the hotel with the passengers. After breakfast the next morning, they visit the citadel, the Mohamed Ali Mosque and Egyptian museum, the highlight of this trip is the drive to Gizeh to see the pyramid and Sphinx and returning over the desert roads to Suez and back to the ship.

The crew also has their share of fun going in this bustling port, where shoes, clothes and electrical appliances, all sorts of souvenirs and electronic toys and gadgets are for sale at cheap prices. The pilot for the trip through the Suez Canal embarks here on the Astor.

The crossing of the Suez Canal has brought all the passengers and crew out on the decks to watch this huge building inching its way inside the gates during four long hours to cross over to Safaga in Luxor. Some of the passengers have covered themselves well to avoid the desert sun's rays while others stand in bathing costumes at the foremost of the ship on the passenger deck. By the time Mela has finished with her work it is already two and the ship is on its way along to the desert, she climbs onto the sun deck for a view over the desert. The bus tours drive along desert streets to Luxor where they are to visit the temple of Karnak and Luxor and go around the Nile River to visit the Valley of the Kings. People taking part to the one and a half day excursion with Arabian dinner and overnight at the hotel are brought back to ancient times of Egyptian Pharaoh and Kings.

Mela and her friends have gone out for a walk round the port area to visit the post office. They see traditional Egyptian bread filled with mutton meat and eggplant called 'falafel', Mela enters one of the shops to taste the local food as they used to do in most ports.

"Could we have two of those please?" Mela asked the man who was stared at her with a blank expression. Nicoleta pinched her in the back and said "Do you really want to eat here in this Luxor palace? Let's get ourselves out of here quick!" Before the seller had time to answer, they were out on the street and Nicoleta told Mela "I agree to that It is interesting to taste local food but not in a place where cockroaches are walking on the table. I called it Luxor for you to look around and see how filthy the place was, and to compare hygienic standards for you to understand not to order anything. I shall pass on Falafel tasting after seeing food served in such a dirty place."

Two days later, in the rarely visited land of Yemen, even more breathtaking and grandiose desert scenery is revealed to passengers at Al-Huhaydah in Djibouti.

Four long days at sea follow the stop at Safaga and the crew go about their routine. Some spend their free time roaming about on the ship while others go jogging and exercising out on the decks. The party makers stay sleeping in their cabins to make up for the late nights spent out ashore. Mela has gone to the crew mess where some crew members have organized a prayer session this night and together they pray for their safe arrival home. In the meantime the ship crosses over to the Indian Ocean, to the beloved precious little pearl for most of the crew, the island of Mauritius. It is the centre of conversations, as each wants to tell about the corner of the island from which he comes from. Members of the English and German crew, overwhelmed by the descriptions of the beauty of Mauritius, its beaches and landscapes are also eager to see this famous so loved land.

The great subcontinent of India, land from where came the Mauritian ancestors, is met in the port of Bombay where a three days stop is scheduled. As usual in places where the ship stays for long, the crew gets time to relax, the overnight excursions leaving few passengers on board. Laure escorts one of the short trips scheduled, going to visit the Gateway of India, monument dedicated to King George V, the Dhobi Ghat, village of launderers, the Tata institute, the Rajami tour, the hanging gardens of Kamla Nehru Park and the mausoleum of Haji Ali. Kristy Ann goes on a night tour for an Indian dinner and classical music on. It is Aline the purser and Esther the shore excursion officer who get the chance to be escort on the two days trip. Excited and happy like schoolgirls on a holiday they had met the night before to discuss all that they had to bring for the trip. The tour bus drove them to the Bombay airport for a flight to Delhi where they spent the night in an excellent hotel after a fabulous Indian dinner to by dawn for their flight. After breakfast served on the plane going over to Agra, the bus takes them to the white Taj Mahal mausoleum. Looking at that love monument erected for Princess Mumtaz by her husband the Shah Jahan, Esther thinks of her love for Mr. Reed and thinks how good it would be to see him again after the trip. They then go on to see the fortress of Arlas, the Pearl Mosque and the Jasmine tour. Breakfast is long forgotten at two o'clock when they at last stop for lunch, they all eat ravenously before taking the return flight to Delhi. There they are brought by bus to visit the old town Jamma Mosque and the Ghandi museum driving via diplomatic and administrative areas. They get time to visit the main shopping centers and dinner on the plane flying back to Bombay.

Laura who is escorting the tour, in the heights of Aarey one hundred meters above is fascinated by Asia's most modern dairy industry connected by huge stairs up to reach a Pagoda surrounded by thirty four columns.

During the day, the members of the ship's restaurant staff have gone in town after serving breakfast, they are coming back to get the tea ready for the passengers and meet the stewardesses going to town after their duty.

"Beware out there in town where the shanty towns may make you weep, seeing thousands of children out on the street at night. The appalling poverty has upset even the most hard hearted of us!"

The crew has been invited to a complimentary tour from two to five in the afternoon courtesy of the Vani Bhawan Indian seaman's club for a tour of Mangalore for visits to museums, the animal shrub gardens. Mela and her friends intend to use their trip to Bombay to bring back home beautiful Indian souvenirs, mainly saris and clothing. They walk in the nearby town along the harbor front to the sari shops where silk and gold embroidered saris are three times less expensive than in Mauritius. In the shops the sales people display a large array of beautiful saris for them to choose from, they even get to go to a tailor to make him stitch the tight fitting blouse and skirt to be worn with the sari for them. Benares saris are in vogue in Mauritius and Mela buys a couple of brightly colored ones for her mother and aunts.

The November heat as they board the excursion bus in the afternoon reminds them of the stifling heat in their country during the summer months. While visiting the temples and museums in the blazing heat, they get terribly thirsty. Mela is dying to refresh herself with fresh lemon and tamarind juice sold by street vendors, but her friends Bianca and Nicoleta and Juliette are watching her "Don't you dare drink from those, have you not heard how dangerous it is to drink water here, it may be contaminated and cause malaria, dysentery or even typhoid?"

She has kept plenty of change hoping to be able to buy goodies from the roadside but cannot use it. She cannot buy a thing to nibble at as her guardians won't let her near the vendors at all. Not even to buy one of those tempting juicy colorful fruits on the roadside.

They visit a beautiful botanical garden with trees are cut in the form of animals and where is found a huge shoe into which children can climb. After the visit, Mela finally gets permission to buy sealed carbonated drink from a seller near the garden gates. Panting and flushed from the long walk in the sun, the German crew rushes to buy a cool drink but they do not have any change, Mela generously gives them her surplus change. A few minutes later they are brought to the Vani Bhawan, the place where the Mahatma Gandhi stopped when he came to Bombay. The seaman's club has arranged a buffet of hot and cold drinks and nice Indian cakes and snacks for their visitors.

Marmagoa is the next Indian town, in this place with strong catholic influence from the French times a kaleidoscope of opportunities awaits the visitor. Aline, the purser is escorting the bus tour to Panaji, one of the most beautiful regions of India. They drive further south to Dona Paula, a picturesque spot where she takes pictures of the wonderful views over the harbor. In old Goa, she sees temples, Mosques, fortresses and cathedrals, and as is the custom for Mauritian Catholics upon entering a church for the first time, she expresses three wishes while praying in the Bom Jesus cathedral. The mausoleum of Saint Xavier is a very pious place where she says prayers for her sick grandmother. The beauty of the fresco at the Santa Monica cloisters fascinates the visitors who then drive alongside infinite rice fields leading to a welcome dip on the idyllic beach of the Indian Ocean.

Mangalore is the third Indian town on this cruise, here again the Indian Seaman club has offered a bus tour for the crew to visit the town. The forewarned crew has dressed in light clothes to fight the heat and carried plastic water bottles. They drive to the Saint Augusto Catholic church and the University building before visiting the Mangala Devi temple. The guide tells them Mangala Devi was the ancient name of Mangalore.

The shore excursion office has organized tours to a typical Indian village for its music and folklore, Laure who escorts the tour is amazed by the show a 'Kambala', buffalo race. The buffaloes with gleaming freshly washed black skin decorated with fancy ropes, mirrors and amulets, paired with the help of a yoke are lined up with their well sculpted owners, ready to enter the arena. Looking every bit menacing their muscles taut, quivering with excitement and their noses flaring, the animals, agitated by the incessant whipping and war cries of the Saarthi, the lone rider behind them, rush past at maddening speed leaving a trail of water flying behind. The spectators hold their breath watching this awful the pairs of heavy snorting animals struggling in the muddy waters, a once in a lifetime experience.

People are warned that during the next visit, of the wildlife in the zoo where is a snake park, it is strictly forbidden to take photos. The carving of Indian musical instruments and weapons can be seen as well as the manufacture of tiles later on the tour.

St Aloysius chapel situated on Lighthouse Hill was built in 1885 by Rev Father Joseph Willy. Similar to Rome's world renowned Sistine Chapel, its magnificent fresco painting and oil canvas paintings beautify the walls and portraits of the Crowing of the Cock and many saints decorating the ceiling delights the eyes that are blessed by their sight.

The ship says goodbye but not adieu to India to sail on south for a day at sea before reaching Madras in the South of India and Mela rejoices at the thought to see the land of her ancestors. After karate lessons in the conference centre, the group were roaming out on the deck to cool off before going in bed. The loudspeakers started to emit an announcement and they all listened carefully "The Captain inform passengers and crew that due to unforeseen circumstances the Astor will not be able to dock in the port of Madras, consequently the ship will sail southwards for one more day to the port of Colombo in Sri Lanka."

Nicolet teases her by saying "No chance to see your ancestors dear but don't worry you will find the same people in Colombo!"

Passengers can participate on the two day excursion for Polonnaruwa in Sigiriya when the ship anchors in the port of Colombo in Sri Lanka. After dinner and overnight in a hotel, passengers set out on the next day after breakfast, to see the rock palace of king Kasyapas and rock paintings representing cloud girls. In Colombo, Laure escorts the tour to the old town where are found the bazaars, Muslim mosques and Hindu temples. Large cinnamon gardens are seen on the way to the town house via the Viharamara Devi Park and the Buddhist temple where a life real statue of the sleeping Buddha lying on its side can be seen. She has generously conceded to leave the longer version of the same tour to Aline the German purser. It includes the visit to Asakaramaya and zoological garden with time for sunbathing on the white sunny beaches. Back in Mauritius in a couple of days, she would have infinite hours of sand and sun on her own little stretch of white beach in Grand-Bay in front of her family bungalow.

Kristy Ann is lucky to get to escort the tour to Kandy which visits the Tea factory and royal tropical gardens of Peradeniya to admire a wonderful variety of orchid, drive to old royal town to the temple with the of Buddha's tooth relic, and return via the Kandy lake to visit a batik factory.

At noon the ship leaves Colombo back to Cochin in India which would be reached on the next day at eight in the morning. The Astor was still in the whereabouts of Sri Lanka and the crew was having dinner and watching the local news when they saw that the place where they had just left a couple of hours earlier had been bombed by the Tamil Tigers terrorist group, causing death and injuries.

Cochin is an Old Dutch settlement a short bus tour discovers the Mattencherry palace, Jewish town quarter with the synagogue, the park in Ernakulam and the court building. Equally short sailing tours through picturesque lagoon and coconut grooves, bring people over Vypeen, Vaalarpadomand and Bolghatty islands to visit Dutch palaces and striking small fishing villages where the people are all dressed in bright happy colors.

The work is tough but Bianca sings Lionel Ritchie's tune *"when the going gets tough the tough gets going"* to cheer up her friends; there is so much to be done in such short time as those passengers who did not depart in Madras now all are leaving their cabins in Colombo. As usual the generous tips and nice words of thanks from the passengers give them courage to go on. While the passengers are out Mela quickly starts on her cabin asking herself how she is going to manage to have so many cabins ready before the arrival of the new passengers. She had finished doing only one cabin when the siren announced the dreaded and hated boat drill. Having to interrupt her work, in such hectic time for a stupid boat drill tremendously disturbs her. She has to bear with it as boat drill is sacred primordial and closely monitored by the security officers. She quickly goes down to fetch her lifejacket from her cabin refraining from her urge to run, instructions are not to run on the ship and never during boat drill. She patiently lines up in her station to undergo the drill with a grim face, fortunately it is not mandatory to smile during the drill as she would surely had caught a fine by the long face she had on. Tonight another of the crew parties is announced, it would be a disguise party. Management wants to cheer up the crew after the rough seas and hard work by organising a costume contest. The crew gets ready each one trying to find an original costume. Nelly lends Mela a large green skirt and a white blouse worn below the shoulders and a head cloth, large earrings and plenty of colourful bangles to dress as a gypsy. Bianca dresses like a Mauritian Indian coolie woman with a blouse above the navel and a large flowered print skirt and a cotton shawl across her shoulders and tucked in her skirt, she wears Indian sandals and the red dot of married women on the forehead along with

Jackie Veerabadren

the feet bangles to go with the Indian sandals bought in Bombay on her feet. Nicoleta appears in a wonderful dress in a cloth printed with all the flags in the world sewn like a sailors dress with the sailors collar and a matching hat, she wears long white socks and shoes. The one hundred dollar prize is awarded to Nicoleta whose costume has been by far the best.

Almost two days at sea while moving south to the paradisiacal island of Male in the Maldives Archipelago. On this tiny island the morning excursion is guided on foot to see the president's palace, the mosque, the museum and fish market. In the afternoon boat trips depart to the pearl white sand beaches for swimming and snorkeling among the coral gardens and exotic fishes. There is also the possibility to hop around the islands to Furuna, famous for deep sea fishing, enjoy a buffet lunch on Kurumba Island with its native vegetation and wonderful beaches for swimming and snorkeling and the trip ends by seeing the fishing village of Himma Fushi.

"My God girls, have you seen the prices at the duty free shop on Bandos island, It's simply crazy the waitresses have bought so many nice things at such cheap prices.'

After morning duty, off they go to Bandos, but Mela wants to swim in this wonderful blue lagoon and lie in the hot white sand. They agree to go first to the shops and then to come with her to the beach.

"Get out of the sea now Mela, you have three o'clock duty and it's already one thirty, by the time you arrive and shower it will be time for taking duty."

But Mela cannot bring herself to leave this paradise so soon and still lingers on until the others turn their back and go taking her bag and clothes along forcing her to follow. She quickly puts on her shorts and goes back with her wet swim suit on. She arrives on ship at three and has only time to get off the wet things put on her uniform and brush the sand from her feet before going to duty. Fortunately the girl waiting for her to take over is never in a hurry to go. She stays on to chat for another twenty minutes and Mela thinks, I would have had time to take shower, but nevertheless I am glad to keep the sea water and sand a couple of hours more, I shall shower after duty at six.

The excitement mounts as the Astor sails further south in the Indian ocean after two days of rough seas another island comes in view.

"Unique by a thousand miles Seychelles presents its rare black parrot, giant Aldabra native tortoises and preserved endemic vegetation of which the famous coco de mer. Drive round its numerous islands and through its lush tropical vegetation with centenary Sandragon trees, dive in its warm lagoons filled with multicolored tropical fishes and lie on its soft beds of white sand to feel the nice burning of the sun's warm rays'

The excursion office has been announcing Seychelles making passengers queue up at the office to buy their tickets to paradise. Mela and her friends are impatient to finish work to go out as they have been told that there is here very nice dancing clubs by the name of Kacholo and Kapacha. The people from Seychelles also speak Creole like the Mauritians but a heavily English accented Creole which has always been funny to Mauritian ears. They cannot wait to go out and meet the Seychelles 'Dalons' and 'Bouledoux' as young boys and girls are called there.

Passengers have had time to tour around the Island of Victoria for about three hours and the ship has moved on to reach the Island of Praslin in the afternoon. The famous valley de Mai with its unique vegetation, its famous Coco de Mer and corkscrew palm is home to the rare black Seychelles parrot. Bianca and Mela are on duty and they have two hours free to see Mahe. They decide to go out and try and see what can be done in this time. A nice jeep driven by two Seychelles Dalon stops, the men kindly offer to make them tour the island. "Where are the beautiful Bouledoux off to, we are Jamie and Frankie, would you like to have a drive round Victoria?"

"Why not "said Bianca "Anyway we have such a short time it would enable us to see much more than on foot. But the ship is sailing at six and we have to be here before five thirty.

"No problem sister, it is not big here it won't take long to tour the island."

The two Mauritian stewardesses embark on the jeep and off they go to see Victoria and its little coves and beaches sending caution to the winds. The Dalons are very, nice and polite men who bring them around with genuine goodwill and helpfulness. On the way they meet one of their friends to whom they introduce Mela and Bianca.

"Hi I am Solano, and now I know why I have been driving around the whole day, it was to meet you, I have never dreamt of seeing someone as beautiful as you."

Mela was surprised but pleased by these nice words and kept her eyes down but he insisted that he wanted to meet her again and bring her to dance.

"We shall come back on the twenty fifth and shall stay until the twenty sixth; you can come and fetch us to go out then. But for now we need to go back as the ship will be sailing shortly!"

She was anxious to get out of the way as soon as possible as the man's eyes on her were making her really uncomfortable. It was almost quarter to six when they reached the pier, they said warm thanks to their new friends Jamie and Frankie. They were hurrying up the gangway when they bumped into the security officer Mr. Reed. He severely scolded them for being so late back and having been so careless to go out like that with perfect strangers. He had seen then getting on the jeep and had taken the precaution to take its number just in case.

"I can tell you I am relieved to see you back whole, don't you know how dangerous it is to do what you just did, be thankful you met good people but beware you may not always be that lucky!"

When the ship leaves Seychelles at six in the evening, even though she has spent time out swimming in each of the islands Mela has not had enough of the wonder of this paradise. She consoles herself with the thought that in ten days they will be back for more of its warm humid caresses. The ship sails one day more southwards to Nossi Be on the West coast of Madagascar, here passengers have simple buses for touring through the lush tropical vegetation to see extended plantations and volcanic lakes.

The next island of Comoros reached on the next day is as primitive with lively loud markets with its innumerable sellers to where simple buses bring passengers through narrow streets before driving over the volcanic landscapes and stop at a viewpoint.

The ship takes another day and two nights at sea to sail up North to Zanzibar in Tanzania. Here, 17th century fortresses, museum and old slave market can be seen as well as the Livingstone house. The cruise bureau has organized tours to the Sultan palace and the Persian baths and nutmeg and cinnamon spice plantations. While the night falls on Zanzibar Astor departs for reaching the coast of Kenya early next morning, the crew is overwhelmed with work while passengers leave the ship to take the flight home. The buses are ready on the pier for those having chosen to visit Kenya 's sightseeing worth, the Fort Jesus and museum. They stroll in the old town and continue to visit the Uhuru park and temples and markets to the woodcarving village of Akamba for buying the beautiful wooden sculptures made by the locals.

While doing her cabins Mela dreams at the suggestive names of the tours announced over the loudspeakers.

'First call for passengers to Shimba Hills tour, please kindly proceed to the gangway for joining the buses to the nature reserve for admiring the sable antelopes, buffaloes, impalas and elephants.'

'Passengers on the tour to Tsavo Park are kindly requested to proceed to the buses to drive to Nairobi inside Buchuma gate, entrance to Kenya's biggest Safari, where huge elephants colored red from the dust in which they roll share the wilderness with black rhino, Zebras Giraffes, Gazelles, Impalas, ostriches and majestic lions.'

The tour excursion office has a whole array of tours in this fantastic land, Malindi tour follows the coastal roads past huge Baobab trees to the Kilifi inlet to see the ruins of the 14th century village of Gedi and take a boat tour to see the coral gardens and finally to see the old slave market, Portuguese chapel and a snake farm.

The disembarkation and embarkation is over and Mela and Bianca are exhausted from the sixteen cabins they had cleaned and got ready. Even if they do not feel very much like going, they nevertheless decide to wander off the gangway in their uniforms to see he beautiful wooden sculptures. The whole day, passengers and crew have been carrying those pretty things in the ship and they also wish to take a souvenir home.

When she heard the program describing the tour to the Amboseli safari, Mela was carried away by the wonder of this area. Described as the most densely populated wild park within east Africa it hosts large buffalo and elephant herds, families of lions, gazelles and antelopes along with a rich multicolored bird's life. The passengers dine and spend the night in the Lodge there and wake up at dawn at the time when the big cats go out hunting to further the exploration further down the Mzima springs to the hippos and crocodiles and tropical fishes. Mela chooses a pair of embracing giraffes as a souvenir of Kenya symbol of the safari of which she has dreamt so much.

The following days while returning to Zanzibar, Mela has so much work to do and is so tired that she cannot bother to go ashore after duty and once more misses this land.

During the return journey to Seychelles the ship's management informs the crew that they will be allowed to have visitors during their stay on Mauritius. This sends a wave of excitement and expectation amongst the Mauritian crew who feverishly set out to establish lists of the names of their potential visitors. The cabins of all the Mauritian crew members have been put upside down with the luggage being prepared to send home.

The port of Mahe is reached on the twenty fifth at eight in the morning and Frankie and Jamie the Seychelles Dalon have come to meet their friends and invite them to the disco. Bianca and Mela ask them if they can bring along Juliette and Nicoleta also.

"Of course sisters you are our friends and the friends of our friends are our friends also."

The prospect of going out in this paradise has given renewed courage to finish the work early. After a long nice swim in the warm lagoon amongst the tropical fishes Mela comes back on board to prepare for the evening. The minibus which collects them has the entire requirement for a typical Creole evening, with guitar, ravane and maravane and the Dalons start singing typical Seychelles music with the lyrics in Creole mixed with English and playing he instruments. The girls dance and sing along as the happy party reach the nightclub, the Kacholo situated on the heights of La Digue Island. The Creole style house where is found the disco has an outside veranda where the dancers can have a drink and a bite from the barbecue. Nicoleta and Mela have started right away to move to the rhythm of the Sega and are giving a demonstration of their talent kneeling on the floor and lowering their heads backwards to touch the floor. People have formed a dancing circle around them and clap their hands to the tempo. The club owner then picks a huge bunch of pink bougainvilleas flowers from the gardens and offers it to the two girls. He invites them to a drink on the veranda and while the big glass of cold fruit cocktail decorated with a hibiscus flower arrives, he insists that they take something to eat, he advices the Creole burger, grilled meat cooked in a Creole sauce of fresh tomatoes onions garlic ginger, coconut milk and hot red and green chili peppers.

The head full of happy souvenirs of the two lovely nightclubs' Kacholo and Kapacha visited the previous night; Mela finishes her work quickly and goes with friends to the BeauVallon Bay hotel for another swim. Afterwards seeing the barman preparing a nice milkshake she orders one for herself and one for the three other friends. She had asked for the price and the barman had told her it was sixty rupees. The normal price was around thirty in Mauritius but being in a beach hotel and in Seychelles sixty rupees seemed not too bad. When the bill arrived she was shocked to see that four milkshakes had amounted to almost eight hundred Mauritian rupees, almost three times as much as she had calculated. The barman who was a Mauritian who had come to work in the Seychelles seeing her puzzled expression said "It is in Seychelles rupees that we count here and one Seychelles rupees is equivalent to almost three Mauritian rupees."

On Sunday the twenty ninth of November 1987 the Astor was inside the Mauritian territorial waters. Since early morning as soon as the announcement had been made that the island of Mauritius was in view, the crew had been sneaking to the upper decks to see the homeland coast. When the first shorelines of Mauritius appeared in the distance screams of delight were heard on the decks and tears came to the eyes of the children happy to see their mother land and suddenly a huge bushy stream of misty air and vapor explode at the surface of the water.

"A whale, look it is a huge whale exhaling air through its blowhole." Somebody shouted

Welcome back to Mauritius.

EPILOGUE

Mela left the ship for her one and a half months holidays to spend Christmas and welcome the year 1988 in Mauritius. Thinking back she remembers her dreams and expectations on the eve of the year 1987, one year after her dreams had been outlived and she had survived the rough sea roads. Now she was ready to sail the world, to go to the end of it, up to wherever the Astor our fairy Godmother would carry her.

The ship continued to sail, cruising passengers around the globe during which the crew kept on seeing the world and new passengers. Mela boarded the ship in January for a grand cruise in the wake of great explorers which departs like the previous year from Southampton, Lisbon and Tenerife over to South America.

On this marvelous voyage all around South America they again visited Salvador de Bahia but went south to Rio de Janeiro in February 1988 for six crazy carnival nights. They danced along the streets with the locals and went to the Christ redeemer statue on Corcovado Mountain by car ascent.

The Astor hugged the South American coast south to Montevideo and plunged southwards to the famous Falkland Islands before rejoining the South American coast at Punta Arenas in Chile to climb up the coast northwards to Valparaiso Santiago and Antofagasta along this very long country. The towns of Callao in Lima as well as Guayaquil in Ecuador revealed typical Inca culture of which many more souvenirs are taken in the form of knitted decorations and typical ponchos.

More Creole was exchanged with the locals at Haiti in the small island of Port aux Princes. At Montego Bay in Jamaica, the locals persuaded a large part of the crew to have their hair plaited in the Jamaican Style with little beads hanging from dozens of tiny plaits on their heads for twenty dollars. Mela's hair being too long, she did not have it done to her hair as would have found the plaits too painful on her head. On the same night after sailing out of Montego Bay captain Derek Kamp ordered that all the plaits be immediately undone before duty! They went to Easter mass on the Island of Bermuda where very friendly people kissed them and wished them happy Easter. They saw the place where rockets had been sent to moon from port Canaveral.

Seasickness which she had learned to tame had become her faithful travel companion. If the routine of cleaning cabins started to become tedious it was soon forgotten in the ports and she promised herself that she would will herself to work to her bones if needed as long as her force would let her and would not stop until she had seen the whole wide world.

Then one day during the month of June it was rumored that the ship was to be sold, Mela was horrified and did not want to believe that such an appalling thing could happen to them. She had not yet seen even Asia and Australia and the eastern part of the globe. Unfortunately as usual for the most appalling rumors, it was finally confirmed. This would be their last cruise lasting until October when the Astor would be taken over by a Russian company.

Most of the crew returned home to go back to their jobs in hotels while some tried their luck trying to find a job in Europe. Nicoleta went to England where she married a British waiter met on the ship while Juliette went to Germany with her boyfriend. Mela came back to Mauritius; her heart was still weeping her lost fairy Godmother. She had suddenly been changed back from the globe trotter to the unemployed island girl dreaming of escape. Luckily a few months later she found a job in the emerging tourism industry of Mauritius.

Thanks to the fluency in German acquired on the ship by talking so much to her passengers she became a tour guide escorting German passengers around Mauritius. She no longer watched the tour buses from the cabins she was cleaning but she was the local guide when cruise ships visited. One day she did a tour with passengers from the Fodor Dostoyevsky ship and it was the tour manager, a German girl called Siggi who was escorting the passengers on her bus. When she learnt that Mela had worked on the Astor she looked at Mela and smiled.

"I see you were in love with that ship, how about a tour on it?"

Mela was looking at her with a puzzled face and she said.

"My dearest this ship is the ex Astor your ship, in my quality of tour manager I have the pleasure to invite you for a visit and to have a drink on the ship."